A Slow-Motion Disaster

The water had withdrawn past her tidal pool and well beyond where the red sand was exposed even at the lowest of tides.

The utter silence with the ongoing background noise of waves left her ears and nerves wailing.

Even the tourists were quiet.

Lina turned and scrambled out of her now-drained collection spot, trying not to slip on the mat of seaweed and clutching her pack in one hand. She waved the other over her head and yelled as loud as she could.

"Get to high ground, *now*! Call in your support scoot for emergency rescue!"

All the climbers who'd been so active and busy and noisy simply stared, either at her or the widening expanse of beach. Their confused eyes and faces scattered all over the cliff's surface might have been amusing if they weren't in danger they didn't seem to understand.

Running toward her own sky-scoot and wishing she dared change into the boots in her pack, Lina shouted again.

"Get away from the beach! Can't you *see*?"

For everyone who's had a day job
in a tourist town

DANGEROUS DAYS ON A PLEASURE PLANET

KARI KILGORE

SPIRAL PUBLISHING, LTD.

CHAPTER 1

Lina Rundgroff remained generally amazed at her good luck in getting a leisure world on her first assignment out of training. Not everyone who'd studied marine xenobiology and specialized in aquatic zones on human colonies always fared so well on their first time out in the field.

Many of her classmates had ended up on planets with standard mixed-use settlements, or something as focused as supply planets for nearby mining or industrial processing moons or even an asteroid belt or two.

One poor soul—or at least Lina thought so—had ended up on an arid world with not much water to speak of. But they'd seemed delighted with the chance to track down and study how life managed to thrive in such a hostile place.

A morning like this left her feeling almost guilty with her great fortune.

Not that she had any intention of giving it up.

She stood in a rocky, knee-deep pool slowly filling with warm salt water, only a few yards from Scarlet Beach, a brilliant red sand beach that gleamed with streaks of silvery metallic highlights. Her mission report detailed how the ore wasn't considered valuable enough for mining, but the striking appearance added considerable value for the ever-changing groups of people intent on rest, relaxation, and capturing holo-vids none of their friends would have.

The source of that spectacular sand soared above the deep beach and provided another draw for vacationers who could afford the massive amount of credits required simply to reach Sarkans 3. Lighter-than-Earth gravity allowed for easier climbing up the scarlet cliffs, and for long, slow parasailing and gliding for anyone not inclined to such vertical challenges.

At the moment, a noisy group of newly arrived human merrymakers attempted their first ascent, and their shouts and cackles of laughter cut through the soothing sound of incoming waves.

Their eye-wateringly bright clothing and habit of constantly stopping to either activate or cover their specialized body-and-head-based cameras never seemed to vary much no matter where they roamed. Despite greater ease of movement here, Lina suspected at least a few sported the subtle (and expensive) addition of personal grav-pac boosts for the steep ascent.

Grav-pacs that small were nowhere near powerful enough to levitate to the top. They only pushed a few feet away from a surface. But they could add enough of a lift to help, and rumor was they'd make a life-saving difference in a fall if someone managed to slip past the numerous safety features involved.

Sure, that was one of the downsides of working or studying on a leisure planet, as on recreational zones of any planet, moon, or one of the huge pleasure ships that endlessly ferried the truly wealthy from one hot destination to the next.

Tourists.

Their sometimes-disruptive presence helped immensely when it came to science and exploration, of course. Without their potential for adding great fortune to the Sarkans System, no one would have glanced twice at this gorgeous landscape after resource extraction was ruled out.

That potential led to the development of safe and reliable grav-drive flight schedules, construction of two immense space ports, and the discovery of the rich natural resources that awaited.

But tourists could certainly disturb a peaceful setting once they finally arrived.

Ignoring the noisy festivities, Lina happily concentrated on breathing in the salty air around her, accented with the sharp, almost piney aroma of a remarkable species of violet seaweed growing in her tidal pool.

That color showed up perfectly in the clear water with Sarkans 3's sun still rising in the sky.

At night, though, it glowed with a delightful purple light that lasted for weeks even after it was harvested and dried.

It had never been discovered anywhere else on this planet or any other, and not here until the last few months. Which meant Lina was the first to study it in-depth.

Even better was how a similar luminescence seemed to appear in sea life that ingested the weed.

Lina knelt, submerging herself up to the hips, grateful for her pale-blue, instant-dry shorts and tunic. Much as the day was shaping up to be a hot one, the idea of returning to her quarters on her sky-scoot soaking wet still wasn't a pleasant one.

The shorts even stayed light-blue against her dark brown skin under the water, giving her a nice visual contrast for the strands floating with each incoming and outgoing wave, the water a tiny bit higher after each one.

The seaweed felt oddly like smooth silk against her legs, with tickly hairs around the borders and growing in streaks on the bigger leaves. She didn't mind trading that level of sensitivity for protection against the jagged bottom with form-fitting plas-socks around her feet and ankles.

She hadn't yet spotted any of the nine-legged, spiky shelled creatures she most wanted to collect today, or much of anything else besides the seaweed for that matter.

She paused with both hands buried in watery silk, tilting her head to the side and staring out toward the endless oceanic horizon.

Normally the incoming tide brought a bounty of native creatures in with it, all hoping to end up in a tidal pool with a compatible companion. All of them either hoping for a quick meal or the chance to pair off—or more than pair in a few cases —and get started making little creatures.

But right now she didn't feel or see a thing, and the only voices she heard came from fellow humans.

No oddly harmonic songs from creatures on the wing, or grunts, mumbles, and shrieks from land-dwellers that often congregated at the beach for a relatively easy feast.

Only those oblivious people scaling the cliff.

And a sensation of something deeply wrong all around her.

A feeling no one who'd trained to work in and around water would ever ignore if she wanted to live a long and healthy life.

Lina stood and turned to look around, absently brushing water drops off her legs, knees, and shins.

But her shins should still be enjoying the seaweed's watery caresses in a knee-deep and rising pool.

Instead the weed was collapsing into a thick mass, sure to go as rubbery and dry as it did during low tides.

Not only the tidal pool was draining when it shouldn't.

Now the ruddy beach was extending itself past the rocky outcrop as the water withdrew.

All of Lina's muscles seemed to go rigid to the point that her lungs protested their confinement and her heart stuttered in her chest.

A tsunami, even without a whisper of an earthquake warning?

Or was this related to a phenomenon neither she nor anyone else on the science teams understood well enough? Not only to adjust to the needs of their newest vacationing arrivals, but to keep themselves and everyone else safe on this remote world.

The rectangular black screen of her secondary wrist-comm didn't show any kind of notification, and Sarkans 3 usually did an excellent job of warning of any kind of unexpected weather. Most tourist-focused planets did.

She looked down long enough to sling her collection pack around from her shoulders, meaning to grab her comm-stick and check for a planet-wide weather warning that didn't reach the level of full-scale comms.

But what she saw when she again glanced toward the horizon made her forget all of that.

CHAPTER 2

The water had withdrawn past her tidal pool and well beyond where the red sand was exposed even at the lowest of tides.

The utter silence with the ongoing background noise of waves left her ears and nerves wailing.

Even the tourists were quiet.

Lina turned and scrambled out of her now-drained collection spot, trying not to slip on the mat of seaweed and clutching her pack in one hand. She waved the other over her head and yelled as loud as she could.

"Get to high ground, *now*! Call in your support scoot for emergency rescue!"

All the climbers who'd been so active and busy and noisy simply stared, either at her or the widening expanse of beach. Their confused eyes and faces scattered all over the cliff's surface might have been amusing if they weren't in danger they didn't seem to understand.

Running toward her own sky-scoot and wishing she dared change into the boots in her pack, Lina shouted again.

"Get away from the beach! Can't you *see?*"

Several of the tourists looked down at once, but Lina didn't even glance at her own wrist-comm. Too much chance of stumbling on sand roughed up by the climbers' antics before they got started.

Especially when the dark-blue curve of her scoot seemed to keep drawing away no matter how fast she ran, and her legs and arms felt like she was caught in an invisible and fast-coagulating gel.

Someone finally managed to respond to her—or more likely to the warning on their wrist—just as she finally reached her miniature airborne tractor near the base of the cliff. A confused, angry voice floated down from above.

"Is this a *joke?*"

Lina slowed down long enough to carefully step over the sharp red rocks and spiky violet plants that formed the boundary between the ocean zone and the cliffs, but she didn't bother looking up.

"Just get yourselves to higher ground and you can argue about that later!"

She tossed her pack into the boxy cargo area of her scoot, then flung one leg across the ridge of her seat. The scoot's decidedly old-fashioned design meant she had to straddle it and hold tight to two handlebars as if she rode one of the foot-cycles people used to get around on land all over Sarkans 3.

But instead of using her own already-burning muscles to turn two or more wheels and struggling to get herself far enough down the pea-graveled road to avoid whatever was coming, her palm activated the scoot's own grav-pacs.

At her harder-than-usual pull back on the handlebars, it shot soundlessly into the humid air, rising past tourists who mostly still didn't have enough common sense to keep climbing.

Lina couldn't have saved more than one, possibly two if she was willing to risk her scoot tipping over.

But thank science and all the deities of self-preservation, one woman wearing a vivid pink skinsuit had anchored herself to one of the cliff's near-invisible support cables and was speaking into a comm-stick. The woman's eyes were fixed on the horizon where it appeared most of the sea had disappeared to.

As Lina rose more carefully past the top of the cliff, she saw the bulk of a rescue-scoot approaching in a hurry over thick clumps of purple and green trees. The big scoot would arrive before she could manage to get even the sensible woman out of harm's way.

She rotated her own scoot to face what was left of the water, then tapped the airbrake. Even with the sun's warmth, the breeze a few hundred meters up chilled her hair and damp skin, but she wasn't about to dig into her pack long enough to grab a jacket.

She settled for rubbing her hands on her dry shorts before turning around long enough to retrieve her comm-stick. Folded, it wasn't much wider or longer than her index finger. The last thing she needed to make whatever was happening worse was for it to slip through water-slick fingers.

The matte-black surface normally only displayed symbols and a few words of text.

Right now, the whole thing flashed from white to yellow to red, and tiny purple waves marched across the background.

Lina gave a practiced twist, and the comm-stick telescoped to the size of her palm.

The obvious emergency flashing didn't stop, but she could read lines of text on the much larger surface.

COASTAL EMERGENCY!!! REPEAT, COASTAL EMERGENCY!!!

Evacuate inland or to high ground immediately. Call for rescue now if needed.

Extreme danger, potential tsunami waves and possible loss of life and property.

The text started to repeat, so Lina tapped the back in her personal sequence to acknowledge the alert and switch to normal interface. She was safe from any kind of wave at this height, unless its velocity was enough to stir up too much wind for the scoot to handle on a lower-gravity world. But she was also in an ideal position to observe and report back to Planetary Science, weather, and rescue teams.

She almost dropped the comm-stick anyway when it buzzed in her hands.

She had no idea it could even *do* that.

This time the text read itself out loud in a flat, but somehow intimidating voice.

SECURITY ALERT!!!

EVACUATE IF NEEDED BEFORE COMPLYING.

Report your current location to Sarkans 3 authorities at once.

Refusal to comply will carry immediate consequences, regardless of planetary status.

Lina frowned, trying to keep an eye on her comm-stick and the nearly invisible sea at the same time. She'd only been on Sarkans 3 for a couple months, but she'd never had to report her current location to anyone.

Sure, the tour groups kept up with their members by requiring location-sensing bracelets and necklaces and rings and such for those who didn't have implants, partly in an attempt to avoid liability if someone got lost or hurt.

But other than that, the general attitude seemed to be no one would protest as long as folks were sensible and well-behaved.

Something besides the bizarre water withdrawal had to be happening.

And maybe they were related.

The comm-stick finally responded to her repeated efforts to switch to her normal interface by presenting her with a scrolling list of messages she'd missed, almost all in the past few minutes.

She tapped the latest one from her research supervisor without reading any of the rest.

Between one uneasy glance at the still-distant line where the ocean should have been and the next, a tiny version of her supe's reddened, scowling face appeared on the screen.

The Director of Planetary Science for the Vatten Continent, Ris Murray was normally easygoing and calm, if sometimes a bit energetic in his communications style, and a real pleasure to work with and learn from. But right now, Lina was halfway convinced saltwater was about to steam out of his ears.

He looked as if he'd been enjoying the bright sunshine without taking the highly recommended sun-protection pills in advance.

"Report at once, Lina! Where are you? Didn't you know there's some kind of coastal emergency going on?"

"I *do* know, that's why I just commed in. I'm up beyond the cliffs on my sky-scoot at the moment, trying to figure out where an entire sea might have disappeared to."

Ris scrubbed both hands over his face. The relief was obvious when he looked back out at her.

"That's the question of the day, isn't it? No trace of a storm or seismic activity on any of the sensors. You're the last of my crew to report in, so now I can rest assured each and every one of you are indeed smart and able to fend for yourselves. See any wandering tourists in need of evacuation?"

Lina turned and held the comm-stick up, tapping to switch to the outward-focused camera. She gave Ris time to see the bright yellow rescue scoot hovering bare centimeters from the cliff, collecting the last of the climbers before switching the focus to the front camera.

"They're handling themselves pretty well. What have you heard? All I know is the water disappeared and Planetary Security is demanding we all check in."

Ris blinked and his mouth dropped open.

"You got that on your public comm? I'm still only seeing the evacuation notice."

"I did. Maybe using the training center's comm lets them know where you are so you don't have to report."

Motion in the distance caught Lina's attention.

"I'm seeing something out there," she went on. "Stand by."

She resisted the temptation to fly out and get closer, but it wasn't easy. With only a little training in personal rescue techniques, she was hardly equipped to help with what could be a large-scale event.

"Don't pull that 'stand by' nonsense with me," Ris squawked. "Tell me what's happening!"

"There's what almost looks like a *ripple* out there, but it doesn't seem to be fast-moving. Could be distance distortion, or simply that much water being displaced and creating clouds and steam. Nothing below me so far."

"Hang on, now I'm getting confirmation," Ris said. "Officially no signs of a quake or storm causing this."

Lina nodded, still focused on the increasingly active horizon. It was a true shame her pack didn't include something as basic as a set of digital binocs. Her day's job of examining samples and creatures right in front of her shouldn't have ever needed them.

"The line is getting closer, and a bit choppier. Still a ways off, but it doesn't seem to be resolving into a high wave so far. And it's not moving as fast as that much water should be."

She glanced over her shoulder to give her eyes a chance to focus elsewhere and realized the rescue scoot was still there, hovering a little lower than she was.

And the sensible, pink-clad woman she'd noticed before did indeed have some kind of device pressed to her own eyes.

"Another update," Ris said. "Seems the water is being...controlled somehow. Like it's caught in a gravity field? But that might not mean it's safe there yet."

When Lina looked back up, she spotted movement above the incoming water. More scoots, by the way they darted around.

"I think they've got observers above it," she said. "Still advancing. Churning like crazy, like it's boiling, but yes, still controlled. Below me is still as dry as low tide, though, so I'm not seeing waves."

She realized how tightly she was grasping the scoot's handlebar by how badly her forearm ached.

But letting go didn't seem like a good idea.

If that was some kind of artificial control out there, what would happen to her if it abruptly stopped and she couldn't get out of the way fast enough?

"Okay, the water's getting higher, gaining enough volume to make a real wave. But now it's lowering again. Like whatever's keeping it from crashing back is adjusting for the continental shelf. Are you getting any kind of live feed on your end? I don't have anything that will record at this scale."

If Ris was either in his office or the primary monitoring room at the Planetary Science compound, he'd be in front of several full-sized comm screens, with at least one tied in to Sarkans 3's official channels.

"Getting the evacuation notice on all channels. Let me see if I can switch to the tourism stream. They might have left the observation cams on in all the... There! That's got to be from the observers, right overhead. The water looks half-frozen, like it could stop at any moment."

Lina heard an odd, churning roar then, as if the sound of a thousand waves had been captured, slowed down, and magnified.

And she caught a whiff of what smelled like the aftermath of a gigantic lightning strike. Her nose tingled with the strength of it.

"Almost back to the normal low-tide zone now," she said.

"Not much higher than a typical wave on a stormy day, but you're right. It looks almost like a model of a wave, or a drawing. It has a solid edge where it should be—"

Just then a deafening crack ripped through the air.

CHAPTER 3

LINA LET GO of the scoot's handlebar to cover one ear against the painfully loud noise.

The water's weird stasis broke, sending a big wave tumbling toward the boundary between the cliff and Scarlet Beach.

Thankfully no one still stood down there.

She and anyone left would have been dashed against the sharp rocks of the tidal pool, yes. And her sky-scoot might have taken a nasty tumble.

But the extraordinary disappearance of an unimaginable volume of water turning into what amounted to an oversized wave sneaking up during the wrong tidal phase made no sense at all.

"I'm guessing you saw that?" she said to Ris. "Kind of messy, but not what anyone would expect with that much water displaced."

The blare of a proximity warning made Lina jump.

She twisted the comm-stick closed without thinking, shoved it into her tunic pocket, and grabbed both handlebars.

One of the bright-orange observation scoots was barreling toward her, with several people aboard waving their arms.

She twisted the handlebars to jet forward and out of the way, thankfully at a different height than the rescue scoot. The tourists were a wide-eyed and open-mouthed blur knotted together in the middle of the flat cargo section.

Except for one.

A pink skinsuit stood out from everyone else's brown and gray and black.

The sensible woman gripped the scoot's railing, staring out toward the still-uneasy sea.

Catching sight of Lina watching, she smiled and shrugged, as if acknowledging she was stuck on a literal ship of fools.

"Lina?" a tinny voice cried from her own scoot's console. "What happened? Report at once!"

Lina smiled back, then toggled the scoot's microphone.

"I'm here. One of the observation ships suggested I get out of the way, so I did. I had to stow my comm-stick. Anything else on your side?"

"Not a damn thing. Looks like someone finally realized the observation feeds were still live. Now it's showing the coastal emergency message and nothing else. Wait, now I'm getting the 'report to authorities' message too, or at least the tourist feed is. You better do that yourself before someone decides to report you missing."

"I don't think I'll have to. Looks like all the planetary authorities are right here."

A swarm of gray official scoots converged on the beach from

all directions, their cargo areas enclosed unlike the others already crowded into the same space above the red cliffs.

A painfully loud voice tried to again drive Lina's eardrums into her skull.

"ALL NON-OFFICIAL VESSELS ARE DIRECTED TO LAND IMMEDIATELY AND AWAIT FURTHER INSTRUC-TION. REPEAT, ALL NON-OFFICIAL…"

Deciding Ris would be able to hear that, possibly over the open air if not through the comm connection, Lina scanned the beach for an open space.

Less debris and mess than she expected littered the area. Only a handful of good-sized logs and clumps of knotty seaweed in many bright colors, no worse than after an ordinary storm.

The road had fared much worse, with heavy drifts of red sand scooped up and left behind by the puzzling wave. Maintenance crews would have a time scraping that away and settling the pea-sized gravel back into a smooth, drivable surface.

Under the continued sonic assault from the dark gray scoots, she slowly descended into a relatively flat spot just inside the beach wall. It had trapped huge amounts of the smaller bits of sea debris as the water receded, leaving the roadside coated with muck.

More than Lina would have liked was half-rotted, and the reek of that combined with what she suspected were more than a few dead sea creatures set up an unpleasant atmosphere under the warming sun.

Just as she stepped off her scoot and tried to locate her tidal pool—hoping it hadn't been completely filled in with sand—a child's piercing voice managed to slice through the sudden silence as the official announcements stopped.

"Look, fishies! *So* many fishies!"

The little girl was on the road side of the wall, jumping light-gravity high and pointing at the ground. Her kid-baggy blue-and-green skinsuit showed bulges that had to be grav-pac boosters, which made perfect sense if she'd been with the climbing group.

She looked to be about nine at the oldest, and black curls that were surely a nightmare to untangle bounced around her shoulders. Even from a distance, Lina saw bright blue eyes and a sweet face wreathed in a round-cheeked grin.

The rescue scoot had landed not far from Lina, and now the group of milling tourists gladly seized on the focus the girl provided by swarming toward her, babbling excitedly.

"They don't seem to have a clue how lucky they are to be above water and breathing."

Lina turned and found herself nearly face-to-face with the woman in pink.

Her light-brown arms were crossed, and curiously pale green eyes watched the group as they gathered to peer at the road.

Unlike most of the rest of her group, she wore a sensible pack like Lina's, and her belt was stocked with binocs, water-grip gloves, and a short-term rebreather. She sounded like she'd learned Terran Standard as an adult, but her words were clear and easy to understand.

"I expect most of them would rather not know," Lina said. "But we really should give them a little direction about what to do with the fishies. I'm Lina Rundgroff, with Planetary Science."

The woman laughed and nodded.

"Yes, the fishies are certainly in need of rescuing, in more ways than one. I'm Tes Gannison, one of Sarkans 3's overwhelmed and overworked tour guides. We can recruit darling little Musa to help, since she's by far the best of this bunch when it comes to following directions. Her grandparents are sweethearts, too."

The two of them—with Musa's enthusiastic help—got the tourists to stop holding up the gasping sea creatures to admire and photograph them and instead start carrying them down to the beach.

Which had resumed its normal ebb and flow as if nothing had happened.

Lina was about to offer to help Tes get the group rounded up when a frowning security official pulled her aside. She'd obviously come from the cooler zone around the spaceport on Mount Bewaker going by the long-sleeved jacket and long pants the same dark gray as their scoots, and the beads of sweat rolling down her pale, angular face.

A patch on the chest proclaimed she was Agent Manhoff, but Lina wasn't about to presume they were on casual terms.

"Your name and planetary authorization?"

Lina grunted, surprised and dismayed that she'd forgotten to report in. At least a solid hour must have passed since she started doing her part to prevent a mass-die-off of creatures caught on the wrong side of what seemed to be an unnatural tidal wave.

"Lina Rundgroff. You can contact my supervisor in Planetary Science to confirm—"

"That's not my job, is it? You were told to report immediately along with everyone else on the planet. Explain your delay."

Tes spoke from behind the official, smiling at Lina.

"Lina was helping keep this tourist group calm, Agent Manhoff, and got us all organized to save..."

Agent Manhoff closed her blue eyes and slowly turned to face Tes.

"And your name is?"

"Tes Gannison. I reported in immediately, and called in the rescue scoot."

The tight line of Agent Manhoff's shoulders relaxed, and some of Lina's tension drained away.

"The tour guide," Agent Manhoff said. "You were the first to report in, and you probably saved lives even if the big wave never quite materialized. Not that anyone on this overly *relaxed* planet seems to know why."

Tes slowly walked toward Lina, and Agent Manhoff obligingly turned to keep them both in sight.

"Then it's good we had someone in Planetary Science here the whole time," Tes said. "That's where the answers will come from. I never would have gotten anyone to move if it weren't for Lina raising the alarm."

Lina shook her head, but before she could remind them she was *biology*, not weather or geology, Agent Manhoff armed sweat off her face.

"I know that's vital to both of you, and I'm sure you'll figure it out. But I'm a lot more worried about finding the murderer."

CHAPTER 4

At the word *MURDERER*, chills ran down Lina's arms and back, uncomfortable in the hot sun.

That was one of the big selling points for Sarkans 3 as a research posting. No crime to speak of, and no murders since settlement.

The safety of the planet was an even bigger selling point for tourism, so it was no wonder Tes paled under her tan.

"What happened?" she said.

Agent Manhoff shook her head, then glanced around. Several other gray-jacketed people were talking to the rest of the tourists several meters away.

"This isn't to be shared around," she said, "especially not with the tourist-types. They don't understand what it's like to live here full-time, and I doubt they'll care once they leave. We wouldn't have come down here for the wave, strange as it was. You saw how fast the rescue scoot got here, partly thanks to the quick call."

After another scan of the beach, she stepped closer and lowered her already quiet voice, enough so Lina had to strain to hear her over the ordinary low roar of the tide coming in.

"The real reason we wouldn't bother with coming down here after a wave like that is the system performed the way it was supposed to." She held up one hand, apparently noticing the inner wave of disbelief that crashed through Lina's mind.

"Even in your lines of work," she went on, "you have no idea what we've put into place to make Sarkans 3 safe. Predictable, even. We have no idea what caused the initial event, and you better believe that's one of our priorities. I'm not alone in arguing that people who live here permanently should know more about how the planet runs, but we're not there yet. So I'll just tell you one of the safeguards performed its first true test today. And it performed flawlessly."

Remembering how the massive potential tsunami had seemed slow, controlled somehow, as it made its way to shore, Lina couldn't argue that something had worked. With her mind teeming with questions Agent Manhoff didn't seem inclined to answer right now, she fell back to one thing she could focus on.

"Did you say figuring out what caused the event is only *one* of your priorities?"

Tes spoke a beat later, and she sounded every bit as breathless and surprised as Lina.

"Exactly what is your job, Agent Manhoff? Assuming you can tell a lowly tour guide, of course."

"My job is to help maintain our high standards of planetary safety and security," Agent Manhoff said with a tight smile. "Same as anyone in Planetary Security. Sarkans 3 isn't your typical leisure world. Most people don't know that, not even people who vacation here, or live here. But many people who couldn't safely travel anywhere else come here *because* of our high standards. Besides tidal control, there's more protection here that you don't see than you do."

She put her hands on her hips and stared down at the red and silver sand before looking up, her face hard and set.

"So you can imagine the uproar when a dead body turned up in one of the arrival scoots that returned itself to the spaceport. While almost everyone on Sarkans 3 was focused on that blasted wave."

This time Lina's stomach knotted to go with the chills.

She'd been delighted to step into one of the gaily decorated arrival scoots right after she'd arrived at the spaceport. Rather than the single colors of the ones around her now, these were painted with vivid scenes from around Sarkans 3, and often draped with items from close by.

Hers wasn't much bigger than the scoot she used for work, with room for her to sit on a proper bench and space for her luggage. Strings of flowers and seashells had drawn her right to it. All she'd had to do was tap her comm-stick against the smooth panel in front of the bench, and the scoot had delivered her to the Planetary Science compound she'd be calling both work and home.

Others were large enough to handle a group as big as Tes's, including their luggage.

Once their living cargo was safely deposited, the arrival scoots took themselves back to the spaceport. All so much safer —and more secure—than letting new arrivals fly themselves in unfamiliar gravity on a brand-new planet after a long journey.

The idea of a dead body was bad enough. But having it

anonymously dumped in one of the cheerful scoots was somehow worse.

"You're sure it wasn't natural causes?" Tes said. "Or some kind of accident?"

Agent Manhoff shook her head again.

"I know the guides don't want news of an actual murder out any more than we do, Ms. Gannison. But there was nothing natural about the way the body was shoved into the cargo hold of that scoot. Or the shape the body was in."

Lina hated to bring up another horrible idea, but she had to.

"Any way it could have been some kind of wildlife? I'm not an expert on land animals, but I've heard there are a handful of forest and mountain predators here that rival our particularly nasty deep-sea beasts."

Agent Manhoff managed a sickly smile.

"I appreciate what you're both trying to do. But I'm not aware of any wildlife that enthusiastically uses a knife, are you?"

"So you don't..." Tes started, then paused for a deep breath. "Do you know who the victim was?"

"I wish I could refuse to tell you because it's secret. But at the moment, we honestly don't know."

Lina covered her mouth, willing her active imagination not to venture down that grisly road. Because then she'd have to wonder how even the smallest, most-altered remains could be unidentifiable with so many bioscans and registries for everyone on the planet.

"Could you at least tell where the scoot came from?" she said.

Agent Manhoff scowled in the general direction of Mount Bewaker.

"That's the real trick whoever did this pulled off. Every vessel on this planet, no matter how small, has a tracking beacon for travel, and an emergency beacon in case it crashes. They're supposed to be impossible to disable or interfere with. This scoot was somehow modified so both of its beacons dropped off the networks."

She turned back to Lina.

"It delivered an arriving tourist to one of the lodges near here and took off again, empty. On course to return to the spaceport. Then it vanished from all tracking until it arrived with a dead body aboard. The beacon didn't switch back on until it landed."

"And the tourist it delivered?" Tes said. "They've been questioned?"

"That's happening right now," Agent Manhoff said. "But before you ask, there are no indications they were involved."

Lina watched one of the rescue scoots slowly rise past the scarlet cliffs before it drifted off along the coastline.

"Don't we need to warn the tourists and the residents about the murder, and that scoots can be hijacked?"

"None of that is general knowledge yet," Agent Manhoff said, "and some of it might not ever be. The official line from Planetary Security is we know what to watch for now, and that's enough. Part of our job, they say, is to keep a panic from starting. Not to create one all by ourselves."

Lina got the strong impression Agent Manhoff didn't agree with one word of that official line, but didn't quite believe she could deviate from it. Her sour smile before she went on only added to that idea.

"I told you because I want people who understand what an unusual society we have here to know what's going on. And you both meet new people all the time, see how they interact, what they say and do. They're much more likely to talk about things—to even directly *tell* you things—they'd never say around a security agent."

An orange light flashed in Agent Manhoff's hip pocket, and she pulled out a thicker version of a comm-stick. She only held it while she stared at Lina, then Tes.

"The truth is we *were* ready for a tidal event, even one with no warning. But we've been so focused on making sure crimes like this can't happen that we're not all that well-prepared now that it has. If either of you sees or hears anything..."

"We will," Lina said, surprised at herself for answering for Tes. "I hope it gets sorted out fast."

Tes gave Lina an odd look before nodding.

"You know at least as well as I do how strict the background information requirements are for all of our tour groups. Sounds like you probably know more about them than we do before they ever get to the spaceport. But if anything unusual shows up, I'll make sure you know about it."

"That's all anyone could ask."

Agent Manhoff turned and walked away, unfolded comm-stick in hand.

Lina's chills finally got big enough to result in a shiver.

"You okay?" Tes said. "I've got jackets and robes on the scoot for the tourists who aren't ready for the conditions."

"I'm okay, thank you. It's going to take me a while to adjust to the idea of controlled tides. Last I heard, that was only experimental on unoccupied planets. I had no idea any systems were deployed around human colonies."

She rubbed her arms, only then noticing she'd shattered the

screen on her wrist-comm at some point. It hardly seemed worth replacing with such limited capabilities.

"And honestly," she went on, "I truly hate the idea of a murderer running around loose on Sarkans 3. I took one of those arrival scoots myself only a couple of months ago. Alone."

Tes watched Agent Manhoff rejoin her group near the big security scoot.

"I'm not thrilled about that myself. Listen, I can usually get a pretty clear report from weather operations since we have to be so sure of conditions for our tours. Though as it turns out, I guess we were a little too worried about high tides or sneaker waves. Think you can get the same from geology or whoever might be investigating that initial wave?"

Lina held her breath for a few seconds, willing visions of herself stepping out of the scoot on her arrival day and coming face-to-face with someone with a knife to dissipate.

"I hope to get myself on the investigating team since I was right here when it happened. Think you'll have time to compare notes once your group settles in for the night?"

Tes smiled and waved a hand at the tourists, now gathering around the rescue scoot.

"They'll be off my hands as soon as I call in our regular transport scoot to take them back to their resort. And after I talk to them long enough to see if anyone might have any idea what happened out there today. Hopefully we can get their climb rescheduled, but they're generally booked nearly solid, so it won't be for a few days. Are you going back to your work site once all the furor dies down?"

Lina looked out toward the beach, where what looked like thousands of footprints now marked the scarlet sand. They'd saved dozens of fishies and other sea creatures that would still be there to discover and research another day.

But her tidal pool was nowhere to be seen in the otherwise flat expanse.

"Not here, at least not for a while. I figure it will eventually drain out again. Until then, or until I get another site approved, I'll have time on my hands, too."

CHAPTER 5

Lina welcomed the chance to get back out into the field the next morning, especially since she was cleared to take one of the bigger research scoot-boats that were normally reserved for senior biologists.

She'd spent most of a long afternoon and early evening worried about being grounded and confined to the important but relatively dull Planetary Science compound for days, if not weeks, after such a bizarre event.

Her idea about having the advantage because she'd been a witness to the wave and its aftermath turned out to be true. As did Tes's expectation of having downtime away from her herd of climbing tourists.

So the two of them met the dawn already settled on calm waters several kilometers out from Scarlet Beach, with a pale-blue sky overhead and clouds around the horizon that promised cooler conditions.

The sparkling-green vessel itself looked more like the boat

side of its function, with a seating area protected by a curving glass screen and a waist-high wall around the cargo area. Most sky-scoots moved and maneuvered too slowly to worry about that much wind protection or keeping things from falling overboard, but the ability to travel at much higher speeds through salty water changed the safety requirements.

A far-larger control console than Lina was used to operating took up the front section, giving her access to an array of information she had to force herself to look away from.

None of her weeks of training on the water had included watching live-updating images of the ocean floor, current and water temperature fluctuations to a nearly microscopic degree, and instant identification of known life forms under the surface, not to mention the positions of almost every other watercraft, sky-scoot, and satellite.

The idea of eventually helping fill in the blanks for all the *un*known creatures in the seas of Sarkans 3 that only showed up as generally fish-shaped blobs and congregations of dots gave her a quiet thrill that once again let her know she'd chosen the right profession.

The back section of the scoot was huge, with more than enough room for several divers and their gear if they'd been available. As it was, even the impressive baskets of food Tes had brought were dwarfed by the space.

Lina matched the coordinates on her comm-stick and compared them to what the scoot reported, verifying that they were as close to the start of the rogue wave yesterday as technology could get them.

"Not that I'm complaining, but tell me why we have enough to feed a crew of ten?" she said, walking toward the back. "Was this meant for a tour group that canceled because of the wave or something like that?"

Tes abandoned her own seat at the front and followed. Today she wore a loose sea-green tunic over a matching skinsuit rather the vibrant pink she chose when she was working. She rolled her eyes and lifted the woven-grass lid of the smallest basket.

"Not exactly. None of the tourists insisted on changing plans today, not when no one was hurt. That they know of, anyway. These feasts before us were gifts from all the tour companies on the planet, even the ones I've never worked for. I suspect a few security organizations that Agent Manhoff would be familiar with contributed as well."

Inside the basket was a mouthwatering selection of colorful fruit Lina recognized from Sarkans 3, perfectly fresh and ripe, and several that she knew had to have been brought from other worlds at staggering expense.

Besides the amazingly fragrant fruit, she saw freshly baked breads, containers of cereals full of exotic super-nutri grains, and individual glass jars full of juice, several kinds of milk, and more kinds of sweeteners and spreads than she would have guessed existed.

She selected a plump, green-skinned sphere that smelled sharp and sweet and earthy at the same time, to go with a fist-sized roll that was still crisp and warm from the oven.

"From the reaction I got," she said, "I wouldn't be surprised if a planetary government or two was involved. Ris, my supervisor, just about fell out of his chair when I told him we'd spoken to a member of security from the spaceport."

Tes grabbed a covered bowl of what looked like mossy green

rocks, but when she added a sprinkle of fizzy black liquid to it, they expanded into soft noodle-like shapes.

"Was he in on all the secrets about this place? About security and tidal control and all?"

"He knew a hell of a lot more than I did," Lina said. "And I got the feeling he was glad I was willing to get involved in the investigation so he wouldn't have to. After he cleared my credentials for higher-level access—which *he* insisted upon doing, not me—he told me the basics of the tidal control for the planet."

She bit into her fruit, sighing at the succulent golden flesh that was as full of stimulating compounds as the strongest old Terran coffee or tea brew.

"The secret is the control units all along the seabed, and they've been there for decades. That was one of the first things the original planetary developers did. Anchor and activate safeguards for the water. Ris says they work by using hydrostatic tension to hold the water molecules together until it's safe. Which is entirely outside of my area of expertise, and his too, even if he wouldn't admit it. But neither of us can argue with what happened yesterday."

"Wow. Between that and the way Agent Manhoff was talking, we may have been blissfully ignorant of how important this watery rock truly is. Wonder how much we don't know."

Lina nibbled her roll, smiling at the crispy exterior and fluffy interior and the rich, nutty flavor.

"Probably plenty we'll never find out if security has their way. But for now, we're supposed to try to work out what happened out here yesterday. Before you ask, no, I haven't heard a word about the murder from anyone besides Agent Manhoff."

Lina wished she hadn't spent so much time contemplating that herself every time she turned over during the night.

"It's like it didn't happen," she went on, "even at a public spot like the spaceport, which makes the kind of control they have over Sarkans 3 even scarier. No hints on who it was yet or a motive, either. As far as what *we* might be able to help with, I'm not really sure where we should start."

Tes paused with one of her breakfast noodles held between a pair of silvery chopsticks halfway to her mouth.

"I haven't heard another word about that either, even with such a gossipy and generally paranoid bunch as tourists and their guides can be. I'm not sure whether to be reassured by what Planetary Security can do, or convinced that I'm nowhere near paranoid enough myself. Okay then, what could have set off a wave like that? Natural or...assisted."

"An earthquake is most likely," Lina said, "or some kind of major storm. Possibly a meteor impact. And we have confirmation from planetary authorities that none of that happened yesterday. So unless Sarkans 3 has somehow exempted itself from the ordinary laws of geology and physics, that leaves us with something assisted, as you say."

Lina waved one arm in the general direction of Mount Bewaker, where Agent Manhoff and everyone else in security worked to keep their spaceport and the rest of the planet safe.

And apparently kept plenty of secrets while they were at it.

"The spaceport's data that I've seen doesn't show any unusual flights, and that's with tracking every vessel down to the very smallest ones. My little sky-scoot is tracked through the satellite surveillance network, and the rescue scoot you called yesterday is, too. Pretty much the only thing that won't show up on the regular tracking maps is something as tiny as a personal waterski scoot or a foot-powered cycle. Even those have emergency beacons in case they crash."

Tes grabbed a sealed glass bottle full of brown liquid that had to be a brew made from ancient Earth coffee beans as she walked back toward the front of the scoot.

"Doesn't this thing have finer sensor devices? If it can see fish, surely it can detect any kind of vessels."

"Sure," Lina said. "The first problem is the sensors point in the wrong direction unless we reconfigure everything. Toward the water, or under it. Changing that would mean basically turning the scoot upside down. The second is no surveillance or weather scoots were out here yesterday until after the water started to recede. No reason to be. It seemed like a typical lovely day."

"And the observation scoots? The ones that were broadcasting the feed from overhead?"

"The trick with those is they're more-or-less automated. They keep an eye on the water, the weather, interesting wildlife nesting areas on land. Everything gauged to build up interest for potential tourists, and apparently people who want to vacation somewhere incredibly secure but still interesting. I'm sure you know more about how they're supposed to be used than I do."

Tes snorted and rolled her eyes as she walked back toward the baskets. She returned with two handfuls of sparkling golden orbs Lina had never seen before.

Besides packing a massive amount of smooth, rich, barely sweet flavor, each bite of the bizarre fruit left her feeling calmer and more relaxed, but still alert.

"Yeah, sadly I do know what those scoot vids are like," Tes

said. "Those damn things have a way of finding the areas of Sarkans 3 that are difficult to access to say the least. And once we get there, having a group of tourists makes them too crowded to be safe, or chases away the animals we're there to see. That or the specific weather conditions they're after are so rare we'll never manage to catch it on purpose."

"And again," Lina said, "nothing all that interesting was supposed to be happening yesterday, or at least nothing worth sending one of the observation scoots out on a new course. We learned in training that only one person in Planetary Science has been relieved from duty so far in the seventeen years of human settlement here, and that was for trying to tamper with an autonomous observation scoot. That violation is taken very seriously, because like we saw yesterday, those might need to be deployed anywhere on the planet."

Tes popped the last golden fruit into her mouth and ran her fingertips over the complex set of controls for the scoot.

"So we're out here on an impossible mission is what you're telling me."

"Not impossible," Lina said. "But I'll give you improbable. My plan is to test for different types of energetic fallout to see if maybe a bomb was detonated, or maybe a ship we're not familiar with was involved. I'm told it's quite the long shot by people who don't have any better ideas."

Tes rubbed her hands together and grinned.

"Sounds like fun to me! The tourists seem to get excited about our little outings, but the truth is they all seem to want to go to the same places and do the same things. You don't have to ask me twice when it comes to something new."

CHAPTER 6

Lina grinned back at Tes and reached under her seat. She brought out a bulky steel case that had required signing a dizzying number of digital forms before she left Ris's office late the night before and finally headed back to her cozy cottage for a restless attempt at sleep.

As annoyed as she'd been at all the bureaucracy, the chance to try out advanced tech out on the open water on a beautiful day more than made up for it. And finding a companion who might be even more enthusiastic was a stroke of good luck she wasn't about to ignore.

"Believe it or not, there are sensors that aren't built into this beast of a scoot. Ris had these sent over from the spaceport security group. From the way he talked about the conditions he had to agree to, it might have been easier if we'd asked Agent Manhoff for help."

She held her palm flat against the center of the case, then tapped a code sequence into the same spot. With a whirring noise and a ripple of blue light, the top section of the case popped open.

Inside was a collection of bright yellow balls of various sizes, all of them sleek and reflective for now. Along the back section of the case, several folded handles they wouldn't be using today waited for missions on foot.

"What *are* these?" Tes started to reach into the case, then drew her hand back. "They look like the bombs you were talking to me about."

"Not quite, but I'm sure someone in security could manage it. Or the people they're on the watch for could. They're energy sensors designed for use at crime scenes, basically. There's another case full of little hoverpods, kind of like tiny scoots that operate by remote control. Apparently they're often deployed in situations too risky for people."

"Are they safe for us to touch?"

Lina nodded as she picked up one that fit into the palm of her hand.

"All they do is receive. They're inert right now, but they're programmed to detect those energies I was talking about. Thankfully they were programmed before we got them, because I'd have no idea how to even start doing that."

Tes picked up a handful of much smaller spheres.

"Me neither. Do we just throw them in?"

"At first," Lina said. "Some of the bigger ones are designed to pick up a wide range of energy signatures that aren't safe for people. I'm not thrilled something like that could already have been in the water for so many hours affecting sea life, so I hope we don't find anything. Once we get data from those, we can switch to the more precise units."

Tes shot her a cocky smirk.

"And you know how to do all of this?"

Lina laughed with her, and the companionable pleasure of it shifted a good bit of her worry toward excitement. She'd worked and studied so hard for so long that even a work assignment with a different rhythm felt like a vacation.

"Only because I got detailed instructions from security. That and a long and even more detailed explanation from Ris about exactly what will happen if I lose or damage any security assets. I'm not sure whether he was including me in that list of assets or not."

Tes held one of the spheres up, turning it so it sparkled in the sun.

"If he's anything like my supervisor, he probably considers you a Planetary Science asset no matter what you're working on. I got an earful from the tour company before they let me head out, too. So if the big ones come back as safe, do we get to put the rest in the water ourselves? As in go for a swim?"

Lina flattened her comm-stick so she could review those directions.

"We do get to go for a swim if all is clear. But not quite like that. Are you comfortable using a breathing apparatus in case we need to dive?"

Tes grinned like Musa, the little girl with the fishies on the beach the day before.

"I haven't for a while, not since I got into climbing. But every tour guide learns how to work in every kind of terrain on the planet. I'd love a refresher."

"I actually haven't gotten to dive since I got to Sarkans 3," Lina said. "So here's hoping for that all-clear."

Deploying the sensors was easy enough that Lina read the instructions several times, wondering why Ris had seemed so anxious. It came down to selecting one of the largest balls—almost as large as her head—before activating a control unit hidden in the open lid of the case.

A few quick taps to activate it sent a ripple of colors across the ball's surface, revealing finer-than-hair circuitry she hadn't noticed before.

The sensor didn't *hum*, exactly, but it did feel like it exuded a fine layer of static against her hand.

"That's it?" Tes said, reading over her shoulder. "You just throw it in the water now?"

"That's what it says. I'd say more drop it over the side since we're already in the right spot. Why don't you do that and I'll watch the results?"

Tes's eyes widened, and she took the ball right away.

"Feels like it wants to get into the water as much as I do. Here goes."

She dropped the sphere over the side, then giggled and dashed back to peer at the readout.

The static text disappeared, and a list of words and phrases popped up. They ranged from green to yellow to red, and the status lines rising and falling beside them matched. Lina recognized notations for several biohazards, like toxic algae or poisonous bacteria, to go with ordinary compounds and creatures.

She'd have to look up the rest if they showed up in the results.

"No serious problems from our side of the equation so far," she said. "But that's only reading on the surface. Now the sensor should submerge itself and check all the way to the ocean floor. It's not terribly deep here."

Tes scurried over to the side of the scoot and back.

"I saw it drop out of sight. This won't show what we're looking for, right? Only whether it's safe to get in?"

"Exactly. We can drop the smaller ones in first, since those are specialized instead of checking across a broad spectrum like the big one. If those find a source and we can't see it, then we'll get to chase it."

The shifting lines on the display finally stabilized, and a bright green line appeared across the list.

"Not one thing that should keep us from going in," Lina went on. "Just what I expected in these waters, but now we know for sure. Let's get these others out there and on the job."

CHAPTER 7

THIS TIME, Lina and Tes only had to drop a few handfuls of the smallest sensors overboard, where they bobbed for a few seconds, then disappeared.

The case's screen cleared yet again before showing another stream of words Lina didn't recognize. Rather than progress lines, what looked like a simple on or off appeared beside each.

Most of the indicators switched to green at once.

But one stubbornly flipped to red and stayed there.

"Look, there *is* something," Tes said, pointing. "Some kind of...drive exhaust emission? What could cause that out here?"

Excited as she was by finding something so quickly, a surge of doubt made Lina wish someone from security was out here with them after all.

"I think that's from a grav-drive. The kind that gets the big interstellar vessels to Sarkans 3 and everywhere else in the galaxy so quickly. But we're a hell of a long way from the spaceport out here."

Tes had her comm-stick out and tapped a search before Lina could manage.

"That's what I'm seeing. That kind of emission doesn't even happen around the spaceport, though. Because the landing and launch areas are shielded. You don't think one of those is... I don't know, lost out here or something?"

Lina shook her head slowly.

In her mind, she was already dropping over the edge into the water.

But she wanted to make absolutely sure this was safe.

"I'm not about to guess on that one. But I know who we can talk to before we take a chance on getting closer."

She crossed the deck and got behind the big control panel for the scoot. Even though she had Agent Manhoff's code stored in her comm-stick, she wanted the bigger screen for this.

Tes had barely settled beside her when Agent Manhoff's serious face appeared on the screen. She was indoors, with a cool blue light somewhere over her head.

"Got something?"

"I think we might," Lina said. "We're out in the open ocean where the wave started yesterday. This doesn't make sense, but we just detected grav-drive energy emission."

Agent Manhoff scowled and shook her head.

"That's not on any flight path, and even if it was, no emissions would be present. You didn't get any other unusual compounds out there? Something to indicate a ship might have crashed?"

Tes glanced at Lina, who nodded for her to go ahead.

"This is the only thing that the sensor's detected," Tes said. "Is it safe for us to go in the water to pinpoint the source?"

"The source couldn't *be* anything but a grav-drive," Agent Manhoff said. "And I'm sure we would have noticed if a ship big enough to have one of those went missing. Any vessel that crashed would be sending out an emergency beacon signal. Any registered ship, anyway."

"Could an unregistered ship have a grav-drive?" Lina said. "Maybe one that's small enough to slip through your detection?"

Agent Manhoff's eyes went unfocused for several seconds, and Lina managed to keep herself quiet.

"It seems unlikely," Agent Manhoff said. "But I'm not willing to say it's impossible. There's an outside chance it could be a crashed ship if it was small enough to slip past us. No one would make a ship that small for interstellar travel, though. It simply doesn't make sense."

Tes winked at Lina, then repeated her question.

"Is it safe for us to get in the water here to see what we can find? There are a bunch of lifeforms concentrated in the same area, both known and unknown to the sensors, so this kind of problem could easily work its way up the food chain over time."

Agent Manhoff blew out a breath with her cheeks puffed up.

"That kind of exhaust has never been shown to affect humans, no. Not that we've tested getting into water with it. I'd be a lot more worried about trees and other life forms that build up layers of their dead cells instead of shedding them, so considering the food chain does make sense."

"But not our nails or hair?" Lina said.

"Not as far as we can tell. Or at least the levels are so small they're not detectible, probably because those grow a lot faster than trees do. Grav-drives have been in use for a few hundred years already. You know better than I do, Lina, that problems in humans or other lifeforms would have shown up before now. You probably know the kinds of sea life that would be in a lot more danger than you are if what you're thinking is true."

Lina nodded. "Anything that grows a shell. Especially things that someone might end up eating later on. Can I send you the energy signature? Is that something you can investigate to see if a ship might have been in the wrong place yesterday?"

Agent Manhoff's brows drew down, but she didn't quite frown.

"That all depends on how big the drive was. Something unregistered that's strong enough to cause a wave to form like that should have caught our attention before now. On the other hand, if there *is* a ship like that loose on Sarkans 3, I damn sure want to know about it. You do your dive, and get out of that water as fast as you can, just in case. Send me that signature and I'll see what I can find out."

The screen switched back to the usual readings of current, depth, and creatures under the scoot. Despite her lingering unease, Lina smiled at the brand-new dots pinpointing the sensors they'd deployed.

The sprawling concentration of sea life still surrounded the problem sensor.

"What do you think, Tes? Low risk isn't no risk."

"You're talking to a tour guide who takes a different, usually inexperienced group climbing up a different steep rock face every few days. Not to mention putting myself in the path of tourists who've decided I might want to *enhance* their experience during my off hours. I'm not exactly the right person to do a risk evaluation."

Lina sent the energy signature to Agent Manhoff, then smiled at Tes.

"I suppose someone who chooses to catalog new sea creatures on a planet where an impressive number of sea predators have already introduced themselves isn't the best either. So I say we jump in and see what we can find out."

CHAPTER 8

FOR SOMEONE who claimed to be hopelessly out of practice in the water, Tes took to it in a matter of minutes.

Lina had to remind her the trick of settling the slippery, transparent bubble of the diving mask over her head—covering her eyes, ears, nose, and mouth—by puffing out her cheeks to get a good seal. But after following that tiny hint, Tes dove neatly into the clear water with barely a ripple.

Lina could see her swim down with easy strokes, hesitate long enough to look around, and flip herself back toward the surface. By the time Tes popped back up, shoulders and chest free of the water, Lina floated beside her.

The water was pleasantly warm and silky against her skin, with more buoyancy than usual because of higher salt content.

All of Sarkans 3 seemed determined to make things easy for human visitors, or to at least make things *seem* easy.

That was the real risk, of course, and the real struggle.

It was far too easy to forget how that ease still masked the same dangers if you weren't paying attention.

"Getting a good comm signal?" Lina said into her own bubble.

She only felt the soft outline of the super-flexible mask in a thin line where it contacted her skin. Everywhere else, all she felt was a slightly humid pocket of air.

"Clear as the open air." Tes's voice was a touch too loud, a typical problem with people who were used to speaking through regular comm-sticks.

"You can pretty much whisper with this setup." Lina's smile made the bubble flex, but it showed no signs of slipping loose. "They're coded together, so I'll still hear you even if we can't see each other."

"In other words, stop shouting. Sorry, I forgot about that part. How long will the air last with these?"

Lina shrugged, as if she didn't already know the exact capacity of the high-end models.

"We've easily got an hour as long as we don't get into heavy exertion. For swimming to the bottom, having a look around, and getting back to the boat, that's plenty of time. But no trying to race the big fish. No sign that any of the usual predators are hanging around in the bunches of unidentified creatures down there. Just the friendly ones."

"I'm not making any promises if a big fish dares me to race," Tes said. "But I'll do my best to behave."

Lina pulled a seaworthy comm stick out of her utility belt, where she'd also stowed an emergency beacon, a scarily sharp utility knife, protective gloves, and the biggest sample collection kit she could manage. Out of all the *just-in-cases* she'd clipped into place, she hoped only the last one saw any use.

After a few taps on the comm's waterproof surface, an echoing chime sounded in her ears. By the way Tes drew back and then smiled, the dual transmission was working.

"This beacon function is about as old-fashioned as it gets out here, besides dropping anchor. The closer we get to the sensor, the closer together the pings get. It should be glowing like crazy down there too. This water's shallow enough that darkness shouldn't be a problem, but don't forget you've got a chest lamp."

Tes pushed herself out of the water up to the waist and tapped the white square strapped just above her breasts.

"So between the two of us, we should be able to find the problem. I say we're ready to go, right?"

Lina laughed at Tes's enthusiasm and nodded.

"Willing to at least follow my lead? Not that I'm a dive expert."

"Lead away. From what I can tell, no one is a dive expert when it comes to looking for stray grav-drive emissions the day after a rogue wave that happened for no reason at all."

"We'll be the first. Let's go."

She ducked under the water, took a second to get her bearings, then dove toward the not-too-distant seafloor.

The water temperature changed in layers as she descended, growing gradually cooler. They'd never reach dangerously cold water in the tropical zone and at swimmable depths, but the adjustment felt great against her skin.

Swarms of brilliantly colored fish swirled and congregated around them, peering at the awkward human invaders with eyes of every shape and size. Lina hadn't yet had the chance to catalog many of her own discoveries, but immersing herself in a crowd ranging from barely larger than a grain of rice to approaching her own length only made her more determined.

One specimen that looked like a pink and green collection of scarves caught in a whirlpool seemed especially curious, flowing in circles around them.

"That's not one of the predators you mentioned?" Tes said.

"Not of us. But the tiniest critters should watch out. Since it's just the two of us, I'll admit it's kind of annoying to finally be getting out here and seeing new species, but I don't have the time or enough tools to properly record them."

"You'll get back to it sooner than you think. And *I* think I see our test site not far below. Can you tell what it's in the middle of, besides a bunch of fish?"

The pings had indeed gotten much closer together in Lina's ear, and she spotted the glow herself now. What looked like dozens of the scarf-like fish resolved into hundreds of smaller fish, all of them ignoring the bright white orb in their midst.

They gathered in an odd shape, as if they were following the contours of some kind of structure. It seemed too linear and angular to be natural, but Lina knew better than to make assumptions in such an uncharted sea.

"I can't tell yet," she said. "Not without getting closer. The scoot's sensors couldn't identify much down here besides realizing there are a bunch of living things. You doing okay?"

"You bet. I'm sure my arms and legs will be complaining tomorrow, but right now this feels fantastic."

"I wouldn't be surprised if you feel it in your abdomen and back more than anywhere else. Stay close in case one of those predators shows up. And before you ask, I have an alarm set back on the scoot to warn us in case one does."

When she was within a body length of the sensor—close enough to see light through the fins and even the bodies of the still-unconcerned fish—Lina slowed her strong kicking except to keep herself from floating back up.

What she glimpsed of the underlying shape through all the activity was even stranger close up. If she angled her face away from the sensor's light, it seemed to have a faint glow all its own.

"I'm going to deactivate the sensor so we can get a clearer look," she said. "So far no signs of a renegade grav-drive engine."

"I'll keep an eye out in case a star-faring fish cruises by in one."

The scarf-fish had apparently lost interest in the bizarre sight of humans swimming this deep, but now it swooped back in to investigate, scattering many of the smaller fish as it swam. Their bodies felt smooth against her body, and their feathery fins tickled.

But Lina hardly noticed, because even before she could deactivate the sensor's light, she got a sudden, clear idea of what was below them.

"I think it's a reef. A coral reef, but not like any I've ever seen or read about."

CHAPTER 9

Lina reached down carefully, sensor forgotten, mindful of the many varieties of coral that packed a sting in their tiny bodies.

The earliest surveys hadn't reported any terribly venomous lifeforms in this zone, but numb or agonized fingertips wouldn't exactly make their work more pleasant.

Besides, the number of fish brushing their bodies along the structure even now didn't seem to be reacting to anything.

When the fish moved away from one section, she finally got a clear view of what she thought she'd seen earlier.

"This is *angular*," she said. "Not curved like most organic forms. Everything is straight lines and right angles. Like an intelligence was at work rather than the reef growing on its own."

Tes reached out and gently touched another section of the reef.

"It's like tiny building blocks. A few minerals form like this, but I've never heard of anything in the water being that sharp-edged."

Lina shooed more fish away, wondering if the lines and boxes were only in a certain area of the reef.

No, everywhere she looked, she saw more evidence of unnaturally straight lines.

But pale, tiny creatures popped out of minuscule square depressions as her hand moved closer, then settled more deeply inside.

"It sure acts like an active coral reef. I'll have to get samples of these creatures analyzed to make sure, but this seems to be entirely natural. These might be all over the warm zones of Sarkans 3."

The line of barely visible individual constructions was formed out of perfect boxes, and when the reef shifted to grow over a rock, the adjustments up and down were an unmistakable stair-step effect. Even the sideways growths and adjustments showed a brick-like structure.

"Is this because of the grav-drive?" Tes said. "Or whatever reads as one down here?"

"I wouldn't think so. If anything, some kind of energy signature might make growth more chaotic. Like a honeybee without a queen. That's the lifeforms I know of, anyway. Things could be totally different here. But the basic way reefs work is they make those tiny hideaways and leave them behind. That's how the reef expands over time."

Tes's gasp was clear through the masks.

"So it could absorb the energy, just like Agent Manhoff said trees do. Something *is* down here, or something *was* down here."

Lina bought a little time by getting the boxy sample kit off her belt, then pulling out a small glass tube. She gently brushed a few of the tiny creatures inside before flipping the black stopper into place.

Then she carefully dug out several of the miniature boxes that certainly acted like coral with her utility knife, and popped them into a glass sample box.

All the ordinary activity keeping her hands occupied let her mind at least attempt to sort through what they were faced with.

"You're right, Tes. Whether this is coral or not, it has the same bonelike structure. So that means it could be holding what the energy source left behind. Or, the energy source could be close by."

After she re-stowed the sample kit, she tapped the comm again to verify what it and the scoot were reporting. She knew this was the only sensor that responded to the grav-drive, but she wasn't going to make assumptions with something this strange and possibly important.

"You don't see the same thing anywhere else, do you?" Tes said.

"No other sensor picked up the same energy signature, and this one hasn't changed its reading. Let's swim in a circle around this reef and check for signs of anything buried that doesn't look like it grew here. There aren't any wave-control pods showing up right here, otherwise the wave yesterday never would've stayed together long enough to build up like it did."

They swam to their left far enough to see the reef structure gradually flatten along the sea floor, then switched and went in the opposite direction, accompanied by a curious and energetic fishie escort the whole time.

A series of what looked like hundreds of tiny balconies built and stacked onto each other rose up at one point, the whole structure a few body lengths tall and almost as thick. At least a dozen creature-covered arms spread out from the central tower.

All of it with the distinctive right angles and straight lines that didn't much make sense where they were.

"It looks like a castle from a fairy tale," Tes said, letting herself drift higher toward the top of the tallest part. "How long did something like this take to grow?"

Lina waved her arms to keep herself from drifting too far up.

"Back on Earth or a typical watery world with coral? Thousands of years to get this big. The scale might be different here, but I doubt it would ever be a fast process."

"So either the energy got here recently," Tes said, "or whoever planted it here had a longer-term plan than I can imagine."

"And I don't see signs of anything like that. Besides this weird coral, everything else is perfectly ordinary ocean floor. But I've got another idea."

The two of them headed back to the still-glowing sensor, and Lina reached through dozens of almost perfectly round black fish to retrieve it.

"You're going to swim away to see if it stops responding?" Tes said.

"You got it. Then even if someone somehow managed to slip some kind of buried grav-drive underneath what has to be a very old reef, we'll at least know how far its influence reaches."

Lina wasn't surprised to see the sensor's light fade as they moved in a straight line away from the reef, then slowly get brighter when they returned. The alert perfectly followed the skeletal growth, even over the thinnest outliers.

"No doubt about what's triggering it," Tes said. "At least in this area. I don't suppose we have enough air to swim further out to see if anything else lights it up?"

Lina glanced at her comm, then out at the seafloor around them.

"Probably not. I don't see any big formations from here. I'd say we get back up to the scoot and start circling to see if anything like this shows up on the main sensors. It picked up a mass of some kind of lifeforms for this, but had no idea what was down here."

Tes grinned through her mask.

"There's one blank you're already filling in. Once you get this sample entered into planetwide systems, will they know how to find it everywhere?"

Lina blinked, struck by the idea that hadn't crossed her mind yet.

"You know, I think they will. That might help us locate a different reef so we can compare the two and see if the grav-drive energy is changing them. Hang on a second."

She swam back down to the reef, searching for a small piece she might be able to break off. She finally spotted an extension jutting out at a right angle from the main body over a rock. It was several layers thick, but not yet attached to anything underneath.

It took much more force than she expected, but she finally managed to jam the knife at the correct angle to pop the finger-length section loose. The still-glowing piece fit inside her sample box, but only just.

"Sorry about that," she said quietly, but Tes heard.

"Apologizing to the reef for knocking a chunk loose? Makes sense to me."

"Yeah, that and taking a bunch more of them away from home. This should have enough older growth on it to see how long ago the grav-drive exposure happened."

Tes swam down herself and examined the break.

"Looks like several layers to me. Also, fair warning, if word of this kind of formation gets out, you'll be overrun with tourists desperate to dive and capture the new discovery before anyone else does. Most of them only with photos, but we'd have to watch the souvenir scrapers constantly. So you better get it examined and sampled as quickly and quietly as you can."

"We'll head out as soon as I recall all the other sensors and we get them back into the scoot. I figure we might as well have lunch while we wait for them to surface. Diving's hungry work."

CHAPTER 10

Sitting in the darkened primary monitoring room in the Planetary Science compound might not seem anywhere near as exciting as diving or cataloging creatures on Scarlet Beach to one of the tourists, and on most days, Lina felt exactly the same.

The sprawling room was kept cool to accommodate the sometimes-large crowds of tourists attending educational presentations about sea and coastal life all over Sarkans 3, but the rows of tables and chairs were empty that afternoon. Rather than the headache-inducing mix of sweat and dueling perfumes that usually accompanied a large group, the only aroma was the earthy acidity of Old Earth-style coffee.

Pretty much the only thing her research supervisor Ris would drink when he was anxious, which he very much was right then.

And still, today, at that moment, there was nowhere else in the settled colonies that Lina wanted to be.

The chance to solve the mystery that only kept getting deeper was too tempting to resist.

Despite not expecting much luck, they'd spotted two more of the weirdly linear reef growths not far from the original. The tell-tale clump of lifeforms on the scoot's sensors led to deploying the spherical sensors again, but not more dives.

Both Lina and Tes agreed it was more important to get the samples analyzed quickly, no matter how tempting more time in the water might be.

Only one of the reefs showed weaker signs of grav-drive energy, but it was enough to create a rough map of where the strange phenomenon might have been centered.

In a straight line that perfectly matched the origins of the rogue wave from the day before.

The largest monitor in the facility—nearly twice as tall as her and several body lengths long—showed an amazingly detailed and moving map of the sea where she and Tes had been that morning.

The wandering, bright yellow path they'd taken in the scoot was vivid against the dark blue of water, and countless pink clouds showed all the lifeforms currently in the area.

A flashing red outline marked where the energy signature was strongest, which of course matched the newly discovered coral reef.

And pacing back and forth in front of the monitor, occasionally glaring at it as if he could bend cold reality to his will, was the reason for multiple silver mugs scattered all over the long demonstration desk at the front of the room.

In a state of agitation, Ris was in the odd habit of forgetting he already had coffee any time he stepped out of the monitoring room, then fetching himself another.

His wavy auburn hair stood up from constantly running his

fingers through it, and his Planetary-Science-blue shirt and pants were rumpled.

All the other women and men normally present in the facility had disappeared before Lina and Tes got there, apparently convinced Ris was on the verge of launching into some kind of screaming meltdown.

If their warning stories to Lina were only a little exaggerated, it wouldn't be the first time.

But she had a strong feeling his energetic response was more excitement than anger, at least today.

"And you didn't detect that energy signature anywhere else besides that reef?" he said for at least the third time.

Lina winked at Tes, who leaned against one of the exhbit tables and smiled, as she had been since Ris started his endless pacing. Lina's own excitement kept her from getting too terribly annoyed with the repetition.

"We didn't have the equipment to do a full survey," she said. "But none of the other reefs we located had that strong a response to the sensors. Agent Manhoff said grav-drive energy seems to accumulate in things like trees and—"

"Yes yes, and shells and such. I do wish this Agent Manhoff had been able to join us today to explain herself a bit more. But I appreciate you taking time away from your own duties, Ms. Gannison."

Tes shook her head and rolled her eyes, smiling at the same time.

"Please call me Tes. And I've been granted leave to help for as long as you and Lina need me. The Tourism Authority is extremely interested in understanding what happened yesterday. Probably almost as interested as Planetary Security."

Ris stopped in the middle of his route, turning to stare at Tes with his hands on his hips. For a moment, Lina was sure she was about to witness one of his rumored meltdowns after all.

Instead he rolled his eyes, then burst into great bellows of laughter.

"Oh I doubt that very much! Even if you had a hundred-thousand tourists clamoring for information and threatening to cancel their previous payments and future plans, I can't imagine every person in Tourism together creating as much noise and fury as *one* Planetary Security agent."

He wrapped his arms around his belly and kept laughing, leaving Tes and Lina exchanging an amused and somewhat puzzled glance. Breaking him out of his distracting rut had to be an improvement.

When he finally caught his breath, Ris stabbed toward the coral reef with one finger.

"And all that nonsense aside, I can't imagine all of them jammed into this room at once would be as delighted with your discovery as I am."

He walked toward the demonstration desk, still laughing under his breath, and tapped the control display for the big monitor. Rather than the sea map, it now showed a microscopic view of Lina's reef sample.

She was relieved he was too focused on other things to notice her blinking back quick tears at the unexpected praise.

Magnified hundreds of times, the coral sample looked even more like the basic structural elements used for human colonies all over the settled systems. Perfectly square walls, offset in rows like bricks, and broken neatly without damaging any of the sides.

"Extraordinary." Ris shook his head and grinned. "Such

microscopic creatures behaving like tiny engineers. I'd imagine the tower you described has incredible strength built right in. And you say the other reefs were built the same way?"

"I didn't say that," Lina said, "because we didn't dive in those areas, remember? We wanted to get these samples analyzed because of the planetary emergency yesterday. But I did map them. The coordinates will take you right to them."

Ris frowned, but only for a second.

"Well, we'll need to do that as soon as we can. Examine the other reefs. For now, I'll send this data to the lifeform identification system planetwide. That will get all the automated systems on Sarkans 3 started identifying where these amazing colonies are located."

"Will that work with the contamination?" Tes said. "From the grav-drive?"

Ris tapped a few more times, and two charts showing the molecular composition of the reef's tiny building blocks replaced the image. Several columns on the left image were higher than on the right, and outlined in yellow.

"The data on the left is from the outermost sample," he said. "Only their most recent layers were affected. And if you look at the older ones, there's no evidence of the energy signature at all. I'll send out both, assuming only the pure sample matches."

"And if the other one shows up," Lina said, "we'll know a lot more about what happened yesterday. If that contamination is commonplace, then something else was behind that wave."

Another voice joined in, with more than a touch of skepticism.

"I find that extremely unlikely."

CHAPTER 11

THEY ALL TURNED to see Agent Manhoff standing in the doorway, looking far more comfortable out of the bright, hot sunlight. Her gray jacket and pants were sharp and crisp rather than wilted by the heat of the beach.

Lina stepped forward before Ris could jump in and demand an explanation for Agent Manhoff's sudden appearance.

"You remember the Planetary Security agent I mentioned? Agent Manhoff, this is my Research Supervisor and Director of Planetary Science for the Vatten Continent, Ris Murray. We were just studying the results of the samples Tes and I collected today."

Agent Manhoff nodded to everyone, then focused on Lina. Behaving exactly the way Ris expected her to, in other words.

"The energy signature you sent me is definitely a grav-drive, but not any design I've ever seen or heard of. This makes no sense at all, but I don't think it would even function for space travel."

Tes stepped in with the practiced ease of someone who dealt with tourists all the time, especially those who hadn't quite recovered from their long journey to Sarkans 3.

"Would you like coffee, Agent Manhoff? Or something else to drink? We have plenty of food from this morning."

Agent Manhoff surprised everyone by smiling, and transforming her demeanor from cold and forbidding to simply grateful, at least for the moment.

"I'd love coffee, thank you. I could use it after the way we've been going nonstop. The two of you saved us a hell of a lot of time, not to mention having to find people with the skills who we could trust with this."

"I'm sure they did," Ris said, taking his chance to speak and waving his own coffee mug toward the screen.

He seemed to have gotten over his fear of Planetary Security.

"Lina and Tes discovering that coral reef is going to speed up the work for Planetary Science as well," he said. "Such an unusual lifeform can give us insight into whole ecosystems."

"How long will it take for the samples to integrate into the lifeforms systems?" Agent Manhoff said. "The more of these reefs we can locate, the easier it is for me to officially pinpoint the source of that wave."

"That all depends on how many sensor scoots are in the water." Ris tapped the display again with the hand that wasn't clutching his mug. "They'll get the updated information within an hour or so. Then it's simply a matter of new surveys taking place. Automated or manual."

Tes handed a silver mug to Agent Manhoff before turning back to the big monitor. It showed a rapid flow of text and symbols that Lina recognized as the update to the planet's life-forms database.

"Most of the tourist expedition scoots are equipped with those sensors," Tes said. "And all of the automated observation scoots are. If you want, I can expedite the message about new surveys so the priority can be shifted for all of them."

Agent Manhoff took a slow sip before responding.

"Getting a head start would be a tremendous help for me. I've got to convince a few of the windbags in security that we've not only got some kind of unreported ship on Sarkans 3, but that ship was quite likely the weapon used against us yesterday."

"But what *kind* of ship?" Lina said. "You said it didn't match anything that's supposed to be here."

Before Agent Manhoff could ask for the data, Ris pulled up the outline of the reefs again. When he pushed out the focus, the outlines of several scoots showed up in addition to the trace Lina and Tes had created that morning.

"I can show the same recording from yesterday," he said. "But I'm sure you've reviewed it already, just as I have. There was no *recorded* trace of a ship being in that area around the time the wave formed."

"We'll have to try to catch it to find out," Agent Manhoff said. "My guess is it's a relatively small ship to evade our sensors, but with an outsized engine to influence that much water. I still don't think it produces un*safe* levels of energy, at least not with normal use. The levels in your reef still aren't toxic to humans. But I'm not sure I'd recommend additional dives until we know more about it."

Lina forced herself not to argue about that. If the energy signature truly was centered on the one reef, and that's where the wave originated, there was no longer an urgent enough need for them to take the risk.

She didn't think Agent Manhoff was talking about danger from the reefs at all.

Agent Manhoff might have turned at least part of her considerable focus to the unidentified body from the spaceport without saying that out loud.

Or to the fact that killing one person at a time might be far too inefficient for the attackers.

"You think they might use it again," she said, staring at the map. "Maybe not there, but somewhere else. Near another vulnerable beach."

"Or a settlement," Ris said. Lina had never heard him sound so shaky.

Agent Manhoff shrugged. "It's possible. I doubt they'd go back to the same spot right away, especially once the lifeforms systems are updated. If they're clever enough to figure out a way to manipulate water on a planet with wave control, we can't assume they're not watching for a big change like that. But I still don't like the idea of someone underwater if they do it."

"I agree with you," Tes said. "But I have to warn you there's going to be resistance to that idea from Planetary Tourism. Thousands of people have dives planned over the next few days, and most of them are tightly scheduled enough during their time here that they can't delay. The howls about how far they've traveled only to have their vacations ruined would be deafening."

"Even if those dives might *kill* them?" Agent Manhoff snapped.

Before anyone could respond, she rubbed the bridge of her nose with her fingertips.

"No, I understand exactly what you're saying. Some of the people who visit Sarkans 3 are powerful enough that they're not used to having their plans disrupted by hours or minutes, much less denied altogether. Then there's the potentially disastrous publicity if any of this gets out. More attention than many of our guests care to risk."

Ris shook his head, and he looked genuinely mournful.

"I'm afraid it's already out. News of that rogue wave on a well-publicized climate-and-sea-controlled planet was never going to stay quiet for long. Sarkans 3 is supposed to serve as a model for other planetary systems considering using the technology. That wave's got scientists and governmental bodies alike worried. And then you have…"

He paled, and now seemed more stricken than upset.

Agent Manhoff put her empty coffee mug down, crossed her arms, and stepped toward Ris. She stood several inches taller, and right then, she looked about a thousand times more confident.

"And then we have what, exactly, Director Murray?"

CHAPTER 12

RIS MANAGED to rumple his hair even worse as he stared at the live map, then back at the control monitor. Agent Manhoff watched him without moving a single muscle.

He looked into Tes's eyes, then Lina's, clearly pleading for help neither of them was willing or able to offer, before finally answering.

"I'm sure someone in Planetary Security already knows about the absurd theories about this planet and why it's so secretive and difficult to get to. And expensive. Mostly nonsense about some kind of rare natural resource, like a revolutionary fuel source or communications enhancer. The usual rumors about miracle cures being hidden and such, too."

Agent Manhoff's long, slow inhale and exhale set her firmly back in her role as a sometimes-menacing member of Planetary Security.

"And all of those dangerous ideas are quickly debunked by Planetary Science, correct?"

"Of course they are." Ris waved one hand toward the monitor. "As soon as we're made aware of the problem. The difficulty is there are so many factors we don't hear about until the latest absurd theory has already taken hold. They're a lot harder to get rid of once they're established."

"Are you saying that kind of nonsense is flaring up again with the rogue wave?" Agent Manhoff said. "Have these fools decided we're trying to hide the true dangers of the planet? Or are you saying Planetary Science doesn't have enough influence to stop that kind of filth in its tracks?"

Ris looked gazes with her long enough that Lina couldn't stand the tension in the room any longer.

She might be overestimating her relationship with the security agent, but watching Ris and Agent Manhoff posturing over useless gossip wasn't going to help anyone.

"Excuse me for saying so, but isn't that what you just suggested, Agent Manhoff? In wanting to keep this quiet to prevent bad publicity? I'm not saying Tes's friends in tourism should include it in their next round of system-wide marketing, but trying to hide an event that hundreds of people experienced doesn't make sense."

As if they'd planned it beforehand, Tes stepped in with a soothing smile and comforting tone in her voice.

"Besides everyone on the beach yesterday, anyone who's affected by canceled water activities is going to know *something* happened. So, the faster we work together to figure out what that was and keep it from repeating, the better off all of us will be."

For a long several seconds, Lina thought both she and Tes had pushed too far. Agent Manhoff glared at each of them in turn, before turning her baleful stare back toward Ris.

To his credit, he raised his chin and stared right back.

Excitable as he could be, he cared deeply about Planetary Science and the work Lina and everyone else on the team did.

Agent Manhoff finally closed her eyes and nodded. When she opened them, she didn't exactly look happy, but she no longer seemed about to have the kind of fit of anger people warned Lina that Ris was capable of.

"Yes, we're all on the same side here," she said. "And none of us wants another incident. Do you have enough of your coral sample for me to take some back for analysis? I'd like to have a direct example of the energy signature we're dealing with."

Ris gave away how worried he'd been by nearly stumbling over himself to leave the room. And he actually gathered several of the half-empty coffee mugs as he went.

"Of course we do, and I'll go right now and get it for you. I'm sure having an analysis from a different perspective is a great idea in a case like this."

As soon as he was gone, Lina covered her mouth to keep from giggling out loud, and Tes didn't fare much better. Even Agent Manhoff pursed her lips, but she refused to laugh.

"I see your supervisor hasn't lost his healthy respect for Planetary Security," she said, raising one eyebrow.

"He lectured me within an inch of my life about taking out your sensors," Lina said. "We've got those ready if you need them back now."

"No, you might need them again. I doubt anyone would go to the trouble of creating a ship like the one we're looking for and only use it once. Far too much time and resources had to go into it for that."

Lina held her breath for a second, then plunged ahead with yesterday's horrible event that no one had mentioned yet.

"Any more information about what happened at the spaceport?"

Agent Manhoff's eyes shifted toward Lina while the rest of her stayed frozen.

"Nothing more than what I told you two yesterday. Which, as I said, is as far as this sort of information needs to go."

Tes spoke with an equally tight and controlled tone in her voice, and Lina couldn't help imagining how shocked her usual crowds of happy tourists would be to hear it.

"You'll notice neither of us mentioned it until we were alone, Agent Manhoff. And I'm sure *you'll* understand why Lina and I might be concerned about what happened."

Agent Manhoff nodded as her face softened into worry, and enough fear that Lina felt more afraid herself.

"I do understand. Even though some of my supervisory agents don't seem to have a grasp about how…overextended the rest of us are, trying to investigate both an unnatural tidal wave and an even more unnatural death."

She stared up at the ceiling, then slowly rotated her neck as if to ease tense muscles before turning back to Lina.

"If it eases your minds at all, the fact that we still haven't identified the victim makes it unlikely any residents or tourists will be targeted. But that doesn't mean I'm any less concerned about people swimming with the possibility of water manipulation on this scale. No matter how upset they might get at the *burden* of restricting their leisure activities."

"May I?" Tes pointed at the control display, waiting for Lina to nod. "I don't know where all the major water activities are planetwide tomorrow without looking it up, Agent Manhoff, but I can show you the main locations on this continent. If you *do* plan to suspend tourist events, it really would be best to give plenty of warning so those of us in tourism can make other suggestions."

As she tapped and adjusted the map view—bringing Scarlet Beach into the center before zooming out—Agent Manhoff reached for her comm-stick, which was flashing red instead of the yellow from the day before.

At the same time, the map whirled to another location on Sarkans 3. This one nowhere near the tropical zones around the equator or the coastal attractions on any continent.

The red and silver was replaced by stoney gray and stark white.

"Isn't that a long way north for water activities?" Lina said. "Looks more like a place for skiing or climbing."

Tes held up both hands and stepped back.

"That's not where I was aiming at all. Can Ris control the map from somewhere else in the compound?"

"Not Ris," Agent Manhoff said. "And the adjustment didn't come from here. It's another planetary emergency. This time it's not water, not like you're thinking. It's snow."

CHAPTER 13

By the time Ris made it back to the primary monitoring room, no one was especially interested in the rest of the coral samples, or even the mystery body from the spaceport.

The horrified look on his face made it clear he knew something had happened, if not what.

Agent Manhoff had taken over the controls to the big monitor without protest, zooming in to a single snowy mountain and the brown bulk of a good-sized building marked with the label *HIVERN*.

Across the bottom of the screen, words as frightening as the coastal emergency from the day before scrolled across.

Mountain Emergency!!! Repeat, Mountain Emergency!!!
Evacuate snow or ice regions immediately. Do not remain within any avalanche zone under any circumstances.
Call for rescue NOW if needed.
Extreme danger, probable loss of life and property.

The same warning flashed on Lina's comm, and Tes's a few seconds later.

"Do those lodges have big enough scoots to rescue people?" Lina said. "For everyone on the planet?"

Her winter sport and recreation experience was brief and limited to her childhood. Her own preference for water she could swim in rather than ski or skate across had taken hold quite early on.

Tes held one hand to her chest as she stared at the screen.

"I'm not sure, but I doubt it. The number of people in Hivern fluctuates too much with groups only there for the day. I've led ice climbs several times, but we've never needed a rescue. I'd never needed a water rescue before yesterday, either."

"The problem is getting a scoot into the area without disturbing whatever's controlling that snow," Agent Manhoff said, her face and voice grim. "Whether it's the same as what caused the wave or not, we have no idea what might tip the whole thing into motion."

The satellite view couldn't get the right angle to show the threat onscreen, and none of the observation scoots were transmitting, at least not to the public.

Planetary Security had apparently learned from the first attack, even if they still had no idea how to stop it.

But Agent Manhoff hadn't hesitated to share the information she was getting as the potential disaster unfolded.

"Has the avalanche moved at all?" Ris said. He sat in one of the usual tourist seats, elbows on the table, hands in his hair. The forgotten sample box waited in front of him along with a fresh mug of coffee.

"Not yet," Agent Manhoff said. "It's still…poised there above the lodge, a lot like the wave was out at sea."

"But the avalanche controls aren't meant to hold that much snow," Tes said. "Are they? I thought they were only supposed to stabilize the slope for a few hours until a team could get there to safely release it. Enough time for people to get out of the way, so even if they fail, no one will get hurt."

Agent Manhoff tapped the controls a few times, and the view on the big screen changed. Now they were seeing from ground level outside the lodge, from not far above a crowd of people.

All of them were dressed for the conditions, with heavy jackets and pants, most of them wearing gloves, hats, and scarves. Their breath rose in plumes before dissipating into what had to be well-below-freezing air.

The scene seemed fairly typical at first, with the ground covered with well-tracked snow, and all the trees and bushes in the area equally draped. At first glance, it looked like a marketing video for some kind of outdoor winter festival.

But rather than what should have been piercing-blue skies above a mountain close enough to fill the horizon, what looked like a churning white cloud hovered along the ridge line.

Not because specially equipped scoots were putting on some kind of snow show, or because a storm was rolling in, or even because an avalanche had recently been safely released.

The avalanche had been set off, all right, from that mountain and several others surrounding the lodge.

And as far as anyone knew, only the safety systems were keeping all of them from sweeping down and burying the lodge and everyone in and around it.

"That's how avalanche controls work, yes," Agent Manhoff

said in response to Tes's question. "They're only supposed to buy enough time for either safe evacuation or for a team to get in there and clear the snow load. They've never been tested in a situation like this. If the attackers *are* still controlling the snow, which seems likely with that much mass hanging suspended, they're controlling us, too."

"But *why?*" Lina said, gripping the edge of the desk. "And *who* is doing this?"

Agent Manhoff looked up and into her eyes.

"I'm sorry, Lina. So far we don't entirely understand *how* they're doing it. Until we figure that out or they decide to tell us, all we can do is try to get those people out of the fallout zone. Without setting off the avalanche ourselves."

While Lina watched, a bright-red scoot slowly approached over the crowd. For their part, they seemed convinced that the more they stayed quiet and still, the better their chances of surviving the day would be.

The only sound coming through the video feed was bursts of wind and an occasional crunch of feet in the snow.

And a low, rumbling howl that had to be the massive waves of snow poised to destroy everything in its path.

"Are you seeing anything that might be causing this?" Ris said. "Or what might have and then fled the area?"

"Not so far," Agent Manhoff said. "Either they have the source of the disruption buried, or they're...*hidden* somehow. Invisible. Doesn't make much difference right now whether that means they're controlling the snow with ships but they aren't in the area, or they set this up years ago to operate on its own. We're right back to trying to control the damage while trying to reach people who are in desperate need of rescue."

"Then let us help." Ris's face was pale but determined. "This is hardly a ski-rescue outpost, but we do have a large group of young people eager to experience whatever they can during their time here. Finding enough winter gear will likely be a problem, but if they can take turns with the security and safety staff of that resort, they should be fine."

Agent Manhoff nodded. "That's acceptable to me."

"I'd like to help, too," Tes said.

And the biggest surprise of all to Lina's mind was Ris agreeing at once.

"Great, we'll get you suited up and call in our rescue scoot. It's nowhere near as large as what they're trying to land there now, but it can carry enough people to hopefully make a difference. Lina's authorized to go as well, of course. And we can transport you and anyone else at the same time, Agent Manhoff."

A great wall of the unknown crashed in Lina's mind, probably very much like the multiple avalanches surrounding the lodge.

For once, Agent Manhoff seemed surprised with no idea of what to say. But she managed to open a smaller display window with a catalog of the Planetary Security scoots available and ready for launch, along with offers to coordinate the responses between the two agencies.

Leaving Lina desperate to slow the motion before all of them got so caught up that they couldn't turn back.

"Didn't you say no one knows how to get a scoot in there without possibly breaking whatever's holding the avalanche so steady?"

"We may have to risk it while we're trying to learn more,"

Agent Manhoff said. "Even getting a few people out might stop this attack from being so effective."

Lina frowned, unhappy for once that she'd caught what someone else was trying to keep hidden.

"They're famous people, aren't they? Or wealthy, or powerful. The ones in the avalanche's path. That's why you want them rescued no matter how high the risk."

It was her turn to face Agent Manhoff's glare, but not for long.

"Planetary Security is working to rescue every single person in that valley, as I'm sure Planetary Science and Planetary Tourism would do as well. If you honestly want to know more, deactivate your comms or leave the room."

Ris finally got his hands out of his hair, smacking both of them flat on the desk.

"I'm *quite* sure I misunderstood you, Agent Manhoff. I find it hard to imagine you just asked me to sever myself from communications not only in the middle of a planetary emergency, but in the middle of my own compound. We do have a presence and expertise in cold weather climates as well as Sarkans 3's many bodies of water. Surely it would be a terrible crime to keep me from coordinating both of those when they're likely to be critical in saving lives."

Agent Manhoff's smile was sharper and more uncomfortable than her worst glower.

"No, you heard me clearly. I understand your priorities, and I agree with them. You're free to leave us the room. Or we can leave if Lina and Tes agree, and speak elsewhere. I'd say for all of less than ten minutes. If we stay here, I'd need to *see* you disable any comm links out of the room whether you stay or go."

Lina wasn't sure which of them she was more annoyed with, but she was determined to let them work it out between them. *Quickly.*

Otherwise she'd suggest taking Tes and volunteering for one of the Planetary Security scoots sure to be on the way within minutes.

Ris finally stood, gripping his comm-stick so tightly Lina was surprised it didn't crack. He walked to the front of the room and stopped beside Agent Manhoff, looking up at her, clear-eyed and apparently unafraid.

"If I may?"

She held out one hand and stepped to the side.

After a couple of taps, another small window popped up on the side of the frozen-winter video. Lina recognized Shel and Tam, two of the other instructors she'd met in her short time at the Planetary Science compound. Both were wide-eyed and trying to talk at the same time.

"I'll be occupied here for a few minutes." Ris's voice was calm, though he still held his comm in a white-knuckled grip. "Please monitor the emergency situation, and alert everyone in Planetary Science to stand by in case we're needed."

"But we're not ready for—"

"I'll also be restricting comm to this room for a short time. Be prepared to give me a full report as soon as we're finished here. And yes, you *are* ready."

When that window closed, another replaced it; this one showing a series of red text warnings as he deactivated the room's comm.

By the time he finished, both Tes and Lina had switched their comm-sticks off, ignoring their own stern text warnings, and put them on the desk beside the control monitor. A few seconds later, Ris did the same.

"There," he said. "Now please do speak quickly, Agent Manhoff. I and the rest of Planetary Science stand ready to help in any way we can. But we have our own response to coordinate."

CHAPTER 14

Agent Manhoff looked at each of them in turn, then reactivated the sound Ris had silenced from the video feed.

Aside from the gusty wind and the unnerving bass roar from the barely contained avalanches, the distant snowy valley was eerily silent.

Lina wondered if Agent Manhoff simply wanted the noise to further hide whatever she was about to say.

"Thank you, Director. I'll be as brief as I can, but if we're all going to go down this somewhat illegal road together, I hope you'll call me by my given name. Jemny."

The quiet, almost hopeful way she said it somehow transformed an ordinary request into a gesture of equality.

And maybe friendship.

"I'm pleased to meet you, Jemny," Lina said. "And I'm sure we all know what you're going to say can't go outside of this room unless you give the go-ahead."

Tes and Ris both nodded.

"There are people who've been targeted by both attacks," Jemny said. "They were in your group yesterday, Tes, and they're in that valley right now. All I can tell you—and I'd face discipline if this gets out—is some are planetary leaders from other colonies. We suspect they are indeed the targets, but we can't be certain. Others are equally well-known and powerful, and a handful have suffered at the hands of terrorists in the past. Sarkans 3 *itself* could be the target."

Tes's forehead wrinkled, and she gazed at the winter scene on the monitor.

"I don't always know the backgrounds of people I take on tours. Actually, I'd say I usually don't. Not unless they're naturally chatty and friendly, or the kind who want to make sure everyone knows who they are. Sounds like the ones you're talking about wouldn't say a word."

"They wouldn't," Jemny said. "They know very well that their lives depend on their privacy. The only other thing I'll say is some aren't on Sarkans 3 for an ordinary vacation. They've got business here that could affect everyone on the planet. It's possible that's what drew the attackers into action."

Ris rubbed his chin.

"Why did you decide to tell us so much?"

"Because I trust Lina and Tes. And you're right, Ris, in that we need to work with Planetary Science on this case. There's too much we don't know and too much at stake to isolate ourselves and waste time trying to figure out what you already understand."

She hesitated, eyes and mouth tight, obviously considering whether to say more.

"The hard truth is I've had trouble convincing certain people in Planetary Security that we need to cooperate more often. As far as I'm concerned, this situation is far too serious to continue waiting. I hope that's acceptable."

"It is to me," Ris said. "I had my fill of struggles in my younger days with people wanting to keep everything isolated when working together was the only rational choice. There's a difference between security and stupidity."

"Has anyone analyzed the energy signatures in that valley?" Lina said. "To see if they match what we found in the coral?"

Jemny's hesitant smile reappeared.

"Not yet. That's one reason I came down here. I hoped to collect a small piece of the sample to do that kind of analysis. I thought I'd be working toward tracking down the ship that created the signature, and that we'd be preventing another attack at sea. I never expected there'd be another so soon."

"Or so far north," Tes said. "How long will it take you to do that analysis? And how fast can you get to Hivern to compare them? The tourist groups travel on much higher-speed transports going between attractions than we locals tend to have access to if we're not with them."

Ris shook his head. "None of our scoots are anywhere near fast enough to keep up with the tourism scoots."

"Our ships are." Jemny held up the small glass box with the sample inside. "If you can get me a fast enough report on this sample, I hope I can get us into that valley in time to make those comparisons. Maybe in time to make a difference for the people trapped there."

Lina turned to Ris, trying not to let excitement overwhelm her better instincts when it came to planning and expectations.

"I just trained on our portable test kits last week. I haven't used one in the field yet, but I'm sure I can."

"You're ahead of me there," he said. "All I've had a chance to do with those is making out the training schedules to get all of you up to speed. Are you willing to put that training into practice now?"

Lina answered before she could talk herself out of it, which meant ignoring a solid wall of flashing red warnings inside her own head.

"I'm ready *and* willing. As long as we can find some kind of cold-weather gear, I think we should go now."

Ris pulled out his comm-stick at the same time Jemny did.

"We'll make those arrangements," Jemny said. "I'd suggest the two of you change out of your swimsuits. No matter what kind of gear we can locate for you, they'll never be warm enough."

Less than twenty minutes later, Lina, Tes, Ris, and Jemny met in the transport hub for the Planetary Science compound.

The red stone sprawl of the buildings created a stark backdrop for the sleek, arrow-like form of the Planetary Security ship. She couldn't imagine calling a silvery craft built so much more like a bird than a box a scoot, even if it hadn't been fully enclosed with a broad expanse of windows up front.

It crouched on low-slung landing gear like a predator waiting impatiently to spring into flight.

Lina wore her heaviest pants and shirt, with an inner layer of both she hoped would keep her a bit warmer. At least the bright-blue color should make her nicely visible in the snow.

Tes hadn't fared much better, with borrowed pants from another teaching associate and one of Lina's jackets.

They could just have easily been planning an outing to the spaceport on windy Mount Bewaker rather than diving straight into frigid weather with almost no protection.

Only Ris was properly outfitted, with a heavy, almost painfully bright yellow jacket and matching pants. Turned out he'd spent time before Planetary Science was fully operational skiing at some of the resorts and lodges around the planet.

The knee-high oval of the portable test kit Lina had trained on sat beside the short ramp into Jemny's ship, the shiny red metal of the case vivid against the ship's silver belly.

The whole thing wasn't much bigger than the water-ready scoot she and Tes had taken out that morning, but the smooth, curved design made it clear they'd be going much faster.

Jemny ducked out of the rectangular door, waving them all inside.

"Everything is still steady, but no one knows how long that will last. We need to get moving."

Ris held up one hand, looking apologetic but determined.

"Are we cleared to travel with you? And on this ship? I'm sorry to sound paranoid, but I don't want to delay things even more by getting arrested as soon as we touch the ground."

"You're cleared," Jemny said. "Something else you don't know is I'm not exactly a mid-level agent for Planetary Security. I supervise arrivals and departures to our continent, and I coordinate cooperation with other individuals and agencies. Or at least I try to. That's where I've been running into human brick walls we have to work around. Things aren't usually this extreme, but this *is* my job. On board, please."

"No wonder we were able to get those specialized energy sensors so easily this morning," Lina said. "I hope you have something similar for snow so we don't have to go trudging through it dragging the sensors."

"Or rolling them along ahead of us," Tes put in.

"I've got that part covered. The nearest weather satellites are being reprogrammed to scan the area, but it's going to take time. I've got a testing scoot en route as well." Jemny stepped back inside the ship, but her voice floated out with perfect clarity.

"I'm leaving in thirty seconds whether you're aboard and seated and strapped in or not."

Ris flashed a crooked smile and marched up the ramp.

"I for one believe her. We'll all be better off if we don't have to endure a fast flight crushed against the back of the ship."

CHAPTER 15

THE THRILL of such a quick journey while keeping a close eye on the continuing feed from frigid Hivern didn't come anywhere close to preparing Lina for the shock of arrival in a different season in a much colder climate.

As soon as the shriek of the now-constant wind hit her face and cut right through every layer of her clothing, she felt all the skin on her body try to shrivel up. Every muscle contracted and shivered hard enough to feel like a head-to-toe rippling cramp.

Even the inside of her nose and her eyes seemed to shrink away from the harsh new reality.

But that didn't stop her eyes from aching from painful brightness, or the sharp aroma of snow mixed with woodsmoke from overwhelming her sense of smell.

They'd landed off to the side of the lodge, in theory because that part of the valley was somewhat less threatened by an impending avalanche. The location also gave them a tremendous view of what they were up against.

Despite the appearance of being built out of stone and massive logs, Lina had no doubt the building wouldn't survive if even one of the giant fields of snow hit it at full speed.

From what Ris had told them on the flight about normal conditions around a lodge like this, the pressure built up on each of the slopes would have been carefully monitored every day from when the first snowflake fell until the last melted in distant springtime. All so specially trained teams on specialized scoots could trigger smaller avalanches as needed to keep a big one from ever forming.

Even if they fell behind in their duties—an impossibility on a well-run and highly regulated resort world like Sarkans 3—the odds of this big an area of snow getting destabilized all at once were incredibly long.

No building could reasonably be designed to survive such an impossible event. If all the unnaturally agitated snow slammed into the lodge at once, the impact and momentum would wipe it out of existence like a rogue wave destroying a dried-out sandcastle.

The mountain in front of the lodge towered so high that Lina had to tilt her head back to see the summit. Or where the summit *should* have been if it weren't obscured by a whirling thunderous mass of snow.

The far side and back of the lodge were equally menaced, with walls of furious white tilted in toward them, as if they were inside a gigantic white house with a transparent roof.

Their ship wasn't spared the danger, with a lower but wider mountain carrying its own precarious load overhead. The fierce wind cutting across the narrow valley twisted the snow on that side upward until it looked like a frozen campfire.

From the looks of the crowd gathered close to the front of the three-story lodge, everyone was outside, trying to catch a glimpse of their possible fate rather than risk meeting it inside and unaware. They huddled close together, barely talking, all of them staring at the biggest threat.

The rescue scoot that had tried to land earlier was nowhere to be seen.

In fact, Lina didn't see any kind of ship nearby, either hovering against the deep blue sky or close to the snow-covered ground.

If any other rescue effort was underway, it was entirely invisible.

"They can't get out by walking?" Ris said. "Or in some kind of land vehicle?"

Jemny shook her head.

"No roads into or out of this valley. Everything comes in and goes out by scoot or ship. That's part of the appeal, which I'm sure you know better than I do, Tes."

"Sure. The more remote the location, the more exciting, or private. From what you're telling us, it should also mean the most secure."

"Should be, yes. It has been for several years now. I doubt anyone would honestly blame the designers and builders for never expecting something like this."

"What happened to the other scoot?" Lina said. "The one that tried to land earlier."

A line of muscles in Jemny's jaw flexed. Then she pointed toward the highest peak, right in front of the lodge.

"Right after I cut the video feed, the avalanche on that slope advanced a few hundred meters, then more as the scoot got closer to the ground. When the scoot retreated, the snow stopped."

Lina's stomach knotted hard enough that she forgot her shivering for several horrible seconds.

"Whoever's doing this has to be watching. And they don't *want* these people to be rescued. That or we were damn lucky to get the tourists off the cliffs in time yesterday. How were we able to land?"

"I wish I knew which it was," Jemny said. "More control today or better luck yesterday, or something we can't yet understand. As far as landing, I was monitoring those mountains down to the millimeter during our descent, and so was everyone back at Mount Bewaker. Nothing moved. The current thinking is we were permitted to land because my ship is too small to rescue more than a handful of people."

Tes blinked back tears, which Lina was surprised to see didn't freeze solid. She couldn't tell whether Tes's voice shook from distress or cold.

"So what are we supposed to do to help?"

Ris looked over his shoulder at Tes, then turned his whole body to face her and Lina.

"Neither of you are dressed for this weather. They're halffrozen, Jemny. None of us can think under these conditions, much less figure out what to do. Where are those warm clothes Planetary Security was supposed to provide?"

Jemny shook herself as if she'd just noticed the problem, then pulled out her comm-stick. Before she could speak, a smaller group detached from the crowd and walked toward them.

Lina could have cried herself at the sight of thick winter clothing in their arms.

"I'm terribly sorry," Jemny said. "I asked the lodge to have things ready for you, then I let the scene here distract me."

"That's understandable," Lina said. "As soon as I warm up enough for my hands to function, I'll start the analysis on whatever's working in this valley."

She was about to ask if Tes wanted to help with that, but Tes gasped.

A small form pulled ahead of the group walking toward them and darted across the snow. Something about the round-cheeked little girl seemed familiar, especially the way she nearly bounced, her steps longer and higher than the planet's lighter gravity could account for.

"Musa!"

Tes ran forward herself and caught the girl mid-bounce, resulting in a spinning, giggling chorus of greetings from both of them. The two of them turned back toward Lina and the others, with Tes holding Musa's hand.

"What in the world are you doing here?" Tes said. "I thought you'd still be showing everyone how to climb."

Musa spotted Lina and grinned. Not much of her face showed through thick, fluffy layers of pink around her head and face, and the matching snowsuit showed telltale bumps of the same tiny gravity pods she'd had on the beach.

"I know you! You're the one who helped save all the fishies. My *grand*parents decided it'd be more fun to see snow instead of sand, and I *guess* that's okay. We got another giant wave, though, so flying all the way to winter didn't get us away from *those*."

An older woman carrying a bundle of winter clothes in the same pink hurried over. Despite being many decades older, her cheeks had the same sweet, rounded look as Musa's, and her eyes were just as blue.

"Sorry about that. Our Musa sometimes gets a little too busy for her own good. Here, let these women get into some warm clothes before they turn into icicles."

"That's okay," Tes said. "Musa was just telling us about finding another giant wave all the way up here in winter."

The woman rolled her eyes as she handed the clothes to Lina, but her face and voice were tight with fear.

"All we wanted to do was get her away from that craziness yesterday, but I'm afraid we've been struggling to do that almost all the days of this darling child's life. We thought bringing her so far north would keep us in the clear. But I think it's worse than where we were. Are you going to take us out of here?"

Lina's heart sank, and she felt guilty pulling a wonderfully thick jacket on and zipping it up.

"I don't think we can fit too many in our ship," she said. "But we're going to do our best to find out what's happening and stop it."

The woman nodded and held one hand over her heart. Then she reached for Musa's hand that wasn't holding tight to Tes's.

"Come on, sweet girl. We need to let these nice people work so they can figure out why those big waves keep following us."

Musa resisted for a second before letting her fingers slip away from Tes. She rolled her eyes in a perfect miniature example of her grandmother.

"Then what will we *do* here, if the waves are gone?"

Tes watched them walking away, shaking her head.

"As if I wasn't already determined to make this stop happening." She took the pants and jacket Lina held out. "*Thank* you.

Go ahead and get started. The second I get a little warmed up, tell me what I can do to help."

Jemny stood off to the side talking to two people who had to be more Planetary Security agents by the way their eyes kept moving, taking in every single detail of the wintry landscape.

Lina turned to Ris, relieved to have his steady—if a bit stodgy—presence in the middle of so much unfamiliarity and tension.

"Let's get your tests started." He held the small glass box with the coral sample in one gloved hand. "Of course we could wait on input from the weather satellites or the testing scoot, assuming they're online in time. Or we could call up the results of the analysis we already did, but that might not be ideal in this situation."

He raised his eyebrows in an expression she'd learned meant he wanted her to finish his thought.

"But we don't have access to that full suite of testing out here," she said. "It will be faster to test both with what I *can* access and compare those than to try to narrow down that huge batch of data."

Ris nodded with a half-smile, and Lina turned to find Tes already holding the oval of the portable test unit. She was wrapped from head to toe in puffy pink, and she already looked a whole lot warmer.

Lina's own shivers had died down considerably now that she was similarly encased in a thick insulating layer of her own.

"Okay, let's set up the test. Jemny said she could patch this unit in through her ship's more powerful sensors, then I can use that to compare the energy signatures. I'll take her up on that, since we can use all the help we can possibly get."

Despite her outward confidence, Lina was terrified to have the whole situation riding on her shoulders. If she missed one factor, or somehow managed to anger whoever controlled the massive amounts of snow, all of them might not make it through the day.

And dwelling on that wouldn't do a blasted thing to improve the nightmare situation.

CHAPTER 16

Lina once again shivered from head to toe, but not because she was still as shocked by the brutal conditions in the winter-locked valley.

The pink garments Musa's grandmother had given her somehow managed to trap and hold every bit of heat her body generated, to the point that moving around too much would make her miserably hot.

Only her nose and eyes were exposed, and that wasn't nearly as intolerable as long as she turned her face away from the wretched wind.

The problem was, with every step she took away from the lodge and the fragile shelter of all the people still gathered there, the more she felt exposed.

Threatened.

Targeted.

Not only would she be the first under the pounding destruction of snow if everything broke loose while she was out there.

But she was deeply afraid of triggering whatever controlled the avalanches and condemning everyone else to their own deaths.

The only thing for it was to keep a grip on her portable testing kit, keep her eyes on the invisible path ahead, and keep moving.

So far neither the ship's sensors nor her kit's had picked up any trace of the enemy keeping the vast wall of snow at bay, which made no sense at all. The expenditure of power had to be tremendous to hold back so much mass and potential velocity.

The wait for an incoming testing scoot or repurposed weather satellites was far too risky to be tolerated.

The kit's palm-sized screen already showed the numbers and lines of the results from the coral reef sample on one side. But the other side—set to detect any sort of energy in use nearby— had so far only shown an occasional twitch that disappeared right away.

Lina fought the impulse to look back and see how far she'd crunched across the snow from the relative safety of Jemny's ship. She knew the speed of a tsunami of snow would easily outpace her, even from the front of the lodge.

Especially in a situation and climate like this, a sliver of distraction could spell disaster.

She kept her eyes moving as often as she dared glance away from the monitor, hoping to spot some kind of motion either in the sky or somewhere on the mountains around her. Some sign of what must be holding so much snow in such a fragile stasis.

The churning rumble deepened as she walked, concentrating itself in a thrumming spot behind her breastbone. She would have known something was wrong here if she'd been delivered with her ears completely blocked and her eyes covered.

As she continued to walk, the woodsmoke smell around the lodge fell away.

And Lina recognized the tingling, lightning-strike sensation that she'd caught the day before, when the slow-moving wave had almost reached the shore.

That had to be at least the same *technology* at work, if not the same energy source.

She slowed as the hard-packed snow beneath her feet grew slushy, almost as if she was walking into the beginning of spring.

But the air around her was colder than ever, sneaking its way through her shell of protection.

Lina stopped, finally catching more than a quick spike of movement on her monitor. The electrical tingle in her nose spread until she felt it in her throat, and tasted the explosive charge on her tongue.

She stepped forward again, and the wavering analysis progress bar finally started moving upward.

Another half step dropped it from green back to yellow, so she moved back, settling her feet in the half-melted snow.

Maybe the energetic surge she tasted and heard and felt with her own body agitated the frozen blanket on the ground past its integrity point.

Too late, she wished she had something like the coral with her, or some kind of tree or shell or something else that could absorb the possible grav-drive blast. A stand of evergreen trees was too far to the side to risk losing contact with whatever her sensors were picking up.

Another was far enough toward the looming tower of snow that she'd have to step into its literal shadow to reach one.

No amount of understanding or reassurance in the world could convince her to do that.

One eye on the progress bar—more than halfway to completion—she kicked at the slush. Nothing but flattened grass and a few bunches of last season's ordinary deciduous leaves, all of it likely too soft and half-decayed for testing.

Then she spotted a slender pinecone, no longer than her index finger and not much thicker. Or at least what she knew as a pinecone from her studies of Earth species.

Surely close enough to accumulate something like grav-drive energy.

Please let it be close enough.

Neither her training nor her experience with the testing unit told her if the analysis would have to start from the beginning if she broke contact with the source.

But either the trembling building around her ribs and stomach was gnawing fear that wasn't going to let her stay so close to danger for much longer, or her body was losing the fight against the force strong enough to keep such a horrifying threat at bay.

She used her teeth to pull off one glove, wincing as the wind drove an ache deep into her jaw and seemed to flay every bit of her flesh off.

Holding her breath, she did her best to hold the kit level while she knelt, reaching with her already achingly cold hand toward where she'd seen the pinecone.

The percentage on the progress bar ticked from ninety-eight to ninety-nine.

Closer to the ground, Lina's teeth chattered, but she couldn't tell whether it was from the surging energy or the thundering bass thrum all around her.

Her numbing fingertips brushed gritty soil, half-melted snow.

Then the sharp, prickly edge of what she *needed* to be the pinecone.

The progress bar refused to move.

She clenched her jaw in an attempt to keep her teeth from shattering.

Her thigh and back muscles protested staying hunched over, but she still couldn't get a grip on whatever her fingers kept slipping away from.

After another stab that felt like it drew blood, she finally risked a quick glance down.

She'd been picking at the thinnest end of the pinecone, and only managing to tear tiny wedges away.

The brown triangles stood out against the slushy white, along with a few shocking red drops of her blood.

Lina moved her hand back and finally grabbed hold, scraping her tender fingers through a crust of ice underneath.

She stood and looked up again, feeling the muscles of her neck creak with tension.

The shadow of the impending avalanche—the line she'd been too terrified to cross—was now only millimeters away.

Was someone advancing the wall on purpose?

Or was that awe-inspiring control finally slipping?

All her breath left in a grunt as the progress bar finally reached 100%.

Instead of looking at the result she'd wanted so badly, Lina gripped the pinecone tight in one fist, the test unit in the other.

And she turned to run.

CHAPTER 17

With every step back toward the lodge, Lina's back and neck and head cringed away from the icy weight that her entire body expected to land at any second.

Her heart pounded too hard for her to hear her gasping breaths or her feet impacting the snow, but she still felt the rumble in her bones. Sheets of sweat formed under her clothing, but her cheeks and one ungloved hand felt like blocks of ice scoured by the wind.

The dark shape of the lodge and the bright arrow of the ship seemed to be a hundred kilometers away.

She fought a mad urge to look down to make sure she hadn't somehow detoured onto a frozen lake that kept her feet spinning but never brought her closer.

The sight of a small person once again bounce-running away from the group and toward her nearly stole all her breath.

But the idea of sweet little Musa getting any closer to the

horrifying tidal wave of snow made Lina dig into her run that much harder.

Several other people streamed forward now, but none of them could catch the little girl who probably thought the whole situation was a fantastic new game.

Lina finally half-knelt, half-fell to her knees, hoping the little-girl-rocket streaking toward her didn't tumble them both backward.

"Lina! You ran faster than the giant wave!"

"I hope so, sweetheart. Let's get away from it just in case."

Thank all the joys of youthful energy, Musa turned and ran back toward the crowd at once, saving Lina the possible embarrassment of not being able to pick up a small child. Her thighs trembled and burned, and her lungs were full of fire from trying to drag enough of the frigid air in.

She staggered back to her feet, checking her grip on the testing unit and the possibly all-important pinecone.

She promised herself she wouldn't do it with the lodge and Jemny's ship almost within reach, but her head and shoulders turned without her approval.

Her muscles fully gave way and her knees hit the snow again, hard enough to rattle her teeth in her head.

The avalanche was indeed moving again, but in slow motion, and in an odd direction. The pure white mass settled rather than leaning forward, as if a gigantic mountain was gradually sinking into the sea. The bottom of it expanded in all directions, with nowhere near the explosive force she'd feared only a few seconds ago.

Even the nerve-racking noise had shifted into a gentler rumble.

At least until an ear-shattering alarm rang out across the valley.

Someone shouted almost directly into Lina's aching ear.

"They're going to cause another avalanche with that blasted racket."

Hands gripped her arm on that side, joined by another pair on the other.

"That much snow might still make it this far. We've got to get her out of here!"

Lina forced her attention away from the oncoming snow and her lungs' demands for more air, frozen solid or not.

Tes on one side, Jemny on the other. Both looking grim and determined, keeping their eyes on the horizon in motion.

They'd just managed to drag Lina to her feet and get her turned when she let out a yell of her own.

"The pinecone! Don't let the snow bury it!"

Lina still had the test unit gripped in one fist, but she'd dropped the tiny bit of evidence.

If that snow swept through the whole valley—a slow meter at a time—they might never find another one.

Jemny scowled, shook her head, and kept dragging.

But Tes let go and darted forward.

She picked something up and returned, holding it so Lina could see.

"This?"

"Yes!"

Lina tried to take the pinecone back, but Tes shoved it into the breast pocket of her own pink suit.

"I think I'll hold onto this for now," she said over the alarm's continued braying. "We won't get another chance to go back for it."

Lina somehow got her feet under her enough to help for the last several steps.

The group of people in front of her had drawn back against the long front wall of the lodge under a sheltering roof, and they stared off to the sides as well as straight ahead. Lina finally noticed the avalanches on both sides were slipping downward as well.

As soon as they made it into the crowd, the alarm cut off.

Ears still echoing the painful tone, Lina tried to speak in a normal voice. Trying to catch her breath at the same time only made it harder.

"What happened? Did the avalanche control kick back in?"

Ris appeared in front of her, trying to retrieve the test unit. He had to reach down and straighten her fingers, gone stone-like from fear and cold.

"The control field has been on the whole time," he said. "But whoever is behind the attack was overriding it. We don't know why, but the attacks stopped. We're in the middle of an unexpected high-stress test of the system."

The thunder moved closer until it sounded like it came from all around them and even overhead. Ahead the snow wave was so near she couldn't see the sky at all.

She twisted to the side, thinking of the true isolation of the lodge and scared to death Jemny's ship would be buried until this hemisphere's spring.

But as the smaller snow load on that mountain finally ground to a halt—along with the other crawling avalanches—the ship and lodge were spared. A sparkling cloud of white continued the movement, not quite blocking out the sky as dislodged snow filtered into the air.

Lina let Jemny and Tes gently lower her to the stones below, not that she had much choice. All of her muscles had turned into warm liquid that wasn't capable of the simple job they'd done throughout her life of holding her upright.

Musa crept forward and onto her lap with a contented sigh.

"The giant wave almost got us. But you stopped it, Lina."

Before Lina could protest, Ris turned the testing unit toward her.

"You did it! A full reading on the energy signature out there, right before it disappeared. A near-perfect match for what you found at the coral reef."

"What about the pinecone?" Lina said.

Ris shook his head, staring at her as if he thought she might have oxygen deprivation.

"It's here." Tes stepped forward with her hand held out. "I'm afraid I crushed it more than I meant to, but hopefully it will still be enough."

Ris grinned as he took the mangled specimen from her.

"It will do just fine. Brilliant thinking, both of you."

A confused and frightened mutter broke out in the crowd on their side of the lodge, where a small bit of the sky was still visible. A slow-moving shape was dark against the blinding landscape.

"And there's my testing scoot," Jemny said. "Right on time, as soon as we don't need it anymore. That means the weather satellites should be online for no good reason right about now, too."

Ris was too delighted with having so much data on hand to tolerate such gloom.

"Nonsense, every bit of information we have will help. If nothing else, we can direct the scoot to hunt for more pinecones so we can map out how far that energy field went."

Tes handed a mug of something steaming hot and fragrant with spices to Lina.

"That kind of search will have to wait for a while," she said. "Looks like the whole valley is under a couple of meters of snow now."

With a few sips of the wonderfully sweet and rich milky drink warming her belly, Lina scooted herself and Musa away from the lodge's wall. Seeming to understand the situation, Musa hopped up and held out her hands.

With help from her, Tes, Ris, and Jemny, Lina got unsteadily to her feet and shuffled forward.

Her muscles were still unusually warm, but they'd taken on the twitching she'd noticed before after way too long either kicking in water or climbing on land.

No injuries, but if she continued to insist on abusing them, a series of debilitating cramps would ensue.

The towering ridgelines around them now stood stark and gray against the blue sky. The avalanches had dislodged a whole winter's worth of snow into the valley.

A choppy, glittering sea of white at nearly Lina's eye level filled the land all around them.

Even if there had been roads, they'd be useless now.

"Any chance the rescue scoots will be able to land?" Tes said from right beside Lina. "I'm probably not the only one who's ready for a change of scenery."

Lina carefully poked at Tes with her elbow.

"You were so eager to get up here, and already wanting to leave."

Musa piped up from her perch in front of Lina.

"I guess we can go somewhere else. But the giant waves will probably just follow us *again*."

Jemny's eyes met Lina's, and the meaning in her cool gaze was perfectly clear. And Lina couldn't help remembering Musa's grandmother talking about trying to keep her safe from insanity almost all of her life.

Unless they could extract more data than matching energy signatures from the test unit and the pinecone, the unpleasant idea of letting Musa, her grandparents, and the others who'd been both here and at the beach yesterday go somewhere else might be their best chance to catch the attackers.

CHAPTER 18

After the terror and relief of the avalanche collapse, watching several bulky black snow-rescue scoots following the sleek blue test scoot into the valley was a bit of a letdown.

At least to the tourists, and very much to Musa.

Lina was relieved when Musa's grandparents and all the rest decided to enjoy one more fantastic meal at the lodge before departing. Besides wanting to make space for the investigation that was about to get underway, word was all the employees at the lodge were happy to take advantage of their chance to relocate for a while.

Turned out they were every bit as shaken by having their peaceful existence hijacked by a still-unknown force as Lina and her friends were.

For their part, the generous offer of a meal with all the guests took a backseat to the chance to circle above the shockingly bare mountains as soon as possible.

None of them turned down the subsequent—and insistent—

offer of several baskets full of enough food to rival Tes's breakfast feast the day before. The aroma alone explained why the tourists insisted on one more chance to enjoy the lodge's hospitality.

But when they got airborne in the rescue scoot and got a good look at the snow-choked valley, none of them could manage to eat.

Lina hadn't gotten a detailed look at the landscape when they arrived in Jemny's ship, but she'd seen enough to know they'd been through more than a relocation of snow.

The stands of evergreens and deciduous trees she'd seen during her terrifying walk were nowhere to be seen. The mountains showed a similar absence of any kind of plant life as well.

Even moving slowly, the avalanches had scoured everything in their path down to the stone and soil.

Once they got over the first ridgeline, the precision of the attack was breathtaking. On the opposite side of the mountains, snow still lay thick and undisturbed with plenty of trees peeking through, as if nothing had happened so close by.

Lina hoped any animals in the area had time to get to safety, even as she knew that probably wasn't true. Not with so much snow held unmoving over such a huge area.

She'd shed her pink snowsuit in the scoot's warm, enclosed interior, vowing to get it cleaned and returned as soon as she could.

Rather than only a couple of seats up front and an empty cargo area in the back, this scoot also had a row of seats around its whole length. A line of sleek monitors was set into the wall below huge windows, perfect for observing the subjects of testing below.

Lina was struck yet again by how many adaptations the

equipment on Sarkans 3 was capable of, for so many different climates.

Ris, also freed of his heavy winter gear, waved everyone up to the front of the scoot. He stood beside Jemny, who'd refused to let anyone else pilot the craft. All it took was one flash of her Planetary Security ID, though Lina suspected the flash of command in her eyes was what actually sent the original pilot scurrying into the lodge.

"There's your result, Lina," Ris said, tapping the big display in front of him. "That seedpod you found is a near-exact match for the coral as far as the type and levels of grav-drive energy. Only a slight degradation in the frequency. Close enough that I'm confident in saying the difference is because of the materials themselves rather than the energy."

Lina peered at the bars and lines, noting only a few small variations between the two.

"It's a pinecone, or close to it. I'm glad to have a match, but how's that going to help us catch whoever's doing this? Or figure out why they gave up today?"

Tes touched her shoulder.

"We're still not sure they *did* give up. Isn't it possible their ship or whatever they're using failed?"

"Yes, it's possible," Ris said. "I'm not ready to scratch anything off the list. The most important thing is getting the data programmed into this scoot's sensors and into the weather satellites. We'll share it with everyone with testing authority as soon as possible."

Jemny glared at him, one eyebrow raised.

"Everyone with security clearance, you mean."

Ris waved one hand at her, and both of them smiled.

"I thought you already sent the data to the satellites?" Lina said.

"I did, but only the one set. Your handheld testing unit got a third, with another slight variation. Having three will make a huge difference. That way they can search for the energy signature in a range of materials, since coral and pinecone are so different. I suspect your handheld picked up the energy in a narrow band over the air rather than after it settled into something else. Those variations teach us more than one way it can show up."

Tes leaned forward and examined the screen, where all three energy signatures were now displayed.

"Are the satellites able to scan something so close to the ground? Or underwater? Not that we're sure what form another attack will take."

This time Jemny spoke without taking her eyes away from the scoot's protective front window.

"The satellites will see plenty, no need to worry about that."

"I hadn't worried about the satellites at all," Lina said. "Not until just now, thinking about how much they might be observing all the time."

"I hope we'll have another tool at our disposal," Ris said, "to use with scoots or satellites. The sensors have the data range now. Could you please fly in a search pattern over the ridgeline, Jemny? I'm hoping we'll catch the way the energy was distributed, even after so much destruction."

Something in the way Jemny went still and silent caught Lina's attention even before the scoot gradually slowed, then stopped, hovering in place directly over the center of the ridgeline.

Rather than turning her intent gaze toward the half-normal, half-scoured landscape, now Jemny focused on the large comm-stick in her hand.

The unrolled surface flashed with red and black alerts that somehow made Lina's flesh chill all over again.

"What's happening, Jemny?" she said quietly.

CHAPTER 19

Jᴇᴍɴʏ's broad shoulders slowly rose and fell, and the silence in the scoot grew heavier with every breath. When she turned toward Lina, her face was hard and cold.

"There's been another murder."

"Murder?" Ris gripped Jemny's arm. "*Another* murder?"

Jemny favored him with a grim smile.

"Looks like you're advancing to another level of security clearance whether you wanted to or not. While we were focused on the tidal wave the other day, a body showed up in one of the spaceport's autonomous tourist transport scoots. We still haven't identified the victim."

Ris let go of her arm and covered his eyes for a second. Lina was dismayed to see his hand trembling when he lowered it.

"And the same thing happened today?"

Jemny tapped her comm-stick, enlarged one of the alerts, and read it.

"Almost the same thing. This time it was one of the observation scoots that returned to the spaceport. The ones that appear to do nothing more than fly around the planet recording video for tourists."

"So they captured another kind of autonomous scoot and redirected it." Tes put one hand over her stomach and stared out toward the devastated valley. "One that's considered highly secured. Lina just told me how only one person has been relieved from Planetary Science duties, and that was for interfering with an observation scoot."

"That was for only *trying* to interfere," Ris said. "No one has ever succeeded before. The operations of those scoots are vital to maintaining tourist safety all over the planet, and almost as important to us as we continue to explore."

"And they're *essential* to Planetary Security." Jemny rolled her comm-stick up and slipped it into her pocket. "That's the real reason why the penalty is so high for tampering with them. They form part of the network we use to observe conditions all over Sarkans 3. It should have been impossible for anyone to take control of one at all, much less without us knowing about it the second the scoot deviated."

Lina wasn't sure which question she wanted to ask first, or which she dreaded to hear the answer to more.

"Did the scoot remain undetected until it landed at the spaceport?"

Jemny nodded.

"Just like the first time, both its tracking and emergency beacons were disabled. It simply dropped off the networks for a couple of hours. Observation personnel and systems have been focused on the tourist transport scoots, not the ones that aren't normally used for people at all. No one had a clue until some poor tourist mistook it for one of their normal transports."

"Without giving too much detail," Lina said, "is there any chance of natural causes this time?"

Jemny gazed at her for several seconds: long enough that Lina didn't need the answer anymore.

Then Tes came up with a third question Lina was afraid to hear the answer to.

"Do they know who this person was, at least?"

"Not yet." Noticing Ris's horrified look, Jemny went on. "Not because the body was that damaged, though there was more than enough. Neither victim was registered on any planetary systems, they have no implanted or wearable sensors, and they don't show up on any other registries we have access to. Which means they've gone to great lengths to stay unknown."

Tes spoke almost too softly to hear.

"Or they've been *forced* to stay that way." She shrugged and shook her head. "Hazard of the profession. Sometimes people on vacation tell tour guides things they'd never tell anyone else, and lots of them talk in front of us as if we're not there. I've never been sure whether it's because they know they'll never see us again, or they figure we don't know anyone in their normal lives. On my most cynical days, I think it's because they're drunk. That or they think I'm too unimportant to worry about."

Jemny's eyes flashed, and her furious expression made everyone draw back.

The controlled calm of her voice was worse.

"Do you mean to tell me Untraceables have been part of your *tour* groups?"

Tes held up one hand.

"Not that I know of, Jemny. But more than one tourist has talked about discovering people either seeking employment or hiding on their lands that don't show up in any registry. The support staff traveling with them talk even more. The Untraceable are still people, not things, no matter how rare they are, or how many laws their existence breaks. They'd escaped from… unauthorized settlements."

Lina's heart seemed to drop through the floor of the scoot and back down into the frozen valley.

She'd read about the horror stories from ages ago, in the early days of human colonization far away from Earth and the original solar system. Registration hadn't been required back then, nor had sensors.

The governments and corporations involved had no problem with colonies who didn't want or need support or communications beyond their initial setup. If they could survive—or even if they couldn't—they were left to forge their own way.

That all changed when truly abhorrent practices were discovered on some of the most secretive planets.

"I thought those settlements didn't exist anymore," she said. "Didn't they go away with the establishment of the Galactic Tribunal?"

"That was the intention," Tes said. "I was taught the same thing. But I've heard about escapees from too many reliable sources to doubt it's still happening. I know of more than one who went on to report the colonies to the Tribunal, but I don't know what the outcome was."

"I'd never seen evidence of that despicable practice on this planet." Ris looked and sounded shaken. "Or heard of survivors being here. But I have heard of other Planetary Science officers who discovered and helped rescue people from those sorts of colonies. Do you think that explains the murders?"

Jemny rubbed the back of her neck, then turned to face the rest of them.

"No one in Planetary Security knows for certain, not yet. But it would explain not being able to identify the bodies. I wouldn't want to speculate too much, but I wonder if settlements like that might be part of the motive, too."

"I understand that you might not be able to answer this," Lina said. "Not that you'd feel pressured to coming from me or any of us. Is anyone in Hivern linked to those settlements? Or to the Tribunal?"

"You're right, Lina. I can't answer you. But I don't blame you for asking." Jemny turned to Tes. "I hope you'll answer me, Tes. Has anyone in the tour groups on-planet right now mentioned the unauthorized settlements to you? Or any escapees?"

"Not any of the current groups, no. But they're not an especially chatty bunch. More often than not, they do keep their business to themselves, and I generally prefer that myself. Which means I rarely have anything unpleasant to report. And yes, if any of them mention Untraceable people or settlements, I'll comm you first thing."

Jemny nodded and started to turn back to the scoot's controls, but Lina had one more question.

"Do you think any of these settlements have the resources or technical expertise to conduct these kinds of attacks? From what I understand, it would be beyond many planetary governments."

"You're right," Jemny said. "Very few governments could do

something like this, and I doubt any of them actually would. You have to move up to the corporate level for the credits needed, and probably for the tech. But don't underestimate the income potential for those kinds of settlements. I'm sorry to say this, but horrifying as it may be, there's still a demand for people who can't be traced. And for people who don't understand how to get help when they need it."

"Or who even know there's a reason to look for help," Tes said. "From what I've heard, sometimes the idea is to make sure the prisoners there—and that's exactly what they are—have no idea their lives could be different. Or else they're too afraid to even consider taking the risk to find out. If we find out about something like that still happening, aren't we obligated to do something about it?"

"We are," Jemny and Ris said at the same time. Jemny nodded for Ris to go on.

"It's not terribly well-known, and thankfully violations are exceedingly rare. But there are procedures to help escaped Untraceable people who are discovered."

"And to deal with Untraceables who stay that way on purpose," Jemny said. "Partly because they're usually the ones holding others captive."

Lina retrieved her thick pink jacket, even though she knew the chill in her bones wouldn't be helped by it.

And no one would be helped by the four of them sitting in the unmoving testing scoot rather than trying to figure out how the environmental attacks were happening.

Maybe that would help solve the murders, too.

"We all have something else to look out for now," she said. "Let's see if we can't solve the puzzle in front of us first."

Jemny looked into Lina's eyes for several seconds, and Lina was reassured by the trust and even respect she saw there.

"Agreed," Jemny said. "If something like that is operating on Sarkans 3, I expect odds are high that capturing whoever's behind these attacks will break open the rest of it at the same time."

CHAPTER 20

THE SCOOT CONTINUED along the stark line between snow and bare rock, now weaving back and forth in a widening angle as it went.

After what felt like days with the aftereffects of such a weighty conversation lingering in the scoot's atmosphere, everyone jumped when the sensors pinged over the devastated side of the ridge.

And only a few seconds later, they pinged again over the snowy part, at the same distance away from the highest point.

The repetition continued as Jemny crisscrossed the line of mountain peaks.

"Did they have two sources?" Lina said, glad to have something else to focus on. "Or something overhead?"

"Maybe some kind of mirrored system," Ris said. "Possibly set up long in advance. I'll call for a team to examine both sides on foot just to be sure, but I doubt they've left anything behind."

Tes turned toward Ris with a smile.

"But now we know what at least one of their patterns looks like. Something else for the satellites to watch out for."

"We need to do a better search of the sea floor," Lina said, "and not only because I'm impatient to get back to warmer weather. We only searched a small area. It's entirely possible there's a wider range, or a double like this one. Assuming there were corals to capture it."

Ris nodded while he tapped away on his comm stick.

"Corals or shells, or possibly the bones of dead fish. Anything that could absorb that energy. Everything we learn narrows down the search and gets us closer to catching them."

Lina walked back to the baskets, retrieving a still-warm bundle of what looked like bright green balls the size of her fist. Once the toasted barleyfruit was roasted and cracked open, the chewy, buttery yellow interior was irresistible comfort food.

She needed plenty of comfort at the idea of Musa and her grandparents roaming Sarkans 3 and in danger. Either the environmental attacks or the unknown murder victims would have been enough to worry about by themselves.

"But we still can't act like we know what's happening, right?" she said. "We're still going to let everyone who was at the beach yesterday and in the valley today go wherever they had planned to try to bring on another attack. Will they at least have enhanced security?"

"They're being shadowed," Jemny said. "But we can't put too many agents with them, or we risk our target knowing about the surveillance. They'll be much safer than they have been."

Tes expertly rapped her barleyfruit against the edge of Jemny's chair, cracking it neatly in two. The heavy bread-like aroma finally got Lina's appetite going.

"The Tourism Authority's looking into the backgrounds of everyone who was there for both attacks," Tes said. "But no connections or patterns so far. If they exist, we'll find them."

"I know none of you want to hear this," Jemny said, "but simply letting them disperse and travel will narrow them down in a hurry. Each time the groups sort themselves out and reform, we have a better chance of knowing exactly who the targets are."

"No, I *don't* want to hear that." Lina had to resist the solid temptation to crack several barleyfruits against Jemny's head. "No matter what anyone did to make themselves a target, assuming they did anything at all besides being on this planet, an innocent like Musa doesn't deserve to take the risk for them."

Ris carefully took Lina's barleyfruit and cracked it himself, handing back two green-filled-with-yellow halves.

"That's why I'm broadcasting this data so widely. So we can spare them the risk if possible."

Lina tried to distract herself by digging her fingers into the warm yellow flesh of her barleyfruit. The fluffy clump looked and felt dry, but it tasted like fresh wheat-flour biscuits drenched in the highest quality butter. After a few of them, she'd have more than enough nutrition and energy for the rest of what promised to be a very long day.

No wonder the winter sport guides in Hivern lodge kept them on hand.

"There's a small chance that broadcasting too widely might cause a problem," Jemny said. She'd set the scoot's autopilot into the same weaving pattern so she could enjoy her own meal break and get something to eat. "What if our attackers have access to the planet's scientific or security networks? They'll know how we're tracking them."

Ris paused with his fingers over his comm stick.

"Do you really think that's possible? That someone who lives and works here could want to cause this kind of destruction? Someone easily could have been hurt or even killed in either of these attacks."

"You know a big part of my job *is* to think of things like this," Jemny said. "Everyone in Planetary Security has a primary focus, but none of us ever forget why we're there. The thing I worry about most is missing my chance to stop a problem before it ever happens."

Tes took her turn to venture back to the baskets, returning with a handful of what looked like strips of thick tree bark. They were actually harvested from just under the bark of a vigorous bush that grew on the same northern continent.

Lightly sweet and loaded with protein, they were the perfect complement to the barleyfruit.

"What if it's worse?" she said softly. "What if these attacks aren't aimed at any one person or group, or even a specific location? What if they're purely random? For no other reason than some awful people causing all this damage because they *can?*"

"Then we have even more of an incentive to stop them," Ris said. "I value your experience, Jemny, so if there's a certain group you think I should exclude from receiving the data, let me know. Otherwise I think we have to take the chance and warn as many people in planetary management or exploration as we can."

Jemny gazed at the scoot's big monitor, watching as the sensors continued to pick up more of the gray-drive's energy signature on both sides of the ridge. A corner of the screen displayed a remarkably lifelike image of what was below them, marked with a series of red dots that matched each ping.

The scoot's processors rendered a line between all the dots, creating a likely path for the ground patrol to follow.

Lina was impatient to run the same kind of survey of the ocean floor.

"Go ahead and send as you wish," Jemny finally said. "I'll get out the alert to put a trace on anyone who accesses the data. I expect every one of them will be nothing more than people as concerned as we are doing their jobs."

"But the more information we have," Lina said, "the sooner we can put a stop to all of this."

What none of them expected was for the attackers to go silent for the next three days.

CHAPTER 21

Lina did her best to walk the line between optimism and fear as the minutes, hours, and days continued to add up after the avalanches.

She and Tes happily took the chance to continue their survey of the ocean floor where the tsunami had originated. They located several more of the mathematically impossible reefs, all of them thriving in their odd configuration.

The twinned pattern was much harder to detect than it had been on either side of the ridgeline, since many of the reefs had such an irregular shape, even with all those right angles. But they discovered enough faint traces to match the approximate distance between two lines of grav-drive fallout.

A handful of abandoned shells that were also contaminated filled in enough of the gaps to create the underwater map.

Even after sending his data to almost the entire workforce on Sarkans 3, Ris didn't have nearly as much luck. Aside from the two areas that had already suffered attacks, the energy signature didn't show up anywhere else away from the spaceport.

But they did confirm that the mysterious unauthorized drive didn't match the standard ones in use all over the planet and throughout the human colonies.

If nothing else, they knew the attacker hadn't likely stolen an existing grav-drive ship and modified it. This appeared to be an independent design based on the same technology.

But who had the funding, technical expertise, and access to do such a thing?

And *why*?

The bright spot in Lina's tense and anxious days was the frequent updates she received from Musa.

Jemny had the brilliant idea to suggest the digital correspondence. It functioned as a way to reassure both Musa's grandparents and Lina, as well as an unobtrusive way to keep track of where they were on the planet.

The sweet videos and photographs were a joy in the moment, and Lina looked forward to every one of them.

Unfortunately they also kept the high stakes of their stalled investigation uncomfortably vivid in the front of her mind.

She and Tes were circling a water-scoot in a massive sweep for more corals or other evidence when yet another planetwide distress signal pinged through.

Tes clutched the side of the scoot and closed her eyes before Lina had a chance to read the alert.

"I was afraid it would be sand this time," she said. "Or a rockfall. But this might be worse."

Lina turned to her, unable to speak.

"It's a potential mudslide," Tes went on. "In one of the volcanic zones."

"So the ground probably has a high concentration of ash. They knew exactly where to strike."

Lina had to try three times to get her next words out.

"Is Musa there?"

Tes only nodded.

The scoot's built-in comm squawked then, and Lina wasn't surprised to hear Jemny's voice cutting through without anyone activating the speakers.

"I'm en route to your location with an agent who'll return your scoot to shore. I've also got clothes for you so we won't have to stop along the way."

"Is someone already there?" Lina said. "Someone who can protect Musa and her family?"

"We have agents there, but with the wind turbulence stirred up and all the dust and debris storming around in the air, it's impossible to get ordinary scoots in or out. They've got a huge mountainside destabilized and hovering over a visitor center."

Lina tried to keep her temper from getting the best of her, but the thought of Musa threatened yet again was too much. Her concern came out as a near-yell.

"Then *why* is there a visitor center in the middle of a volcanic zone in the first place?"

Tes put one hand on her arm.

"The report says the trouble is in the Sopka Valley. That cone has been dormant for well over a thousand years. That's one reason tourists want to go there. They can feel like they're in the zone of fire and see volcanoes everywhere, but it's perfectly safe. Or it has been until now."

"If you know that valley," Jemny said, "you know how high the mountains are around it, and how narrow the gaps are. The altitude keeps most scoots from ever getting there in the first place. The ones that can make it are specially equipped for the strain of going that high on a planet with low gravity to start with."

Lina clenched her fists to stop herself from programming their water scoot to go to this Sopka Valley anyway.

"So what kinds of vessels can get there? Your ship? Or the bigger rescue scoots?"

Tes squeezed Lina's arm, then pointed. Jemny's silvery ship was approaching low over the water and stirring up a plume of spray behind itself.

"Never mind," Lina said. "See you shortly."

The ship's comm had just gone black when it pinged back into life again. This time Ris's worried face filled the screen. He'd had his hands full with data analysis and plotting maps of the attacked areas, but he did his best to keep up with Lina and Tes.

Today he looked like he'd started out the day relatively pulled together, then gradually deteriorated until now he might as well have stumbled out of bed and grabbed wrinkled clothes off the floor without bothering to attempt to smooth his rumpled hair.

"You got the alert? And hopefully a ride to the Sopka Valley?"

"Jemny's ship is just landing," Lina said. "She says it can get into the affected area. Any more clues or theories about how we can catch the monsters behind all of this?"

"Only that the energy signature is getting weaker with every incident. Not enough that they can't succeed, at least not yet. But I can see the changes on analysis."

"We'll contact you as soon as there's something to report."

Ris's eyes widened and he opened his mouth to speak, but Lina tapped the comm off. Her gnawing worry about Musa and her family and everyone else had far more influence over her than worries about offending her supervisor.

She grabbed her pack as the ship pulled alongside them and hovered a few meters overhead. Just as Lina wondered how she and Tes were supposed to get inside, a hatch opened in the ship's smooth belly, disgorging a rolled-up ladder. As soon as it reached its full length, the ladder snapped into place and hung rigid.

Tes joined her on the scoot's wide cargo area and watched two agents they hadn't met before climb down with intimidating grace. Before any of them could speak, Jemny descended several rungs and shouted.

"Your scoot will be just fine. Let's *go!*"

"Ever climb anything like this?" Lina eyed the ladder without much confidence.

"Sure," Tes said. "We use them in several climbing classes and locations all over the planet. Just focus on the rung you're standing on and the one you have hold of, and don't look down."

She swung her own pack over her shoulder and climbed almost as fast as the two agents had descended. She disappeared for a few seconds, then leaned through the hatch with a reassuring smile.

"Do you need us to throw down a safety harness?"

Lina pursed her lips and shook her head. In all her training and experience, she was far more comfortable in and around massive amounts of water than massive amounts of air. But she refused to let anyone else know that.

Especially not if tourists routinely managed to use the things. She spoke more to herself than to anyone else.

"Just make damn sure that ladder stays put."

She held on to a rung at chest height, trying to ignore how the scoot bobbed up and down with the current, almost far enough to force her let go.

Funny how she hadn't noticed the movement until just this second.

Timing it to a swell that brought the ladder closer to the deck, she finally stepped onto the bottom rung and pulled herself up, following Tes's advice to keep her eyes straight ahead and focused on the blue horizon.

She wished the ship's landing wheels and struts were down rather than retracted so she'd have something else to pay attention to, or maybe grab hold of in an unimaginable emergency.

Despite her certainty that the ladder would collapse and send her swinging back and forth until she finally lost her grip and landed on the scoot with a thud, Tes was pulling her into the ship in only a few seconds.

Unlike the first time when they'd ridden to the winter lodge, several other agents crowded into the ship's gleaming white-and-silver seating area. All of them were dressed in what looked like modified, bright-white diving gear. Slick and formfitting, with hoods and helmets hanging down their backs.

Each of them had a solid, much larger version of the flexible breathing masks Lina used for diving dangling around their necks.

"What kind of conditions are we flying into?" she said as the ladder rolled itself back up and the ship's belly hatch closed.

Jemny frowned and shook her head as she turned her attention to the ship's controls. She wore the same protective clothing and gear herself.

The sleek command area was far more streamlined than anything Lina had seen on a scoot, and featured several screens and displays. Jemny seemed to control the ship by touching them without looking.

"The air's full of dust and ash, and we have no idea what else. Volcanic ash untouched for hundreds or thousands of years is reason enough to take precautions. We've got suits and masks for you both. So get ready."

Lina joined Tes, who had one of the strange-looking suits in her hands.

"How long since you dove deep enough to need something like this?" Tes said.

"Not since my early days of training. We had submersibles for really deep water, like we do here. They only had us get into the suits so we'd have an idea what to do in an emergency. Have you used these?"

Tes handed the suit to Lina and shrugged.

"About the same, just the most basic training for emergencies. I'm sure we'll do fine so far away from water, since that should eliminate the chance of drowning."

Lina had managed to roll and tug and pull the clingy suit not quite up to her waist when an idea too big to ignore struck. She half-walked, half-waddled forward to Jemny. They were flying over a stretch of grassy flatlands, but a line of regular, conical mountains rose in the distance.

"Have you been scanning for the grav-drive energy signature around the volcano?"

Jemny glanced at her, eyes narrowed.

"Of course we have. All over the planet, not just there."

"Listen, you might need to change the frequency you're scanning for. Right before you picked us up, Ris told me he's discovered the energy is getting weaker with every attack. We might all be searching for what they used in previous attacks instead of what they're using now."

Jemny drummed her fingers along the top of one of her pristine displays. Then she nodded once.

"Understood. I'll contact him right now and have him send the data and what he thinks we should be looking for this time around. Now I'm going to ask your opinion about him, and I promise you whatever you say won't get back to him."

Lina nodded slowly, hoping she'd be able to be honest about whatever Jemny was about to ask.

"I need someone to coordinate updating the scans we've been running planetwide with the new data. We've been handling that in Planetary Security, but it sounds as if Ris has a comprehensive understanding of what we're looking for. Is he capable of handling a job this big, keeping up with everyone and everything who needs the information?"

Despite her worries about what they might be flying into, Lina laughed.

"Ris is more than capable. If he were here, he'd tell you that's nothing compared to keeping up with regular personnel and all the projects and moving parts in Planetary Science, much less with the tourists and everyone in training. He can get a bit over-wrought sometimes, but his data and management skills are solid. And I get the feeling he'd be pleased enough to take what you're asking seriously without getting arrogant about it."

Jemny nodded, with a faint smile.

"That matches my impression of him so far. I'll let him know and get him started. Since we're not finding a damn thing the old way, it can't hurt. Get suited up and strap in. Conditions on the ground don't favor a gentle landing."

CHAPTER 22

COMPARED to the surreal slow-moving wave and even the terrifying multiple avalanches, arriving in the Sopka Valley was like landing in hell.

At first all Lina could see looked like a shadow peeking through the high ridges of other tall mountains, as if some kind of localized storm had gotten trapped and kept trying to find the way out.

No sign of scoots or ships or any other vessels that could be controlling the attack, at least not that she could see.

But as soon as Jemny's ship flew high enough to slip through a gap in the ridgeline—with its engine letting out a low rumble as it strained into the climb—Lina finally understood what they were up against.

The black clouds raging in front of a towering mountain of raw gray stone that had the obvious cone shape of a volcano were bad enough. The maelstrom followed the slope of the land more than the avalanches had, like all the debris had simply levitated without changing shape.

Even though Lina knew it wasn't erupting, some deep-seated part of her brain kept sending out the alarm that they needed to get away as soon as they could.

Her ancient survivor's mind was convinced explosions and magma were about to rain down on all of them, not to mention fast-moving clouds of noxious gasses.

The dust stretched across the whole valley from in front of the volcano to the nearby mountains, mostly obscuring whatever waited below. Lina could barely make out a broad open space full of brown and green through brief breaks in the cloud cover.

That had to be where Musa and the rest of the tourists were now sheltering, though the valley didn't feature anything as sturdy as a lodge to protect them from the choking mess. The maps they'd studied of the so-called visitor center showed nothing more than an open-air amphitheater with freestanding exhibits.

But when Jemny descended—not into the mass of debris held in the attackers' threat, only through clouds toward the valley—the ship jerked and tilted, and the engine's noise twisted into a high-pitched whine.

Jemny yelled at everyone to strap in as she belatedly did so herself.

Despite all the other agents already employing the sturdy harnesses built into the seats, they still held onto the seats in front of them, and their formerly cool and emotionless faces fell into lines of stress and worry. Even Jemny showed more distress than normal, with grunts of effort and teeth bared in a defiant snarl as she fought to keep the ship steady.

All Lina and Tes could do was grip the thick straps across their chests, brace themselves against their own seats, and hope the ship didn't get tossed sideways and even upside down like seaweed in a stormy high tide.

After several pitches and drops that rivaled anything Lina had ever experienced at sea, the ship finally thudded to the ground in what looked like late twilight. The bright sunlight of the day didn't stand a chance of getting through the storm overhead.

The engine's protests were replaced by what sounded like a thousand furious handfuls of rocks hitting the silvery exterior, along with the wind's chorus of tormented screams.

"Masks on!" Jemny yelled over the noise. "And do your best to keep visual with each other at all times. The energy field out there almost knocked out my controls, so comms and sensors might be useless."

Lina started toward a head-shaking Jemny even as everyone else lined up in front of the usual side-portal. Jemny didn't even look away from the ship's monitors—most already set to the faint blue of standby—before she answered questions Lina didn't have a chance to ask.

"Ris already notified our satellite operators of the new frequency range, Lina. We can't do a thing about that down here, even if we could get signals out. Also got a fleet of high-altitude sensor scoots and transports incoming, and more ships like mine to evacuate the tourists. Hopefully they'll catch a lucky break out there."

"Then what *are* we supposed to do?"

Jemny grinned, all traces of strain vanished from her face and body. She actually seemed *excited* rather than terrified.

"Do what we can to get people to safety, and keep an eye out in case we can do a whole lot more. If any comms do manage to make it through the interference in the valley, the ship will record them. Time for us to get *out* there."

Tes waved Lina toward the portal, pointing to her already covered face.

Lina felt a river of sweat springing up under the rubbery white suit at the idea of nearly sealing herself into the thing, but she pulled the hood into place, then raised her mask. Unlike the gloves that felt like a second skin, it was uncomfortably rigid against her flesh, covering from her forehead down to her chin. The tight fit made her jaw feel like it was caught in a vise.

The way the helmet snapped over the mask only intensified the caged feeling.

But despite her anxiety, she was able to breathe freely through the filtering mask itself.

The agents all carried bags stuffed with more masks and full suits in case any of the tourists were already in distress, along with huge shoulder-mounted lights that looked like they'd pierce through the gloom outside with ease.

Lina nodded and pointed toward the portal.

She was startled when Tes seemed to speak right into her ear.

"Are your ground comms up, Lina?"

"I hear you, but I don't know how."

Tes tapped the side of her helmet.

"Bone conduction between the helmet and the mask." She waved a gloved hand toward one of the agents, now waving their hand in a circle as a warning about opening the portal.

"They said this system is supposed to work better with all the noise and interference out there. I hope so. Clip this tether onto the front of your suit's belt, then clip the second one to the back before you hand it off to Jemny. We're at least going to start out attached."

Lina understood the worry as soon as the portal started moving to the side. An ear-wrenching shriek preceded a whirl-wind of sooty dust, and even through her hard mask she smelled the ozone of a lightning strike mixed with old charcoal.

And the same electrical charge tingled across her tongue as with the first two attacks.

Lina clipped the glowing, wiry tether attached to Tes into a metal ring on her own belt, then did the same to a second one before Jemny took it. They had about three meters to play out between them.

Undeterred by the noise and debris outside the portal, the first agent slipped through as soon as there was enough room. The others spilled out in a rush before Tes looked back and nodded at Lina.

"We'll at least get them back to this ship and out of the horror out there."

And she stepped out and into the furious cloud.

Lina held the portal's sides for a second, fully aware of Jemny behind her and Tes playing out the tether.

She couldn't quite grasp how she'd gotten so far from her peaceful tidal pool, on the day when she'd first met Tes, Jemny, and Musa.

Even more strange was the idea of going back to her ordinary life—before she knew anything about the secret security function of Sarkans 3—when all she thought about was discovering and categorizing as many of the planet's teeming lifeforms as she could.

With pure luck and the team she'd somehow managed to become part of, she hoped to find some combination that would keep her safe and sane.

Her first step into the raging winds of the Sopka Valley drove all of that out of her mind. She didn't have room for much besides her own survival, and doing her best to find Musa.

Steady as she normally was in water or on land, she could only walk hunched over with her knees bent. Otherwise the gale would have toppled her over and left her at the mercy of her twin tethers glowing like eerie fish she'd seen on her deepest dives.

The wind seemed to attack from all directions at once, and she wasn't having any more luck shifting with it than the ship had.

Her visibility extended not much past the tips of her own gloved fingers that now shone with their own white glow, but not enough to help with the gloom. She was more than grateful for her connection to Tes and Jemny. It was all she could do to keep walking without stumbling over rocky ground that she could barely see.

A voice she didn't recognize spoke.

"No lock on anyone out here, sensors can't get through all the static. Lights are worthless except maybe as beacons for each other. We'll walk out our tethers, then walk to the left to try and sweep them up."

Her tethers pulled from both directions, and Lina concentrated on staying as coordinated as she could with the straight line.

Grunts and soft curses made it clear she wasn't the only one struggling with her footing, but they started walking.

The dust was thick enough that the suspended cloud of

volcanic ash and mud hung almost out of sight over their heads, with only a more-deeply shadowed area to give it away.

"When did we last hear from the target group on comms?" another agent said.

"That's not our concern," Jemny cut in, "because this is a rescue-in-any-condition situation. But they were still active less than ten minutes before we landed. We just need to find them."

The walk—silent except for the continued sonic assault from wind and grit—went on long enough that Lina got concerned about how long their masks would hold up. But she was too afraid of any answer to ask.

Getting stranded out here would be horrible, and so would being forced to retreat to the ship without finding Musa and the others.

All she could do was keep going.

And keep hoping.

After completing one circle around the ship, they all marched forward in a straight line before starting the same circuit to the left. Lina decided not to ask whether Jemny had attached another tether behind herself before they ventured so far away from safety.

The second walk around felt like they were moving in slow motion through the billowing clouds of soot and it would be days before they came back around. Assuming they didn't over-shoot somehow and not realize it until they reached the edge of the valley.

And even a small valley like Sopka could certainly be big enough to keep them wandering around so long in the ever-changing wind that the noxious air got them, or the attackers' mysterious source of control over the landslide failed.

Lina was afraid to mention her fears out loud, or admit to the overwhelming urge she had to run and not stop until something stopped her.

Not only because she was ashamed, though she hated feeling like such a potential coward.

If even one of the others was as on-edge as she was, those words could start a panic they'd all get caught up in.

That could all too easily result in no one ever leaving this formerly peaceful valley alive.

All she could do was try not to lose her balance and fall, and watch for the blurry lighter patches that were the only sign of the agents' huge shoulder lights. The illumination of their suits disappeared entirely.

The wind did its best to shove them forward, then back, before switching to battering from the sides.

Her nerves kept trying to convince her that the already form-fitting suit was getting tighter, and robbing what little breath she had to keep walking. Her sweat had long since congealed in the cool outside air, making every movement seem like her skin was covered in some sort of glue.

She first thought the dark shapes on the ground were rock formations, and she tried to force herself to believe that even after she walked too close to pretend.

But time could run out, even for people huddled together trying to protect themselves from suffocating in toxic dust.

"I think… That looks like something straight ahead of me. On the ground."

CHAPTER 23

A TALL FORM like a moving torch bounded in from her left, somehow running over the treacherous ground. Then Jemny knelt beside one of the shapes.

"Got something here! Keep circling in until you reach me, and we'll start taking them to the ship."

Lina saw several dark lumps in a drifting clearing in the dust, too big to be one person, scattered in a loose group. She staggered to Jemny's side, finally tripping over a rock and landing with a tooth-knocking thump in front of one of the rough shapes.

The word Jemny used—some*thing*, not some*one*—worked in a queasy loop through Lina's mind.

Jemny carefully lifted what Lina realized was an arm.

And that arm didn't resist the movement.

"They covered each other, face down to stay out of the dust," Jemny said. "We don't have enough room on my ship for everyone here. If we can find their scoots, we can put them in there to wait for rescue."

Lina's jaw and gut clenched with what she had to say, but that didn't stop the words.

"Maybe we should figure out who we *can* still save and go from there first."

"Some of the agents have med-scanners, but they won't work in this kind of interference any more than our sensors or comms do. So unless you've got an ancient stethoscope or something like it hidden in your suit, I'm not sure how you're going to figure that out."

Lina scooted forward, lifting the seemingly lifeless arm higher. She reached into the shadows underneath and felt a smaller body.

She shifted her grip until she had a slender limb.

Then she started to pull.

"Just move them until they resist. That might not tell us everyone who's still alive, but we'll know who's conscious."

For an endless moment, she was certain all the tourists were already dead. That all the effort to get out here would end up yielding nothing more useful than retrieving corpses, stacking them like logs in the ship or rescue scoots, and going right back to trying and failing to catch whoever kept attacking.

And all of it with no idea why the attacks were happening, which made them even more cruel and senseless.

Then whoever she had hold of tried to pull away, and Lina gasped.

"This one's moving. Grab someone else, Jemny!"

Lina grabbed the squirming person with both hands and

pulled again, while Jemny lifted the body on top of the pile out of the way.

She didn't have hold of Musa, but a little boy around the same age. When he brushed the dust away from his face and started coughing, Lina realized she had no way to keep him from breathing in the poisonous air. If she tried to put something over his mouth after dragging him out into the open, he'd surely fight, and possibly bite her.

One of the agents tapped her shoulder and stepped forward, somehow projecting their voice outside of their mask.

"Keep calm, we're here to help you. Put this on so you can breathe."

Lina waited long enough to see the boy take hold of the mask, pressing it to his dust-and-sweat streaked face.

By the time she turned back, Jemny had moved two more of the adults over to the side, where she seemed to have forgotten about them.

If Lina stopped to help them, Musa might end up suffocating, or getting taken off to one of the now-empty scoots.

Tes touched her shoulder.

"I've got them. Go look for her."

So Lina squatted close to the smaller bodies and reached forward. Three more confused and agitated children wriggled free one at a time, and thankfully each of them managed to take the masks without getting even more upset.

Then a small hand grabbed hers with ferocious strength.

Musa's little face was coated with the filthy dust, and even her teeth were covered with it when she smiled.

"Lina! I knew…" She coughed, covering her mouth and shaking her head. "You came to…to help us…"

Lina yanked off her own helmet and mask, doing her best to take shallow breaths though her heart raced in her chest. Even with that, her throat burned and tickled within seconds, and she was fighting back coughs herself.

"Musa, put this on so you can breathe."

"No you don't," Jemny said from beside her. "I need you functional. Give this one to her, and help me with the others."

Lina scowled at Jemny, but took the clean mask. After she got her own back into place, she helped Musa wrap the more flexible mask from the top of her head to under her chin and waited for her to catch her breath.

"Where are your grandparents?"

A pair of dirty hands reached for the girl, who smiled big enough that Lina could see it over the mask before she went to them.

Tears streaking the cheeks of both adults were just as clear under their larger masks as they knelt to catch Musa in a huge dual hug. Without moving, they both looked up at Lina.

"Thank you for finding her!" Musa's grandfather cried. "When that cloud swooped down and we couldn't see her, we thought the absolute worst. We've already been through too much, then for this to follow us..."

Musa's grandmother kissed where his cheek was under the mask, then the top of Musa's head.

"We're all together now, and that's what matters. We need to get out of the way and let Lina and her friends figure out why this keeps happening."

When they all stood, Musa's grandmother reached for Lina's hand.

"I'm Seerit Sauri, and my husband is Pandar. Thank you so much, Lina."

Lina could only nod as they took Musa's hands and walked away.

"There, she's with her grandparents," Jemny said through Lina's bone-conduction comm. "Now get over here and *help* me."

Lina walked over to where Jemny was still sending children toward a tightly knotted group. Two other agents knelt in the middle, shoulder lights now deactivated but suits still keeping them somewhat visible, looking each child in the eyes before settling a mask into place.

With the horrific noise showing no signs of letting up, Lina couldn't hear what any of them were saying.

A few more adults were sitting up now, most of them coughing despite the shocking white masks covering their mouths with their sooty foreheads peeking through the transparent top. Tes walked toward them with two more people stumbling beside her.

No one who'd been gathered in the valley wore anything close to protective clothing. Their arms and legs showed through rips in even longer garments. Lina hoped it was from catching them on rocks rather than the relentless wind scouring them away.

"We've got to start taking them to shelter," Jemny said. "Looks like this was mostly families with kids. I haven't found any not breathing yet, but some aren't conscious."

"Do you know if the rescue scoots are here yet?" Lina said. "Or at least on the way?"

Jemny shook her head as she pulled a young teenager to her

feet and held up a mask. The poor girl hacked as if her lungs were riddled with disease or extreme old age.

"Put this on so you can breathe," Jemny said with her amplified voice. "See that group over there? Can you walk to them and wait, quick as you can? We're doing everything we can to get you out of here."

Once the dazed girl nodded and walked away, Jemny spoke only through Lina's helmet and mask.

"Still no comms. Unless this forcefield or storm or whatever it is breaks and finally crushes us all, we'll have to get back to the ship and try to get airborne."

Lina clenched her fists even as Jemny reached for another child.

So much damage had been done already.

To Scarlet Beach what felt like a year ago, to the beautiful winter landscape, and now to this valley that should be safe and peaceful even in the midst of the planet's geological fury.

All of that without serious harm or death to people, possibly because someone charged with protecting Sarkans 3 and everyone who visited had managed to interfere.

Lina couldn't pretend animals and habitats hadn't been badly harmed.

Her excitement and idealistic notions of her work and her new life had certainly been damaged.

But it could have been so much worse.

Now they were caught in the middle of another deadly situation, and she had no reason at all to think this wouldn't keep happening over and over and over again.

So far all the countless hours of worrying and investigation and talking had brought them no closer to understanding, or stopping the attacks altogether.

"But *why* is this happening?" she said, too loud and her voice still rising. "Whoever it is hasn't demanded anything. They're just *tormenting* us!"

When the child stopped and stared at her, still clutching his throat and covering his mouth, Lina realized her ears were ringing.

Sure enough, every person she could see through the surging clouds of sooty grit had turned their way.

Only Jemny seemed unconcerned, pulling the boy closer and getting a mask over most of his head to protect his still-shocked face herself this time.

She didn't even look away as she spoke only to Lina again.

"I assume no one told you how to activate the external speakers on your helmet. Squeeze your left fist in exactly the same way to deactivate them, and you'll be fine. I need you to follow my tether back to the ship and let me know if the system's recorded any messages while it's been on standby."

Lina wasn't anywhere near upset enough to pretend she hadn't just been dismissed, or at least encouraged to walk away long enough to get herself under control. But the idea of taking even a quick break from all the noise and dirt and strain of knowing an aerial landslide could crush them at any second was too tempting to resist.

She squeezed both fists to be sure before speaking.

"Got it. I'll let you know how it's going over the comms. And hopefully *only* you."

She turned to go, but Jemny grabbed her shoulder.

"Hang on, disconnect yourself first. Otherwise you'll drag me and Tes along with you the whole way. Neither of those tethers are long enough to make it."

Even with the mask covering most of her face, Lina's indecision must have been plain.

"You comfortable hanging on to my tether?" Jemny said. "Otherwise I can call Tes in and we'll see if the two together are long enough to reach."

Lina bit back quick agreement.

They'd walked out much farther than both tethers would be, easily more than twice that far. No matter how anxious she was, she wasn't about to let Jemny humor her like that.

And she certainly wouldn't agree to hook the longer tether to her own suit even if Jemny offered.

It would be way too easy for everyone to get separated that way.

She wished she could pretend they wouldn't need to evacuate in a hurry, but too many strange things had already happened to even consider that idea.

"I'll make sure to hold on." Lina unclipped her tethers and linked them together, taking the time to make sure the rings on her suit were too small to feed the clip all the way through. "Hopefully we'll hear from Ris before then. He'd be thrilled beyond reason to figure this whole mess out."

Jemny nodded, her body already turning back toward the people who still needed help.

"Right. Take care, Lina. Comms are open, so keep me updated."

Lina took a deep, shaky breath and managed a smile that was only for herself.

"You do the same."

CHAPTER 24

Before she'd taken more than a dozen steps into the whirling muck—carefully holding on to Jemny's tether—Lina felt a small hand grabbing her free one.

She didn't need to look to know Musa had found her, somehow not getting herself lost in the howling wind and thick blanket of grime that took up most of the air in the valley.

"Do your grandparents know where you are?"

Lina bent to catch the girl's unamplified voice.

"They're sitting with the others, but they said I could go with you. Or I think they did. I left kinda fast."

Lina kept the tether centered in her loose fist as she walked, making sure she didn't pull it in either direction. The unlikely possibility of yanking it loose at one or both ends—leaving her and Musa wandering lost in the valley—was far too vivid in her imagination.

What little light that penetrated the smoggy valley faded as they passed back under the mass of soil and ash holding them hostage.

"Did you run off so they couldn't tell you not to?"

Musa waited a long time to answer, which told Lina all she needed to know.

"They know you'll make sure I'm safe. You and Tes and even the scary ones with you."

After several more steps that made it clear just how far they'd ventured from the ship, Lina decided not to waste her opportunity to ask questions. Then she'd get Musa back where she belonged, hopefully inside the ship along with her family.

"Do you remember what happened this time, Musa? Right before the huge cloud showed up?"

"You mean *another* giant wave? We were walking around and looking at all the strange things in the dirt under the grass, like old bones and where trees used to be. Some people were going to try climbing again on the volcano mountains before we left, but they never got to. Because the noise started then, right before the ground flew into the air."

"Noise? You mean the wind we can hear now?"

"Not that. It was so high that I could barely hear it, and it made my head hurt."

"Do you still hear that noise right now?"

"Kind of. It's hard to over the wind. But it's still there."

Lina's mind flashed to what she knew about grav-drive energy, which wasn't nearly as much as she wanted to even after so many hours concentrating on its effects.

And to how Jemny's engine had protested the climb over the tall passes.

Machines and engines normally tried to warn humans when they'd reached their limits.

It was just the kind of odd detail that might make a difference.

"Did anyone else seem to hear the noise?"

Musa shook her head.

"I asked my grandparents, just like I did at the beach and in the snow. They never could. They've told me before about how sometimes old people can't hear as well as a kid like me. Especially since I have magic ears. Do you think that's true?"

Lina barely noticed that she could finally see flashes of the silvery ship through the dust. Her back and hips were starting to ache from leaning toward Musa, but she had no intention of missing a word the girl said.

"Did you say you have magic ears? I don't think I know what that means."

"Just that I had to have an operation when I was a baby, a long time ago. They put a… Well, I can't remember what they called it, but it was like a speaker that made sounds work better. So I can hear like everyone else does. But I never heard *better* than everyone else before. Is that where we're going?"

Musa pointed one dirty hand at the ship, and Lina nodded without thinking. Of course Musa probably wouldn't see her nod, since the ship was the most exciting thing right now.

Just like her grandparents and everyone else probably wouldn't be able to hear something a girl with a hearing aid implant could.

"That's where we're going, at least for a little while. Do you remember if the noise you're hearing stopped when the other big waves stopped? At the beach and in the snow?"

Musa walked several more steps, low-grav-bouncing enough that she was almost skipping, but never letting go of Lina's hand.

"It got really *loud* both times, remember? But when the loud stopped and the waves were gone, the noise was gone, too. Do you think that might help you figure out what's happening? My grandparents said that's why we keep seeing you. I'm glad we do."

"It just might help us, Musa. A whole lot. And I'm glad to see you, too."

They'd arrived at the ship, and for a horrible moment, Lina was convinced they wouldn't be able to get inside once they walked up the short ramp. The rounded port door was flush with the smooth, metallic skin, now coated with a thick layer of black dust.

"Jemny, can you hear me? I have no idea how to open the door."

For several more seconds, Lina worried they were too far away, and they'd have to retrace their steps no matter how much she wanted to hurry.

That or crawl under the ship and huddle there beside the landing struts and wheels.

"Just put your hand in the middle of the door," Jemny said over Lina's bone conduction, her voice clear but strained. "I'll key the release mechanism from here. Should have added you to the ship's security system before we left, sorry about that."

The apology, no matter how casual, got a smile out of Lina that felt great with so much going on.

She let go of the tether and held her gloved hand over the middle of the port. After what felt like hours but only lasted a couple of her breaths, the door clicked and slid to the side.

"Hurry, Musa, so all this dust won't get inside."

They scurried into the ship before the door finished opening, and it closed behind them just as quickly. Lina's suit lost its glow at once, and it was nowhere near as white as when they'd started out.

"Wow," Musa breathed, still wearing her mask. "It's so smooth and shiny in here."

"We're in," Lina said. "And if someone has a chance, please make sure Musa's grandparents know she's with me. Will I still be able to hear you if I take my mask off?"

"You can remove it," Jemny said, "but keep it in reach, and put your helmet back on. We've just about got everyone rounded up. Only a few who can't walk, no fatalities so far. Let me know if anything's on the comms. You'll see an alert flashing if there is, and hear the most irritating *ping* ever invented to torment humans."

Lina slipped her helmet off, pulled her mask after it, and took a slow breath of mostly clean air. Particles lingered from the swirl of dust that had followed them on top of what blew in after they landed.

The same scorched, charged scent lingered, and the constant rattle of debris against the ship hadn't let up.

Musa pushed her mask back over the top of her head and grinned up at Lina.

"Just don't take it all the way off," Lina said, pushing her own helmet back into place. "We'll probably have to go right back out. I need to see if anyone who can send help has tried to get in touch with us."

Musa followed her to the front of the ship and the unfamiliar bunch of screens.

"That was the *other* thing that upset everyone today," Musa said. "When the giant wave was about to start. People talked about their comms not working."

"But that didn't happen before." Lina thought back to telling Ris everything that was happening during the controlled tsunami. She'd been able to patch her portable test kit results into this ship after the avalanches, too. "The whole attack is shifting, no matter how hard we try to track it all down."

Each of the screens was ominously black rather than standby-blue, and tapping them didn't bring any response. No signs of any kind of alert or pings, annoying or not.

Only the endless assault of dust and rocks outside.

Before Lina could ask for help through her bone conduction comm, Jemny's voice crackled into her ear.

"...activate comms on the... ...should start up when..."

"She's not talking right," Musa said, sounding far more amused than Lina felt.

"No, she's not. Jemny, Agent Manhoff, I couldn't understand you just now. And I can't access the ship's comms."

Another series of staticky crackles, then more garbled words.

"...at the ship... ...get them to shelter before... ...wait for us before you..."

Lina retrieved the pack she'd stowed under her seat before getting into the uncomfortable and overheating protective suit. Her own comm stick powered up just fine, showing a series of colorful test patterns and playing the usual soft activation sounds.

But it didn't respond when she tried to get it to function, staying as black as the ship's screens.

"I'm afraid comms still aren't working, Musa. We may be on our own for a little while."

She turned to see Musa peering at the screens and controls up front and carefully not touching anything.

"I don't think *any*thing is working. I got to sit next to the scoot pilot when we were flying to this valley, and lights were everywhere on that one. Don't you think this ship feels like it's dead?"

Lina shivered, and it had nothing to do with the cool interior.

Musa was right.

There was no sign of power on any of the ship's systems or anywhere else. So far nothing worked but the portal they'd come through, and only then with Jemny's assistance.

Even the air inside felt stale, which it shouldn't with a ship on standby. The dust shouldn't have lingered in the air for any length of time if ventilation was functioning, either.

"Maybe Jemny knows how to get it started again," Lina said. "I'm glad to be out of all that wind and dirt, aren't you?"

Musa nodded, then cocked her head, staring toward the curved roof.

"That weird sound is still there, but it's…different now."

"Louder? Or like an engine working harder?"

Even inside the ship, if that landslide let go, Lina didn't like the odds for their survival. If the weight didn't crush them, getting out from under tonnes of volcanic soil wasn't a given.

"I think it's higher now," Musa said. "And kind of jaggedy. Like it's rippling in water."

"Or it's an oscillation. Does it sound like hearing a *motor* underwater? Or like something that's not running very well?"

Musa shook her head.

"I can't tell. Do you think we should try to get Tes and the other ones to come inside and out of the storm?"

Lina tried to look through the ship's forward windows, but she couldn't see a thing besides the seething dust.

"Would you be okay staying here while I try to do that?"

Musa nodded, but her wide eyes looked frightened.

"Jemny, are you headed this way with our rescued people?"

Nothing.

Not even a whisper of static.

Even without any kind of alarm or message, Lina was certain the bone-conduction comm was now as dead as the ship.

CHAPTER 25

Lina knew her heart hadn't actually stopped beating.

Surely if it had, she wouldn't still be breathing and thinking well enough to be deeply afraid.

But convincing herself of that while standing with Musa in a dead ship with no way to operate comms was a tall order.

Musa putting on a brave smile while she once again reached for Lina's hand only intensified the sense of impending panic.

Another glance toward the blank screens up front showed how much of the sparkling black dust floated in the still air, which already felt more stale than when she and Musa walked in. Colder too, and with a stronger smell of cinders and burning things.

Even so, she considered staying right where she was. Doing her best to keep Musa—and herself—distracted while they waited for Jemny or Tes or Ris or someone else to rescue them. After all, what good could they possibly do by wandering right back into the storm they'd just escaped?

Except…

If they did wait here and the others returned, with exhausted or wounded tourists in tow, and found a useless ship, they might be wasting too much time and energy to give them a chance to escape. They might all be better off heading to one of the scoots to wait for rescue.

At least those were usually equipped with enough food and drink to keep their vacationing passengers entertained. And if this group did include someone important or endangered enough to require the kind of retreat only Sarkans 3 could provide—and enough obsession or ill-will to draw this kind of attack—the scoot might be well-provisioned indeed.

She didn't allow herself to consider what she and Musa would do if no one ever found their way back to the ship, much less what disaster might make that possible with someone as tough and focused as Jemny knowing exactly where they were.

Since she was traveling with one excited little girl instead of several dazed and possibly hurt tourists, heading out to warn the others only made sense.

Lina couldn't help taking one more look at her comm stick, but she didn't bother unrolling it to make sure.

Its tubular surface was still active, and completely blank.

"Okay, Musa, I think we're going to change our plans yet again. Is that okay with you?"

Musa rolled her eyes in an adorable imitation of how Lina wished she felt.

"*That's* what we've been doing on our *whole* vacation, ever since the first giant wave. Grandpa says I'm getting all kinds of good practice with life skills. He said I'll know how to…adjust my expectations."

"He's right, that's very good practice, and a great life skill. Since we can't get comms to work and the ship is getting kind of smelly, how about we go find the others so we can let them know?"

Musa let go of Lina's hand so she could pull her mask back over her face, then she bounced in place.

"Let's go! Maybe they already know what's happening and what to do about it."

Lina slipped her comm into her pocket and pulled her own mask and helmet back on, wishing she could borrow a little of Musa's certainty.

"I think you might be right."

She didn't realize how worried she'd been about the ship not letting them back out until the door slid to the side at her touch. Jemny must have activated some kind of automatic function that didn't need regular power.

She was anything but relieved at how much worse conditions were once they stepped outside.

Rather than late twilight, now the sky looked like evening was well underway. She could no longer tell the difference between the hovering wedge of soil that had once been layered over the volcano and the roiling clouds that filled the Sopka Valley.

Everything looked like thick smoke from an oily fire, and the burning stink was awful even through her mask. The renewed glow of her gloves and suit was barely a smudge in the thick darkness.

She doubted even the huge shoulder lights the Planetary Security agents carried would make much difference.

When Musa covered her ears with both hands, Lina almost

went back into the ship to look for another suit, or at least a hood and helmet. The idea of the girl's extra-sensitive ears being exposed to the choked shriek of the gale turned Lina's heart into a clenched knot of regret.

But if they'd had enough suits—or one the right size—surely the others would have already given one to Musa. Assuming she hadn't run after Lina before anyone got the chance.

All she could do was hold Musa's arm and grab the tether that disappeared from sight barely a meter in front of them.

And hope that thin and fragile-looking connection that barely glimmered against an imposed night still led to Tes, Jemny, and the rest of the people stranded in this nightmarish place.

Before they'd taken more than a few staggering, uncertain steps away from the fragile shelter of the ship, she couldn't pretend the artificial storm hadn't gotten far worse.

Now the wind felt like it was actively trying to lift her off her feet rather than shoving her in every direction at once.

Larger rocks and clumps of ash and bits of plants hurtled through the much stronger blast.

She wished even more that Musa had a helmet to protect her delicate skull.

The tether whipped back and forth enough that a sickening certainty started to take shape in Lina's belly.

Even if she was still attached to the currently useless ship, if Jemny and the others were now *de*tached, they were all lost.

"Can anyone hear me? We're out of the ship, headed back to you."

Nothing but the bellowing wind answered.

Lina barely heard Musa's scream as she tripped and landed

hard, getting her hands down just in time to brace herself instead of landing mask-first. By the time Lina knelt beside her, Musa was wailing.

"I *hate* it here! I want to go back to the beach and see the giant wave there instead of this!"

Lina held her tight for a moment, fighting back tears at the despairing sound of her voice.

"I hate it here too. Once we find the others, we'll all get out of this valley, okay?"

Instead of answering, Musa wrapped her arms around Lina's neck.

It was all Lina could do to keep herself from giving in and just sitting there on the ground, hugging Musa and leaving their fates to the cruel winds.

When she finally looked up and paid attention to their surroundings, another shock ripped through her already strained mind.

She'd dropped the tether when Musa fell.

And it was nowhere to be found.

CHAPTER 26

Lina tried to keep herself from breathing too fast, certain that whatever powered the mask's filtering abilities wouldn't be able to keep up with hyperventilation.

Anyway, when faced with a sobbing child, she couldn't imagine anything worse than losing her own composure.

There was no one else out here who could rescue them.

At least no one who'd be able to find them if *she* didn't find the damn tether.

Without letting go of Musa, she shifted onto her heels, then her knees. The girl's slight frame worked with the planet's light gravity to let Lina get carefully to her feet without too much effort. But she did almost wish Musa still had her tiny anti-grav pods concealed under her clothing.

Keeping her balance once she got there with the tempest doing its best to knock her back down and send both of them tumbling across the jagged ground was another matter.

She turned in a slow, shuffling circle, as if her eyes could magically adjust to the horrible conditions.

With the way the tether had been jerking in her grip, it could have gone in either direction.

If she chose the wrong way to start walking, she and Musa might be wandering off to their deaths.

But staying still and hoping it would blow back might not be any more helpful.

Too late, she wondered if she could have fashioned some kind of loop around her waist to run the blasted thing through, so losing her grip wouldn't matter.

She'd been in too much of a hurry to stop and make sensible plans.

"We aren't *lost*, are we?" Musa nearly moaned into her ear. "Are you looking around because we're lost?"

"We're not lost, not like you mean. I just need to figure out where the others are. It's going to be okay."

Lina felt Musa shaking her head. It didn't much matter whether she was rejecting the lie or trying her best not to give in to hopelessness.

Either one fit.

But maybe the two of them together would have a better chance of at least walking in a straight line.

"Did you get hurt when you fell, Musa?"

"No. Just scared. Need me to get down and walk like a big girl?"

"If you can. That way we can keep each other on the right track."

She gently set Musa on her feet, holding on through an especially brutal wind gust.

"You dropped your rope," Musa said right before Lina let go. "The rope back to the ship, and to the other people."

Lina squatted to stay close enough to hear over the worsening howl of the wind.

"I sure did. That's what we need to find now. Think you can help me walk in a straight line so we can do that?"

Musa mimicked Lina, looking in all directions, though she either wasn't brave or steady enough on her feet to actually turn.

"Do you know which way to go?"

"Not yet. But I'll bet we can figure it out."

Musa took her hand and patted it with the other one.

"I bet we can too, Lina."

Lina almost wished she didn't sound quite so confident.

For a moment, she thought again about staying still. Not out of fear this time, or not *only* out of fear.

She could too easily envision Jemny, Tes, and the others moving in one direction looking for them, and herself and Musa moving differently enough to barely miss them.

Then Musa coughed even with her mask on, and Lina realized her own throat was feeling ticklish. She'd thought about it but never got around to asking Jemny how long the masks were good for.

Not that any mask was likely to be designed to stand up to endless clouds of volcanic dust driven at terrifying speeds.

So she stood as upright as she could manage and still keep her balance, held tight to Musa's hand, and started walking.

After Musa stumbled several times, once badly enough that Lina almost fell beside her, Lina picked her up again.

"This isn't because you're not a big girl. It's just that carrying you helps me keep my balance."

Instead of trying to cover up the embarrassment Lina was trying to prevent, Musa giggled close to her ear.

"That's silly, but I'm not supposed to say things like that. I'm supposed to pretend it makes sense so you won't feel bad."

"I appreciate that, but you don't have to worry about making me feel bad. I feel pretty silly a lot of the time anyway."

Lina stumbled over a rock she couldn't see then, and Musa's grip around her neck got uncomfortably tight.

A distraction for both of them was in order.

"Tell me about your vacation. How long have you and your grandparents been on Sarkans 3?"

"Three whole weeks so far, but our trip is for three months, so we've got lots of time left to see things besides giant waves. I liked the first two waves a lot better than this one."

"I think I did too. What are you looking forward to most besides maybe waves that aren't quite so giant?"

Lina took several more shuffling steps before Musa answered. The extra weight actually did help keep her balanced, at least so far.

She felt Musa's back rise and fall with a deep breath followed by another cough.

"My grandparents always get sad this time of year, so I'm looking forward to them feeling better. They remember my parents way more than I do. I tried to tell them how lucky I am that I get to live with them, but I think that just makes them feel worse."

A shiver of curiosity took so much of Lina's attention that she almost tripped again. With everything she'd recently learned about security on the planet and the kinds of people who visited, this might be exactly the kind of thing Jemny needed to know about.

But asking a scared little girl more about what sounded like missing or even dead parents might not be the best idea in the middle of a mystery storm.

A storm that wasn't any kind of bad luck or accident of nature, but possibly created to target someone in this valley right now.

"I can tell how much they love spending time with you," Lina said. "I bet they'll be glad to see you when we finally find them."

"I shouldn't have snuck away like I did. But I knew you'd keep me safe."

Lina froze, head tilted to one side.

She was sure she'd heard a shout or some other kind of loud noise off to the right, but she didn't want to scare Musa before she knew for certain.

"All of us make decisions before we get a chance to think sometimes," she whispered, still straining to pick something out through the wind. "Do you hear anything different now?"

"Did you hear the big noises stop?" Musa whispered right back. "The one that came with the giant wave both times before?"

Lina closed her eyes and nodded to herself, and to Musa if she wasn't too busy being enchanted by their hellish surroundings.

"Do you mean the noise stopped just now, Musa? Like it did before the wave ended the first two times?"

"I think it stopped. But maybe that other noise is just louder than the really high ones and I can't hear it anymore."

Lina strained anew, and she held her breath in an effort to pick out what was different, at least to Musa's magic ears.

"Tell me about the new sound?"

"It's kind of fluttery, like when a bunch of birds fly overhead. But not quite as fluffy. This sounds kind of hard against the air."

Images of a hundred scoots arriving to rescue them danced through Lina's mind, along with a less comforting scene of the bigger rocks finding a place to gather all at once.

Piled up around Lina's feet and knees and legs, and maybe high enough that her slowly failing mask wouldn't matter anymore.

She did her best to block out the heart-stopping possibility of the suspended side of the volcano finally slipping out of its unnatural control. If gravity finally took over, no one in the valley was likely to ever escape it.

"Okay, can you tell where it's coming from? Is it overhead, like birds?"

Musa stopped breathing at the same time Lina did, both of them listening.

"Some of it's overhead. But I think... I think most of the noise is that way."

She let go of Lina long enough to point to the right.

Exactly where the shout came from, at least what Lina *thought* was a shout.

When she blinked and tried to look that way, she realized the visor of her mask wasn't as clear as it had been before the constant wind scoured it.

Not that she'd be able to see whether they were walking toward a worse threat or not through so much stuff thickening the air.

"Let's try this." She turned her body in the same direction. "Keep listening and tell me what you hear, and if we're still going toward it. I hope I can get us inside and out of this awful storm."

Musa coughed several times before she could answer.

"Good. I'm tired of this valley and the storm and all these giant waves. I'll tell you which way to go."

But before Lina had taken more than a dozen steps, she could hear the growing noise for herself.

And it sounded like all the suspended dirt and ash and rocks slowly starting to fall.

CHAPTER 27

Lina struggled with a growing urge to run, even though she knew she couldn't run fast enough to get herself and Musa away from whatever was happening.

The clouds over their heads were too thick and heavy for her to work her lungs that hard, even without the now-invisible wedge of mountainside added to the load. And even a valley that was advertised as cozy and secluded was far too big for her to make it to the dubious shelter of its edge on foot before it was too late.

All she could do was keep going, trusting her feet to avoid hazards she could no longer see, and her and Musa's ears to keep them going in the right direction.

Her fearful sweat left her feeling slick and sticky inside the suit, but it refused to give up on its tight grip. She felt drops running down her scalp under the hood, and she no longer knew whether the haze across her vision was perspiration fog or the damaged visor.

Musa didn't squirm or resist, thank goodness, but her weight was finally starting to drag on Lina's shoulders and back, driving a series of aching cramps deeper into her muscles with each step.

And still the ominous pattering noise continued.

All around them now rather than just in front.

Where she didn't hear a trace of the one shout she was almost certain she'd imagined.

Even as the scorched, electrical smell in the air grew stronger, Lina's throat felt more itchy and sore. She knew Musa was doing her best not to cough, but her slender ribs kept twitching under Lina's arms.

Neither of them would last much longer out here without help.

Help Lina was afraid would arrive too late if it ever got there at all.

She let out a shriek when something smacked against the back of her thighs, but she was too afraid of falling to turn right away.

"What's wrong, Lina?" Musa shouted, her arms squeezing Lina's neck.

Lina only shook her head as she slowed and stopped, working to balance against the never-ending wind.

The impact repeated, this time hard enough to hurt.

Her heart pounded too hard in her ears to let her hear anyone that might be approaching, or anything.

It hadn't crossed her mind until that second, but the oceans weren't the only part of Sarkans 3 that harbored bizarre and frightening predators. Many of them more than capable of taking out one woman carrying a little girl through blinding, enforced nighttime.

Was it possible some kind of unknown beast had been trapped in the valley before the storm fell, or driven down when the mountain's face levitated away?

Lina kept her back toward the source of the latest attack, determined to protect Musa the best she could while standing and fighting at least this one thing. Even if it proved far too much for her in the end.

"I'm going to set you down behind me, so I can figure out what's going on. Can you run in the same direction if you need to?"

Musa squeezed so hard Lina's head pounded, but she gradually let go, loosening her grip with each deep breath she took.

Painful coughs snuck in between each expansion of her little chest.

"You can run with me, Lina, and we'll *both* get away from whatever the bad thing is. We can go right now."

Lina's heart once again broke at how trusting and innocent Musa was, even in the face of the third terrifying attack she'd endured in only a few days.

Many of the adults Lina knew could benefit from such so-far unbreakable optimism.

"Just let me see what it is first. Then we'll run if we need to. But promise me you'll run on your own if I can't."

Musa's chest hitched with the threat of tears instead of coughs, but she put her legs down when Lina knelt.

"I promise. But you promise you'll come with me if you can!"

"If I can. I promise. Be sure to stay behind me."

Lina had half-turned when she was hit again.

But this time her hands were in the right spot to grab for the thing.

She caught something too thin and wiry to be part of any animal she knew of, and too sharp and strong to be a plant. At least any plant she'd ever encountered or heard about.

A few seconds of running her fingers along the thing and finally holding it up close to her mask finally let everything click into place.

The faint glow made it clear she had hold of the tether she'd dropped what felt like days ago.

Her surprised gasp pushed her into an awful coughing fit that left her doubled over, barely holding on to the thin wire that kept trying to jerk away again.

Utterly disregarding Lina's instruction to stay behind her, Musa rushed forward and grabbed Lina's arm.

"Lina! Are you okay? What happened?"

Lina sank to her knees, now trying not to laugh or cry and take more of her own breath.

"It's the rope. The one attached to the ship and to Jemny. We're not lost anymore, Musa. They'll be able to find us now."

Before she could decide whether to turn to her right or left— to look for the others or retreat to the dead ship—the shout rang out again. Not quite clear enough to understand over the unending roar, but definitely human.

"That way!" Musa tugged Lina's arm and pointed right, still fighting back coughs. "I heard someone!"

Lina nodded, now feeling too lightheaded to move in any direction. She shifted until she was crosslegged on the rocky ground, then yanked the tether four times as hard as she could. She held each pull for a couple of seconds before letting go.

Perhaps not the most elegant way to communicate on a world with incredibly advanced and real-time options, but sometimes going back to the basics of how long-ago divers got the job done was best.

That four-pull sequence was the easiest thing Lina could remember of her curiosity about how people managed to communicate things like emergencies for centuries. Long before innovations like simple radio or bone-conduction comms made it all so much easier.

I wish to come up.

If nothing else, Jemny or whoever was attached at the other end couldn't possibly think a random gust of wind created that deliberate pattern.

"Hold on, Musa, come sit with me. We're both coughing too hard to keep going if someone can get to us."

Musa's small body trembled as she settled herself in Lina's lap, but she didn't protest. She was coughing again, and Lina's were hard enough that black dots danced along the edges of her vision.

She shook her head and tried to focus when someone shouted out of the increasing darkness building inside and outside of her own head.

"Lina! I thought we'd lost you!"

She recognized Tes's voice, and Jemny's right behind her.

"Come on, we need to get them out of this dust. How much longer until you finally get this calmed down?"

"Changes in nature are *rarely* instantaneous, Agent Manhoff. We've got the energy field under control already. Even you should know the only safe way to clear a terrible threat is slowly and carefully."

Lina blinked, trying to get her head and eyes cleared enough to see who was speaking. It was everything she could do to keep from dissolving into another hacking, choking fit that would muddle her senses even more.

Because that sounded an awful lot like...

"*Ris?* How did you get here?"

Hands tried to lift Musa away, and someone tried to slip the tether out of Lina's grasp, but she fought them both.

Without much force or energy, but she did her best to hang on.

"It's okay, Lina," Ris said from very close by. "We're taking you and Musa to the medical scoot. Her grandparents are already there and doing well. They're trying to be calm about Musa being out of their sight yet again, but they're sure you've kept her safe."

Lina shook her head, but she finally let go of Musa.

"She...ran to me. Couldn't get...her to go back."

Now Tes was on her other side, gently pulling Lina's fingers away from the tether.

"They know, don't worry. Turns out Musa's always been one to dash off every chance she gets, even when that meant *crawling* off. Might have saved her life a long time ago. Let's get you out of here."

Lina let the two of them pull her upright, but she leaned on them more than she wanted to.

"Wait, did you say... Medical scoot? How? The storm?"

She half-walked, half let them drag her forward.

"I'm afraid all our masks are a bit worse for wear," Ris said. "It's cleared up quite a bit already."

Lina jerked back at pressure against her mask, somehow afraid he was going to try to pull it away from her face.

Instead he only wiped a broad clean line down the middle, clearing away most of a thick layer of black and gray dust.

She wouldn't exactly say the air was back to normal, or even up to the level of a typical overcast day on Sarkans 3. The painful and noisy rocks were no longer threatening to crack her skull, or at least her face shield, but plenty of filth still obscured most of her view more than a few meters away. She could finally see Ris, Tes, and Jemny, and even one of the other agents carrying Musa several steps ahead of them.

Only Ris's suit and mask looked anywhere near new and clean. Everyone else looked like they'd rolled through the ashes of a gigantic campfire, with dull gray obscuring the original white. The formerly white masks almost blended in.

"What happened?"

Jemny walked slightly ahead of them, playing out the tether in one hand as she went.

"One thing is your bone-conduction comms failed, which is one of the *first* things I'll be following up on as soon as we get out of this blasted valley. Probably too much exposure to volcanic dust. That never should have happened, and I'm sorry. If I'd known that was possible, you wouldn't have been on your own going back to the ship."

Lina only then realized she was hearing everyone's voices through the air rather than inside her helmet. Her throat wasn't bothering her nearly as much, either, probably because the dust had settled noticeably in the last couple of minutes.

She was mostly able to walk on her own now, so her feet kicked through a thick layer of sooty gray rather than leaving single lines where she'd been dragged.

"That's all right. Did the dust get to everyone's comms?"

"Everyone lost bone conduction," Jemny said. "But most of us were close enough to stay in communication even when we couldn't see. Thanks to Ris here—or maybe I should say Director Murray since he persists in calling me Agent Manhoff—conditions are improving greatly. If slowly."

Lina felt Ris's ribs jerk as he grunted.

"That's all down to you more than to me, Lina. I noticed the decreasing frequency in the residual energy signature, but you're the one who suggested scanning for it. Thanks to you, and your suggestion I pass it along planetwide, *Jemny*, we were able to pinpoint the source."

"Sources is more accurate," Jemny said. "From what we can tell so far from satellite records, it looks like a modified vessel of some kind overflies the area, leaving a path of grav-drive energy. Then remote sources amplify the energy enough to control the landscape from far enough away that they were almost impossible to detect."

"But we've got them now." Tes patted Lina's arm before gradually letting go so Lina could try taking on more of her own weight. "Once Ris got the satellite scans working on the correct frequency, they were able to locate the sources from the tsunami, then the avalanche."

Ris also slowly let go, leaving Lina to walk slowly but steadily on her own.

"Right now technicians are winding down the function for the units placed in and around this valley. That's why things are clearing up. But they were afraid if they just cut the power all at once, they wouldn't be able to control the mountainside's mass enough to stop a landslide."

"That's what Musa heard, then?" Lina said. "The interference winding down?"

Ris and Tes glanced at each other, and even Jemny's forehead creased above her mask.

"I'd guess she heard the energy levels reducing, yes," Ris said. "And I'm sure you both heard the debris we directed back toward the mountainside. That seemed safest, since it was so recently evacuated."

"I did hear the pattering noises," Lina said. "But Musa hears a lot better than I do. Probably better than most anyone here from what she told me. I think she must have had some kind of hearing implant when she was small."

"I think we'll let her grandparents tell you more about that," Jemny said. "I don't like to admit it, even among friends, but they had a lot more to say than anyone in Planetary Security was aware of."

CHAPTER 28

THE MEDICAL SCOOT appeared like a most-welcome mirage as they walked, with its glowing blue body and flashing orange lights shocking as the gloom slowly lifted in the valley.

Even the wind and horrible noise had finally died down to not much more than a steady breeze that continued to clear out dust and soot. Only an odd rumble in the distance remained to let Lina know things weren't quite settled yet. Her mask wasn't quite useless enough to keep her from knowing the scorched, electrical aroma was lifting as well.

Despite a big group of people gathered around the scoot, she was able to pick out Musa and her grandparents right away. They sat together on one of several ledge-like treatment areas, Musa between the two adults. Someone dressed in a protective suit as blue and glowing as their scoot knelt in front of them, peering at Musa.

For her part, Musa seemed far happier and more relaxed than she had not long ago out in the storm.

A few rescue scoots stood out as well, with a steady stream of tourists hurrying to get on board. Lina wondered how many of them had also been at the other two attack sites. No doubt Jemny and Ris already had that data coordinated and sorted and sent off to the relevant authorities.

And certainly to the relevant marketing experts to figure out how to deal with an unprecedented slam to Sarkans 3's reputation as a safe retreat for those who desperately wanted or needed that reassurance.

A few spots of green peeked through under all the soot: the remnants of what the Sopka Valley had been. Hopefully with time, rain, and a lot of hard reclamation work, it would be restored to its former calm and beauty. Much like Scarlet Beach and the winter wonderland of Hivern before it.

Lina's back and chest ached from coughing, and her legs trembled from struggling to keep her balance in the dreadful storm. Her whole torso still threatened to cramp from carrying Musa for so long.

From the careful, plodding way they walked, Tes and Jemny weren't faring much better.

Only Ris seemed to have a spring in his step. Likely because he'd only arrived after the worst of the physical threat was under control.

It was definitely for the best that *someone* who knew what all had been going on for the last several days wasn't completely exhausted.

Lina was already looking forward to a hot soak in one of the therapeutic tubs back at the Planetary Science compound, then as many hours of sleep as she could manage. She knew the sore muscles would really set in a couple of days later, but she might have the mental strength to deal with that after some serious rest.

But even that had to wait until she understood more about what all of them had just been through.

"I know you've got control of the landslide now," she said, "and I hope figuring out how the attackers used grav-drive energy means they won't be able to do it again. Did you catch them? Do you have any idea who they are, or why they were doing this to begin with?"

"I'm not going to comment on *why*," Jemny said, "but Tes can tell you *how* we got hold of the attackers, since it was her idea."

Tes shook her head, and blushed deep enough that Lina saw it through her grubby face shield.

"It wasn't all me. You gave me the idea, Lina, or the test pods we used in the water did. Remember how we programmed all the small ones to pick out what we were looking for? Once Ris found the right frequency for the attack in this valley, I wondered if something like that might help. Then Jemny took over."

They'd gotten close enough to the medical scoot to see everyone taking off their masks. Some without hesitation and others more cautiously, but no one collapsed into painful coughing fits.

A few flashes of blue sky overhead convinced Lina to pull hers loose long enough to take a careful, still-smoky-smelling breath of cool air. The resulting faint tickle in her throat was a small price to pay for freeing her face and jaws from the tight clench of the mask and helmet.

She slipped the gloves off and tucked them into one of the

suit's pockets, flexing her fingers and savoring the escape from her own sweat.

Tes, Ris, and Jemny did the same as they kept walking.

Jemny waved Tes's comment about taking over away.

"All I did was suggest reprogramming some of our smaller security hoverpods so they worked like your underwater sensors, based on Tes's very good idea. Then they could locate the control units based on their energy signatures. From there, it wasn't much of a leap to follow the same signature to the controllers themselves."

Lina's skin crawled with tingling gooseflesh at the idea of finally facing their attackers after everything they'd put the planet's residents and wildlife and tourists and everyone else through.

She wasn't normally given to violence or likely to encourage someone else into it, but this might be an exception.

"You've got them in custody?"

Both Tes and Ris looked surprised at Lina's words and her voice—cold enough to create an avalanche of her own—eyes wide and eyebrows raised. Only Jemny seemed to take it in stride with a single nod.

That one motion and the hardening of her expression transformed her back to intimidating Planetary Security Agent Manhoff—the one Lina and Tes met in the aftermath of the first giant wave.

"Suspects are being held, yes. Back at the spaceport on Mount Bewaker. If they were indeed responsible for these attacks, they'll be dealt with. I can promise you that. There's more than enough evidence and precedent for a quick trial and an appropriate sentence."

Angry as she was, Lina didn't yet want to know more about what that sentence might be, or even who the suspects were.

She cared a lot more about why.

"That's enough for me, then. It's time to talk to Musa's grandparents."

She was relieved when Ris and Jemny changed directions without her having to ask, and equally relieved when Tes stayed with her. Out of everyone she'd gotten to know during the insanity of the past several days, Tes had been with her for most of it.

And she hoped their friendship would continue long past the eventual return to whatever normal turned out to be.

"Are you okay, Tes? What did I miss while I was wandering around lost in the storm?"

Tes laughed, and the lighthearted sound broke up a satisfying amount of the tension and fear in Lina's heart and mind.

"You wouldn't have been that far off by most measures. I'd say you were walking less than ten meters away from the right direction in the end."

Lina smiled and rubbed her grit-coated face.

"Easy to recover from unless no one can see. In that case, we might as well have been on the wrong side of the planet."

"Exactly. I'm mostly more tired than I've been since my first full day of mountain climbing training. We'd just about gotten everyone up and moving by the time Ris's comm signals made it through, letting us know he had rescue and medical scoots on the way. Then it was easily the longest wait of my life, staring up into the clouds and hoping *we* weren't the ones too far out of place to find."

"How did you get comms?"

But Lina answered her own question right after she asked it by pulling her comm-stick out of her pocket, where she'd stashed it when they left the ship and entirely forgotten about it. The formerly blank cylinder now flashed with bright red notifications. It had apparently given up on the usual beeps and vibrations.

"Never mind," she said. "By the time we got back out into all that noise, I never even heard or felt any alerts. I'm guessing the interference was already dropping by then?"

"You got it. That happened before we could tell any difference except for our comms. So we had almost everyone ready before the scoots started arriving. Except for you and Musa. You gave Jemny a hell of a start with the way you yanked the tether in a code like that. She swears it wasn't ancient Morse code, but it sure got her attention. What did you use?"

"Old diving code, but I read a little about Morse code when I was studying history, too. I guess the diving code fit into my mind better since I was already obsessed with getting into the water. All I said was I wanted to come up, which was true. We might as well have been at the bottom of the sea."

"How *did* you two end up so far off track?"

Lina nodded toward Musa and her grandparents, still sitting on the med-scoot's platform only a few short strides away. They all had their masks off and pink spheres with straws in their hands.

"I'll tell you all about it as soon as we get out of here."

Tes nodded and squeezed Lina's arm.

"I'll see what else I can do to help. And I'll have someone bring you a sphere of that orenda juice. It won't replace the rest we all need, but you'll feel a whole lot better with just a few sips.

One of the few imported crops to this paradise of a planet, and absolutely worth it."

Lina hesitated for several almost-normal breaths after Tes walked away, watching Musa chat happily with her grandparents. Except for the soot coating all of them, they could have been sharing their impressions about a delightful vacation activity.

None of them looked like they wanted to dig into whatever secret in their past might help explain the stress and fear so many had just experienced. A weary part of Lina didn't want to, either.

But she was afraid the whole thing might start up again if as many people as possible didn't understand what got the assaults started in the first place.

Then Musa looked up and saw her, with a little girl's excited grin and wave for Lina to join them, and the decision was finally made.

Lina only hoped the fallout wouldn't be as terrible as the dust and ash and rocks that had so recently settled all around them.

CHAPTER 29

Musa seemed to have regained most of her enthusiasm as she jumped up and trotted toward Lina, but she still clutched her pink sphere of orenda juice.

Someone had wiped the worst of the soot away from her face, leaving it bright and fresh with only a few traces of gray. Unfortunately the tunic and pants she'd been wearing were so coated with dust that Lina had no idea what color they'd started the day as.

Musa's grandparents only watched rather than coming after her. But their similarly scrubbed faces showed signs of exhaustion, as did the forward slump of their bodies. They both managed a welcoming smile to encourage Lina to keep going despite her own weariness.

Musa grabbed her hand and nearly dragged her the last couple of meters.

"Lina! Come hear what my grandparents did while we were lost in the storm!"

Lina winced at the words, but Seerit, Musa's grandmother, shook her head and reached for Lina's other hand.

"Don't worry yourself, Lina, we understand what happened. It's a wonder any of us managed to stay together during all that commotion. And Musa's the one who ran off and scared all of us, aren't you?"

Musa lowered her head and kicked at a spot of grass poking through the ashes, but Lina could still see her smile.

"I never should have run away like that, and I'm sorry for making everyone worry." She looked into Lina's eyes, and an honest-looking frown crossed her face. "I really *didn't* mean to make it harder for you, Lina. You were too busy to take time to look after a little girl like me."

Seerit let out a roughened laugh, then sipped at her juice.

"Hush, Musa, you're only going to make Lina feel bad. She did a fine job of looking after you, didn't she?"

Lina couldn't quite manage to feel bad when Musa had so clearly been repeating what she'd heard.

"It's okay. Musa helped me figure out which way to go. Do you mind if I join you and ask a few questions? Don't worry, nothing official, unless you have information that might help us over in Planetary Science."

Seerit and Pandar moved to the side, making room for Lina to join them, just as a girl not much older than Musa and in equally soiled vacation clothes ran up. She held out a blue bag that bulged with more spheres.

Musa suddenly took on a much older, more serious air as she accepted them.

"Thank you very much, Caten."

The girl stared at her for a second, then nodded before she dashed away.

"She's been on several of the same excursions as us," Seerit said quietly, with an affectionate smile. "I think she and Musa have taken a liking to each other."

Musa scowled and shook her head, even as she glanced in the direction the other girl had gone.

"I was just being polite like *you* always tell me to." She turned a beaming smile toward Lina, but her eyes twinkled. "Would you like some juice to help your throat, Lina?"

"I would indeed, Musa. Thank *you* very much."

Apparently satisfied with Lina's response, Musa handed the bag over, moved a blue cushion from a pile arranged against the side of the scoot to a few strides away, and sat down where she could watch everyone else.

She had plenty to look at, with the dust continuing to swirl upward and out of the valley. The morning's bright sunlight had passed, but more than enough of afternoon's blue sky remained to show how much soot and ash and general debris would have to be removed from the landscape.

No one was actually cleaning yet, not with mostly tourists and a few exhausted tour guides lining up for rescue scoots that could finally land and depart.

Far more interesting—certainly to a curious little girl's eyes— were the bunches of white-suited agents walking back and forth across the flat space that was now visible all the way to Jemny's not-quite-so-silvery ship. Several of them held the same kind of oval testing unit Lina'd used in her brave-mad expedition in front of the winter lodge.

Probably checking for traces of the grav-drive energy signature, even though Planetary Security had suspects already in hand.

Ris couldn't be the only one who thought more data was always a good thing.

When Lina turned her attention to Musa's grandparents, they both smiled in a sad, accepting way.

"I imagine you have questions for us," Seerit said, reaching for her husband's hand. "Going by the number we answered for your friend Agent Manhoff already."

"I'm sorry to put you through more than you've already been through. It really is none of my business."

Pandar shook his head and patted her hand, and the gesture made her miss her own older relatives dreadfully.

"Nonsense. You've been wonderful with our Musa, for one thing. And I daresay you paying attention to everything happening around her kept the rest of us safer. You have every right to know why."

"Or at least a *possible* reason why," Seerit said. "That's the hardest part of terrible things like this. Sometimes we never understand all of it."

Lina set the bag down to get one of the juice spheres Musa wanted to make sure she had, and to buy herself a little time.

Not understanding had been intolerable for her since she was Musa's age, and maybe younger. That was part of what drove her into a career of discovery on a planetary scale in the first place, and on many different planets if she could manage it.

The pink ball was soft under her fingers, and the cool surface felt wonderful. She handed the bag to Seerit and Pandar while trying to puzzle out how to drink from the sealed straw.

"Just bite the end and drink." Pandar demonstrated with a sphere of his own.

The juice was soothing and barely sweet enough to keep from burning Lina's throat as it went down. But the persistent tickle finally felt better, and her mind cleared enough to make a huge difference when it came to trying to understand the last several days.

"I'm not sure I know the questions to ask," she said. "All I'll tell you is I'm worried about all of your safety even on Sarkans 3 if any of these attacks might have been targeting you."

Seerit got out more juice for herself, but she only rolled the pink sphere back and forth between her palms.

"It's possible. Our family has been targeted before, and extensively. I'd so hoped those days had passed for Musa's generation."

Pandar rubbed her back, and the way he gazed at her made Lina look away. No matter what Musa's past held, Lina was glad she was growing up with a lovely example of a close relationship.

"We still don't know why *this* happened," he said. "I trust Lina and Tes and Agent Manhoff to figure it out."

Seerit nodded and leaned against his shoulder for a second before looking into Lina's eyes.

"When it comes to us possibly being targeted, we have to start with my great-great grandmother having primary responsibility for developing the first grav-drive engine. Hardly anyone remembers it was originally called the Cepat Drive, for Ivy Cepat. There are still certain…factions that believe that change in the course of humanity created more problems than it possibly could have solved. And they've been trying to punish all of her descendants ever since."

Lina tried to stop herself, but she knew her jaw dropped.

If that was true—and she had no reason to doubt Seerit—then the people around her right now had every reason to seek out a secretive and usually secure planet like Sarkans 3. Anyone involved with the drive that had made human travel outside the Earth system possible surely had more power, notoriety, and likely wealth than many of the planetary government officials who vacationed there.

"I had no idea. I suppose your family has worked hard to keep me or anyone else from knowing."

Seerit closed her eyes for several seconds and nodded.

"No matter how many name changes or years spent hiding or even appearance changes, word always seems to get out about who we are. I left the company after what happened with my grandson and his wife, but I refused to spend the rest of my life secluded in some private, secure facility like some family members have. Musa deserves a better life than that."

Lina couldn't help glancing at Musa, who was now transfixed by one of the rescue scoots taking off.

"That's how she lost her hearing," Pandar said. "And both of her parents. A primitive but effective bomb, almost impossible to detect, when she was only a few months old. The monsters who planted it swore they had no idea she was with them, but should that have mattered? They were determined to steal her family whether she was there or not."

"I'm terribly sorry to hear that," Lina said. Her stomach roiled at the thought of that original loss in Musa's life, and more in horror at what could have happened over the past few days. "I admit I don't know much about the origins of the grav-drive, but I can't imagine how that kind of crime could have possibly made sense."

"Ivy was apparently a challenging person," Seerit said. "And some of her choices have never sat right with certain groups of people. She worked in an educational setting, but she decided to patent the drive and take it private despite calls to donate it as a public good."

She smiled with her eyebrows raised.

"Her recorded and often replayed response was anyone in the *public* could buy one of the Cepat Drives from her company. Never mind that the costs of those original drives were astronomical, so to speak. So that didn't endear her to those already opposed to her, and it certainly turned more against her. Later in life she either donated or purchased drives for those she considered deserving. Some of them arguably were."

Pandar winked at Lina, and she wondered how many times he'd been part of a conversation very much like this one.

"Dear Ivy also set up a foundation that still operates today. They've done a lot of good."

"She certainly did," Seerit agreed. "Once she'd amassed a fortune that had been unimaginable up until then. Anyway, we can't say for certain any of this was aimed at us. But the fact that whoever did it used a modified Cepat Drive makes me more suspicious."

Lina must have been too exhausted to hide her surprise, because Seerit patted her arm again.

"Don't worry, word of your investigation hasn't gotten out to the general tourist population. Your Agent Manhoff of course knew who we were, so she warned us about what you'd found so far."

Musa glanced back at them with such an innocent smile that Lina laughed right along with Seerit and Pandar.

"I only want to move forward a little bit," Musa said. "So I can *see* better."

"Five more strides," Seerit said. "No more."

Musa popped up like a cork and carried her cushion forward, where she dropped back down and waved.

"How much does she know about all of this?" Lina said.

"Only that her parents died in an accident so far," Pandar said. "And that she has magic ears."

"Agent Manhoff might want to talk to her a little more about what she can hear," Lina said. "With your permission, of course. I think Musa caught when the attacks started and when they were about to end. That might help with making sure this never happens again. She seemed excited about the whole idea, even in the middle of the storm."

Seerit nodded and held one hand over her heart.

"Musa has a lovely ability to see things as a game or an adventure. If you can be with her when the time comes, I'm sure it will be fine. She's a tiny bit intimidated by Agent Manhoff."

"She's not alone." Lina put her empty juice sphere back into the bag and retrieved another before getting slowly to her feet. "But if she's not *too* intimidated, we'd be glad to take you back to your lodging with us. Agent Manhoff's ship is much faster than even the rescue scoots, and it shouldn't be terribly crowded."

Musa once again demonstrated her keen hearing by looking back over her shoulder and grinning.

"I want to go on the fast ship, please!"

Pandar and Seerit laughed.

"We're staying near Scarlet Beach," Pandar said, "so if it

honestly isn't a problem, we'd be honored to go on your fast ship."

"Not at all," Lina said with a smile. "I'll let you know as soon as we're ready. I'm terribly sorry for everything that's happened."

Both Seerit and Pandar stood more easily than Lina had.

"I feel we're the ones who should apologize," Seerit said. "If our being here brought any of this down on your delightful planet, I'll do everything I can to make it right."

Lina took each of their offered hands for a second before turning away.

Musa jumped up again as she passed by, and surprised Lina by rushing forward into a quick hug.

"Will there be any more giant waves when we get back to Scarlet Beach?"

"I certainly hope there aren't any more waves. But we'll get you back there soon so you won't miss anything."

CHAPTER 30

By the time Lina helped as much as she could with getting tourists aboard rescue scoots and out of the valley, she wished for the piles of food from her day with Tes on the sea or after their avalanche adventure in Hivern.

That and several days of sleep might get her back in the neighborhood of feeling like her usual self.

But she'd settle for escaping the constant grit of ash all over her skin and in her eyes, and scrubbing the taste of long-ago scorched earth off her tongue and out of her throat.

She wasn't sure she'd ever get rid of the bizarre electrical charge that seemed to have taken over her sense of smell.

No one had arrived to begin the extensive cleanup the Sopka Valley needed, but she'd heard plenty of chatter. One of the rescue scoots had disgorged an anxious knot of tourism officials who proceeded to scurry from place to place, staring at the damage and muttering to each other in gloomy tones.

Tes was sure they were noting the cost of all that cleanup on their comm-sticks, and possibly offloading the rotten job of breaking the bad news about canceled plans to some poor scheduling personnel.

Or just as likely leaving it to the already stretched-thin tour guides to handle.

Ris stopped just short of pushing Lina and Tes toward the distant oasis of Jemny's ship, promising to keep them updated on anything new that happened in the valley. For his part, he'd summoned a crowd of scientists and students for the rare chance to examine volcanic soil turned inside out and dislodged far from where it had settled thousands of years ago.

Even Musa seemed to have finally exhausted her near-limitless supply of energy as Lina, Tes, Jemny, and Musa's grandparents made the long trek across the valley. Musa held onto Lina and Tes's hands willingly enough, and she kept glancing back to make sure her grandparents weren't falling behind.

But she was unusually quiet, enough so Lina was determined to do everything in her limited power to make sure the next day was fun, but restful for the whole Sauri family. Assuming she was awake herself.

"Is it only us on your ship, Jemny?" Tes said.

They'd come to within a dozen meters of the birdlike vessel—looking more like a charcoal-colored Earth crow than a silver sculpture at the moment.

"Everyone else is either staying to work or shadowing one of the other rescue scoots." Jemny turned a weary smile toward Musa's grandparents. "I'm afraid you're stuck with me as your shadow."

"I expect we'll be in good hands," Seerit said.

Lina blinked her scratchy eyes, trying to catch the thought

that kept dancing around in her mind. Something she needed to ask Jemny, or maybe tell her.

She hoped she didn't need to deliver a warning instead.

"We'll get you to your lodging first," Jemny said. "Then I'll drop Lina at the Planetary Science compound. I think that's where you're heading as well, Tes? Then I'll get myself back to Mount Bewaker."

"That's where our biggest ship landed," Musa said, perking up. "The one that brought us all the way to the vacation planet. But we don't have to go back there until it's time to leave."

Jemny reached toward the middle of the ship's port, where all traces of Lina's handprint had disappeared.

Surely the port was already keyed to Jemny's hand, unlike when Lina had to call for help when she was here with Musa.

When the port was the only thing on the whole ship that worked.

She started to say something, but the port slid aside as soon as Jemny touched it.

By the time Lina stepped inside, it was obvious there were no worries about trying to wake its systems or get them back online. The irritating alert Jemny had warned her about pinged away to itself, and enough blinking lights to cause an instant headache covered all the displays up front.

Even the traces of gray dust that had followed Lina and Musa inside were gone, along with the stale air.

"Just give me a second to clear these blasted alerts," Jemny said. "Then we'll be underway and out of here. Everyone get strapped in and ready."

All the exhaustion Lina had been struggling to keep from swamping her started to trickle into her muscles, bones, and mind. It was all she could do to help Musa adjust the straps for her smaller frame, then settle into the next seat.

With the suspects in custody—and likely already under questioning—she was almost ready to believe the terrifying attacks might be over. Surely Planetary Security had more than enough expertise and techniques to get the motives, and to make sure the methods were permanently disabled.

Then everyone in Planetary Science and the Tourism Authority could get to work putting things at Scarlet Beach and Hivern and the Sopka Valley as right as they could before time took care of the rest. And of course the Tourism Authority could return to making sure all visitors to Sarkans 3—high-risk or ordinary vacationer—had a trip well worth what they'd paid for it and more.

She'd happily leave dealing with any demands the attackers might have to someone else to figure out.

All she wanted at the moment was to keep her eyes open long enough to get back to her own quarters.

Jemny finally looked back at all of them, nodded once, and danced her fingers over the screens. The ship lifted without a trace of the noisy struggle or gut-churning turbulence it suffered landing in the terrible storm.

Once they were airborne, Lina leaned forward enough to get a look as Jemny circled the much-quieter valley below. It still resembled a dumped-out charcoal fire more than a lush landscape, but the swirling clouds were now gone, drawn out by the prevailing winds.

"Can I look around now?" Musa said, looking at Lina.

"That's a question for Agent Manhoff and your grandparents. I'm going to stay strapped in myself, just because I'm tired."

"Should be smooth flying as soon as we clear the gap," Jemny said without looking back. "You'll hear the engines work a little harder because it's so high, but only for a few seconds. As soon as that's over, you can walk around. *If* your grandparents agree."

Lina heard the same low rumble she remembered as the ship headed higher, aiming for the lowest spot in the high mountains all around the valley, then they were through.

A few small scoots circled around the other mountains as well as in the valley, probably trying to map the grav-drive energy signature just like they'd done back in Hivern.

The more data the better, even with most of the excitement over.

Lina sincerely hoped it was indeed over.

Musa turned toward her grandparents, bouncing in her seat.

Then she froze.

She slowly looked back toward the front of the ship with a worried frown.

"Is the engine supposed to be working even *harder* now? I thought you said it would only be for a few seconds?"

Lina realized the rumble hadn't slowed down at all. Even though they were descending through a series of smaller volcanoes—all still covered with thick green forests—the engine sounded like it was still straining.

"No, it shouldn't still be working so hard." Jemny sounded more worried than Lina had ever heard her. "The controls aren't responding the way they should be, either."

A burst of heat surged through Lina, and a frigid chill followed right behind it. She loosened her harness and hurried forward.

"Did the dust cause a problem?" Tes said, heading toward the controls as well.

"Does that mean I can get up, too?" Musa cried, but her grandparents told her to stay put.

"It may not be dust," Lina said. "When I came back to the ship with Musa, everything was dead. Completely dead. No ventilation or lights or anything else. The only thing that worked was the port. Could something have gone wrong while everything was shut down?"

Jemny shook her head, hard.

"This kind of ship doesn't shut down like that, not without the pilot entering a specific sequence. Or it shouldn't. Everything was still on standby when I got back. Are you *sure* nothing was running, Lina?"

"Absolutely. The air was stale, and none of the alarms were sounding. There was dust on the floor, and the screens were all blank. Not standby. Like they had no power at all. My commstick was dead, too."

"That doesn't make *any* sense!" Jemny worked the controls more forcefully, as if she could beat the ship into submission. "Our comms weren't working, but they were still powered on. But something's wrong here. The ship isn't responding to my navigational input."

Musa piped up, now sounding more worried than excited.

"I hear that choppy noise again, Lina. The one you said sounded like a motor underwater? And the really high one, too."

Jemny clenched her fists, then sat back with her hands flat on her thighs.

The rumbling sound of the engine stopped.

She slowly turned and looked up.

The haunted expression in her eyes made Lina's blood run cold.

"When did you hear those noises before, Musa?" Jemny said.

A small, cold hand slipped into Lina's.

"The high one when all the giant waves started," Musa said. "And the noise got choppy when the volcano wave was over our heads."

"What's going on, Jemny?" Tes said, her worried gaze meeting Lina's.

Jemny's somehow blank smile was more frightening than her worst glare.

"Well, it seems the ship is running just fine as long as I don't try to change our course. Unless something changes, we won't be going by the lodge or the Planetary Science compound. We're on a course for Mount Bewaker that I can't alter. To the spaceport."

Lina held her free hand to her heart, which continued to beat despite her certainty it had stopped with Jemny's last words.

What she *hadn't* said was worse.

While everyone was busy dealing with the first two attacks, two unpiloted vessels had arrived at the spaceport.

Each with a murder victim on board.

CHAPTER 31

Lina kept her eyes on the monitors in front of Jemny.

She was afraid if she looked at either Jemny or Tes, she'd give in to the panic dancing around the edges of her mind.

And if she looked at Musa or her grandparents—who'd all felt safer traveling with them rather than on the rescue scoots— she was afraid she'd burst into frightened, guilty tears.

The monitors were enough like the water scoot that she could tell all systems appeared to be normal. She recognized altitude and that they were descending, alongside airspeed, which was increasing.

Several lines of text with green dots or bars beside them probably meant nothing on the ship itself was running in a dangerous state, at least not when it came to strain or malfunction.

Even the wide-field navigational map seemed to be functioning smoothly to her inexperienced eye.

She could see a remarkably detailed image of the jagged,

mountainous land below them in one section, with text overlays of landmarks near their current location.

The Sopka Valley and its odd, crisis-driven familiarity was falling behind.

Another section showed a list of destinations with matching images beside them. Jemny had apparently tried to enter the lodge near Scarlet Beach, the Planetary Science compound, and Mount Bewaker.

Only Mount Bewaker was outlined in green.

The others had no outline at all.

"What happens if you tap the lodge?" Tes spoke quietly, but Lina was sure Musa heard every word.

"The engine fights like we're climbing into high altitudes," Jemny said. "And the nav systems never lock on. Same with any other destinations I can think of, close by or on the far side of the planet. I can't even get us back to the Sopka Valley. Anything besides the spaceport is refused."

Lina pulled out her comm-stick, hoping to get a message to Ris about what might be happening.

The screen was still active, or at least powered on.

But when she tried to get a response, nothing happened.

She knelt down and finally risked looking into Musa's eyes.

"Can you do me a big favor, Musa? I need you to go sit with your grandparents for a little while. As soon as I can, I'll join you. Okay?"

Musa pursed her lips, but Lina could tell she was trying to hide her own worry.

"Okay, I guess. But we're not *supposed* to go back to the spaceport for a long time. Not until we have to leave the vacation planet."

"I know," Tes said with a remarkably natural smile. "That's what we're trying to fix."

Musa shrugged as dramatically as any teenager before walking toward her grandparents.

"My comms are frozen out, too," Jemny said. "And the ship's. They're not blocked like they were in the valley, or turned off like you say the ship was. They just won't respond."

After a quick glance at her own comm-stick, Tes nodded.

"Same here. Can you tell whether we're at least still on the tracking networks, so someone might know what's going on?"

"I can't tell for certain," Jemny said, "since I can't get comms from outside the ship. A vessel this size *could* slip through those networks if our own automatic comms aren't broadcasting our location correctly, or if they manage to send out a false location. Since this is a Planetary Security ship, we won't be able to land undetected like the two scoots did. I doubt anyone will look for our emergency beacon unless we crash. But someone will get a visual on us before we get to the spaceport. And the lack of required official comms will send out an alert."

Lina's chest seemed to constrict around her heart and lungs.

"And if you can't respond and they're not expecting us, what will they do?"

Lina rubbed the back of her neck, shaking her head at the same time.

"They wouldn't appreciate an unexpected Planetary Security ship approaching, especially one that doesn't announce itself and that they can't communicate with. If we're lucky, they'll only send out an interceptor. If we're not, they'll send a ship with destructive capabilities."

"I didn't even know there *were* ships like that on Sarkans 3," Tes said. "I'm guessing it's not exactly public knowledge."

"No one outside of Planetary Security knows, and most people inside don't. They're a weapon of last resort in case of a major attack. I honestly doubt our single ship would meet the requirements for launching those lethal-force ships in a normal situation."

Lina hugged herself, wishing she hadn't taken off her protective suit. Right now she'd trade overheated, sweaty, and covered with soot for feeling like she'd stepped right back into Hivern without any kind of winter gear in the middle of a blizzard.

"But we haven't been in a normal situation since the tidal wave," she said. "And hardly anyone on the planet knows about that, either. We may have done too effective of a job keeping the attacks and murders quiet for our own good. By the time the spaceport authorities notice anything wrong, it might be too late."

The cones and peaks of volcanos below had given way to a series of rolling hills and valleys, equally green and heavily forested but nowhere near as regular in shape. Before Lina could try to focus on a single feature to distract herself, a low *bong* she hadn't heard before sounded from the console in front of them.

Jemny cursed under her breath and clenched her fists again, but she didn't bother moving them from her thighs.

"That's the warning we'll be shifting into high-speed flight," she said. "It means our course has been plotted and locked in, so I'd better make changes now if I need to. Somehow feels like an extra stab in the back since I can't do a damn thing about it."

"Do we need to get strapped in?" Tes said. "Or check on the others?"

Jemny shook her head, then shrugged.

"If whoever is controlling us or took over during the storm follows the usual procedures, you won't feel the acceleration. Should be smooth. But at this point, I'm not willing to promise anything. Except that we'll arrive at Mount Bewaker—unexpected and unannounced—in less than an hour."

Sure enough, Lina saw the landscape beneath them gradually move faster until it blurred into a mass of green. And aside from a slight twist in her stomach that probably had more to do with what she was seeing than how her body felt, she couldn't tell the difference in their speed.

"As far as those other two unexpected arrivals," she said in a low voice, "whatever happened to them happened *before* they got to the spaceport, right?"

Jemny finally seemed to break herself out of her angry daze.

"As far as anyone can tell. They'd both been in that condition for a while, and they weren't in-port for more than a few minutes before the…criminal cargo was discovered. You're thinking we're supposed to be next."

Tes leaned close to the monitors, watching the kilometers tick by.

"Makes sense to me, though I don't love saying so. But which one of us is the target? Or is it all of us, conveniently delivered together in one neat package?"

Lina refused to look back at Musa and her grandparents.

Horrible as it seemed, it was somehow easier to assume they *weren't* the targets.

"Could be any of us, I suppose. You and I figured out what kind of energy the attackers were using, Tes. And Agent Manhoff here is the one who gave us the hint that put us on the case. As far as we know, the only one they're missing is Ris, since he alerted planet-wide surveillance systems."

"That's all fair." Jemny didn't look back at the Sauris, either. "But none of us are descendants of the inventor of an engine that changed the course of human history. It's not that hard to imagine our attackers would be glad to get hold of all of us."

"But they only decided to come with us at the last minute," Tes said. "They could have just as easily stayed with their group like they did before."

Lina forced herself not to raise her voice.

"Does any of that really matter right now? I don't care *who* has us trapped in an enemy-controlled ship, or even why. Not yet. The only thing I care about is what we're going to do to stop it."

Jemny pulled out her big comm-stick again, then ran her fingers over the ship's controls.

"Still locked out of everything. I'm not the kind of person who just accepts any kind of defeat without a fight, much less one that might lead to me showing up at the spaceport dead inside my own ship. But right now, since I'm locked out of the controls of my own ship, I'm sorry to admit I don't yet know what to do."

Tes looked into Lina's eyes, and the fire Lina saw there raised her flagging spirits considerably.

"Well, one of the main duties for a tour guide is solving impossible problems," Tes said. "For ourselves and for our especially demanding guests. I'm nowhere near willing to give up and just wait for the crash or the murderer or whatever they've got planned for us. There's *something* we can do about this. We just can't see it yet."

She didn't bother looking at the monitors, and neither did Lina. Jemny was the expert about how her ship's controls worked. But she might not be quite as used to paying close attention to the areas outside of the front section.

Lina took a few steps away from the front of the ship, trying to play the last several hours and even the last few days back in her mind. Going all the way to the first time she'd stepped aboard this ship, dressed in what turned out to be a pitiful attempt at cold-weather gear.

Several rows of empty seats waited, with Musa's grandparents watching her carefully from two of them.

The efforts to keep the Sauris from getting caught up in fear hadn't amounted to much, but at least Musa currently stared at her smaller version of a comm-stick with a smile on her sweet face.

The back of the ship was taken up with neat bundles of supplies the agents still back in the Sopka Valley had left behind. Probably more of the protective suits, masks, and bright shoulder lights, since Lina hadn't seen them carrying much else.

Except for one thing that had made her own walk through that valley both more secure and more frightening.

CHAPTER 32

LINA TOOK another step and felt a slight ridge under her booted foot.

A smooth, rectangular rim on the textured gray floor, probably meant to keep things like drifts of volcanic dust or maybe scarlet sand from causing problems.

Lina stood on the port she and Tes had climbed through when Jemny picked them up from the water scoot. The self-locking ladder had to be there somewhere as well, perhaps rolled up between the ship's floor and the metal hull.

Her heart and throat wanted to clench in horror at what her mind hesitantly suggested

But she'd had more than enough of horror over the past several days.

If she could prevent even a small amount now, she had to at least try.

Lina walked forward to stand beside Jemny, who again had her unresponsive comm-stick unfolded on her lap.

"Do you know where the beacons are on this ship?" she said, close to Jemny's ear. "Are they accessible?"

Jemny turned enough for Lina to see her frown.

"The electronics are throughout the ship, and I can't access any of those right now. But the beacons themselves are enclosed in the hull."

"On the bottom?" Lina said. "Can someone get to them at all?"

Jemny turned the rest of the way and Lina drew back.

"I suppose someone could with the right tools. Or the right weapon. What are you thinking of?"

Lina took a quick breath, making sure she was still willing to even discuss the possibilities, then plunged ahead.

"Okay then, are any of the tethers we used during the storm still aboard? Or are there others?"

Tes spoke from Jemny's other side.

"I just saw a bunch of those tethers in a storage cabinet, in the back. What are you talking about doing, Lina?"

Jemny threw both hands up.

"Any reason why you decided to rummage through my ship's storage?"

"Same reason as whatever Lina's suggesting, Jemny. Trying to find a way out of this mess."

Jemny abruptly stood and turned, and Lina and Tes stepped back.

"In any case," Jemny said, "*I'll* do the rummaging, if you don't mind. There are several things on this ship that I don't want just anyone getting access too, particularly with a child aboard. Yes, there are tethers, but I don't know what you think you could do with them, Lina. And before you ask, the ship's beacons would be damn hard to get hold of without taking the hull apart."

"Do you think you could force the ship to…" Lina put her hands on her hips, trying to conjure an option. "I don't know, scrape over a boulder or something? Or are any of those things you have aboard capable of doing the job so we can get to one of the beacons?"

"This ship isn't armored and hardened to the same level the lethal force ships are," Jemny said, "but the hull isn't exactly made of fabric. Every fast-flight ship on Sarkans 3 has a reinforced hull, far more than the scoots do, because a crash would do a hell of a lot more damage. But don't forget that the emergency beacons are designed to *survive* a crash. They're not easy to disable."

The landscape had shifted to the tans of a drier area beneath them, but they were still going too fast for Lina to see much more than a blur.

"Well, someone figured out how to disable them," Tes said. "On the two scoots, right?"

Jemny shrugged, frowning. "Sure, on less secured vessels, with less protective covering. And those scoots were intact, nothing removed or damaged. The control beacons were disabled in some other way."

Lina was once again reduced to wanting to shake Jemny to try to get her out of her Planetary Security mental rut, and keep her from acting just like the supervisors she'd talked about being frustrated with.

"But that means something *can* be done," Lina said. "Are the tracking beacons easier to get to? The ones that just relay the ship's location?"

Jemny stared up at the ship's curved ceiling, and for a moment, Lina thought she wasn't going to answer.

Then she realized Jemny had been thinking, not ignoring the questions.

"Part of the tracking beacon structure is exposed inside the landing gear and on the roof. If we could break that circuit or interfere with the signal in some way, it would force the emergency beacon to report a malfunction. Or it *should*. Before today, I would have told you there was no possibility that this ship could be controlled from anywhere but my console."

"Could we get up there?" Tes said.

Despite thinking something similar not that long ago, Lina's belly rolled at the idea of actually stepping outside of a ship in motion.

Jemny snorted and shook her head and jerked her chin toward the port.

"Not that way. It's locked out while we're in flight. The speeds we reach are just too high. Locked out not only electronically, but mechanically."

"What about through the port in the floor?" Lina said before she could lose her courage. "We got in through that one while you were hovering above our water scoot."

Jemny raised her eyebrows and looked toward the floor.

"That *is* the emergency exit, so it has an override not available on the main port. But it's not going to work at this velocity."

Lina saw Musa watching them, her eyes wide and curious. She smiled and turned back toward the windows, hoping Musa wouldn't catch the anger and growing desperation bubbling so close to the surface.

The land had taken on more of a green tone again, but what really caught her attention was the line of deep blue on the horizon. They were fast approaching the sea, which meant they'd reach the Vatten Continent before much more time passed.

After that, Mount Bewaker and whatever waited for them.

Something Musa had said floated to the top of the stormy mess inside her mind.

"Remember Musa talking about hearing a noise when the attacks started?"

"She also said she heard it once we were airborne." Tes said.

"You've got more of the bone-conduction masks and helmets aboard, right?" Lina waited for Jemny to nod. "They seemed to go pretty damn loud to me. Maybe we could try using those to block whatever's controlling the ship?"

Jemny scowled and opened her mouth, and Lina braced for yet another disappointment.

But then Jemny looked toward the storage cabinets along the ship's back wall herself.

"You think the sound is part of the control mechanism?" Tes said.

Lina managed a weak smile.

"I think it makes as much sense as anything else, don't you? I doubt any of the vessel or satellite scans are looking for anything like that."

"No, they wouldn't be," Jemny said. "What I sent and Ris followed up on was focused on that specific grav-drive signature. I doubt anyone outside of Planetary Science would scan for sound at all. If nothing else, we might be able to disrupt whatever they're using if we can get close enough to the ship's sensors, or the tracking beacon."

Tes waved one hand toward the back of the ship.

"I wonder if we can get two of them to feed back and amplify each other? Looked to me like those shoulder lights have good-sized power supplies. That might do the job."

A tiny spark of hope started up in Lina's belly.

"At this point, I don't know what it could hurt. Maybe Musa could even help us tune the sound to match."

She and Tes both watched Jemny, waiting for the one person who could put the whole crazy idea in motion. Like she'd done before in stressful moments, Jemny laughed and grinned.

"You make a damn good point, Lina. What else are we going to do? Stare out at the landscape and wait for whatever these maniacs have planned for us?"

She paused, glancing up at the ceiling again.

"Unfortunately we don't have much access to components from in here. Maintenance is supposed to be done from the outside. But I might have an idea or two about how to slow us down enough for one of you to go after the tracking beacon."

Tes gasped and stepped toward Jemny.

"One of *us*? How did that become the plan? You know a lot more about this ship than either one of us."

Jemny's grin turned wicked.

"True, and that includes navigation and landing, especially around a busy spaceport. Which one of you wants to take on that particular challenge?"

Tes rubbed her eyes before turning to Lina.

"You said there was dust when you came back here with Musa. Do either of you think there's any chance someone actually got inside the ship to override the controls? Because I'd be really unhappy if one of us went outside to try this sound override thing and it turned out there's some kind of sneaky transmitter or something like it *inside*."

Jemny shook her head slowly.

"The door worked for you, right Lina? Even when the ship seemed dead?"

"That was the only thing that worked. It let me in and then back out without a problem."

"Makes perfect sense," Jemny said. "From this ship's design specs, there's no way it would have shut itself down like that without *some* kind of interference. But, the door is one of the few things that would work while the rest of the systems are offline. The emergency port you're about to go through works the same way, and neither one would have let anyone else in before you got here. Even with the power out. Remember when I triggered it to let you inside? That keyed it to your palm."

Tes met Lina's gaze, and they both smiled.

"Sounds like one of us is going outside," Lina said. "If we can get the feedback idea to work. Come on."

CHAPTER 33

JEMNY MADE short work of dismantling two of the bone-conduction helmets, with valuable assistance from Musa's nimble-fingered grandfather. Seerit proudly informed everyone it wasn't the first time Pandar's hobby of tinkering with electronics and recreating ancient tech had come in handy.

Much like when they'd been on the ground in the fierce storm, the bone-conduction comms functioned despite the interference that knocked out normal comms.

Down there, the dust itself had kept the helmets from working correctly.

Up here—and with all traces of dust filtered out once the sabotaged ship came back online—it was a simple matter of setting up a channel between the two sets of thumbnail-sized speakers.

Then bringing them close enough together to produce an ear-shattering squeal of feedback.

"That's *way* too high to match the giant wave noise!" Musa cried, hands over her extra-sensitive ears.

Tes yanked the tiny speakers apart.

"I'm so sorry," Lina said. "Maybe Jemny has some kind of helmet that will fit you."

But Seerit was already digging into the small backpack Pandar carried.

"We keep protection for her, especially for leaving planets and reentry. Here you go."

She held out a compact set of earmuffs decorated to look like bright yellow flowers with colorful butterflies perched on the top.

"They might look like toys," Seerit said, smiling as Musa jammed them over her ears, "but they're designed to filter out noises above or below frequencies that might be painful for her. I've got them set so she'll still be able to hear us. I've also got ordinary earplugs for everyone else if you like."

Tes, Lina, and Jemny joined Musa's grandparents in inserting regular blue earplugs before testing the feedback once again.

"Can you sing the right note, Musa?" Jemny said. "I can always pull out a third helmet for you to wear and connect it to the feedback pair. That way you can help us from inside."

Muse frowned, but she looked more nervous than afraid.

"I think so." She pulled off the earmuffs and listened, tilting her head to one side. "It's really high, maybe too high for my voice."

Jemny blushed, but seemed to set herself and keep going.

"Do you know about music scales, Musa? Where the same note can be lower or higher? Like this."

She adjusted her stance, took a deep breath, and sang out

such a clear, pure, beautiful tone that Lina's jaw dropped. Then she hit the same note an octave higher.

With a quick scowl at Lina, Jemny did the same thing several more times, moving up a scale, then back down.

"Make sense?" she said to Musa.

Musa nodded, grinning at Jemny with no trace of fear or intimidation.

"You sing a *really* pretty song. I don't think mine will be as nice as yours, but I think I can make the two sounds that match."

And Musa did exactly that with three different notes, her voice as light and sweet as one of Sarkan 3's songbirds that Planetary Science was only beginning to investigate.

"That's perfect," Jemny said, beaming. "Your song is very pretty, too. Now can you try again and match your voice with the sound you hear?"

Musa nodded, her eyes going distant as she listened for several seconds.

This time she adjusted her voice up and down, clearly zeroing in on the correct note.

All at once, she smiled while she was still singing, nodding at Jemny.

Jemny nodded back, settled into her balanced singing posture again, and matched the note.

Lina was hardly an expert or much of a musician herself, but she didn't hear a trace of dissonance between the two voices.

"That's *exactly* what we needed, Musa," Jemny said. "We can use this to try to match the tone you're hearing, and maybe even use it to block the control itself."

Musa raised up on her toes a few times, then darted forward

and hugged Jemny around the waist. After a quick startled look, Jemny returned the hug.

Musa dashed back to her grandparents, giggling the whole way. Her child's-too-loud whisper surprised a matching giggle out of Lina.

"She's not all *that* scary."

Seerit caught Lina's gaze and smiled, one hand over her heart.

"I don't think she's scary at all," Seerit said. "But she might be if we give her a good reason to be. So maybe we should wait back here while they get ready."

Lina stood shoulder to shoulder with Tes, waiting for Jemny to face them.

Her exaggerated eye roll was more than worth it.

"You really do have a lovely singing voice, Jemny," Tes said. "I had no idea."

"No one who knows me in Planetary Security or for any other reason on this planet knows, and I'd appreciate it staying that way. Nothing more than a hobby from when I was about Musa's age."

After a pointed look toward the ship's front windows, she started making adjustments to the disemboweled speakers.

Lina followed her gaze, and most of her curiosity and amusement about Jemny's singing fled to the back of her mind.

The blue of the sea was beneath them now, without a sliver of land yet visible. Since they were over the largest body of water on Sarkans 3—larger than any of Earth's oceans—that wasn't surprising.

But it also meant they were running out of time.

Tes seemed equally subdued, but she still smiled at Jemny.

"I hope you'll tell us more about that when this is all over.

Because there's no way that voice was only trained for a little while, then neglected for years."

Jemny only grunted, but she didn't say no.

After a couple more of the ear-splitting tests—accompanied by her glorious voice—they had the feedback set to the same note Musa heard, and the helmet controls secured into that position along a section of trim taken from one of the storage cabinets.

Jemny and Pandar had the whole thing attached to a bridge made between two of the big shoulder lights faster than Lina could follow.

"I suggest everyone make sure your earplugs are secure," Jemny said. "Might want to cover your ears with your hands, too. I'm going to try the right note with the power pack in this lamp. It's going to be a whole lot louder than it was before, but I still doubt it will make any difference from inside the ship."

She shrugged, then smiled.

"I figure it's worth a try before anyone climbs outside while we're still moving."

As soon as everyone's hearing was protected as much as it could be, Jemny held up three fingers. Then she lowered them one at a time before activating the feedback.

Even with her hands firmly in place over her earplugs, Lina winced and jerked away at the deafening shriek.

Jemny held the bizarre speaker-lamp rig up toward the ceiling, then right above the rectangle of the floor's emergency hatch, before deactivating the awful wailing noise. She dashed forward to the ship's controls.

Lina hadn't realized how tense her shoulders and the rest of her body had gotten until the sonic attack stopped.

Before she could even lower her hands, Jemny was shaking her head. She waited for everyone to remove their earplugs before speaking.

"Still locked out, and comms are still useless." She glanced at Musa, who still had her earmuffs on. "Since we don't yet have an unwelcome guest aboard to make this match the runaway scoots and their criminal cargo, I can't say for sure what's going to happen when we get to the spaceport. The two of you coming back to the ship might have interrupted someone's plans for a different scenario. But the required deceleration sequence has already started."

"If someone wants to…" Tes hesitated, glancing at Musa. "If the goal is to create the same criminal cargo for the third time, why would we be slowing down? Wouldn't skipping that step get the job done and make a bigger statement at the same time?"

"It might," Jemny said. "But we still don't know what statement they're *trying* to make, if any. And if we were to go barreling toward the spaceport at our usual velocity, there are systems in place that would solve the problem before we ever got there. Especially with nonfunctional comms."

At that idea combined with what Jemny had said about lethal force ships, any hesitation Lina had about the loose plan vanished.

"Then we need to get ready for me to take this rig outside. I'll trust you to tell me when we're going slow enough to be safe, Jemny. And you, Tes, to hook up one of those tethers like you would for a tourist coming down a mountain."

"Hang on," Tes said, "since I do have climbing experience, why wouldn't I be the one to try this crazy scheme?"

Lina reached for one of the bone-conduction helmets that hadn't been dismantled.

"You could, but I have no idea how to help someone going up or down a mountain. I'm guessing you could operate the tether and talk me through it a lot better than I could manage trying to make sure you don't fall."

Tes pursed her lips and shook her head. But she headed toward the fresh coils of tether she'd pulled out of the supply closets.

Lina did her best to keep breathing instead of drowning in the fear that now clutched at her throat.

"I don't suppose there are steps build into the side of the ship?" she said to Jemny. "Or maybe anchor points for the tethers along the top or bottom?"

"Unfortunately not," Jemny said. "All the ship's hardware systems are accessed using the normal methods like ladders. It's not designed for moving maintenance. I'm afraid all we've got are magnetic packs, kind of like the grav-packs some of the tourists use."

She frowned and shook her head.

"Well, not *exactly* magnetic, since there's nothing metallic in the hull. But they're matched to the components of the hull in a similar way. They're strong enough to let you maneuver in an emergency, but it won't exactly be easy going. That and a parachute in case you slip *and* the tether fails."

"Well, I'm not designed to sit around and wait for things to get worse," Lina said. "Even if my mind is trying to convince me about six different ways a second why I shouldn't be doing this. Let's get me suited up and ready to go before I come up with a good enough reason to refuse."

CHAPTER 34

By the time Lina got back into a fresh protective suit, the ship's decreasing speed was obvious with a peek out the front windows.

Even with nothing below them but water, the scene was no longer a blur. The occasional whitecap stood out against the mass of choppy blue.

But their approach to the Vatten Continent was made obvious by a darker line against the vast horizon of the sea.

They were running out of time.

Which meant Lina didn't have the luxury of running out of courage.

So she tried to avoid looking out the windows at all.

She forced herself to breathe evenly by counting to five on each inhale and exhale while Tes meticulously attached the new tether to Lina's suit. Through the front and back belt loops, but also in an improvised sort of harness pattern around her shoulders and legs that should keep Lina from dangling and spinning helplessly without being able to grab hold of anything.

Not that she had any *interest* in keeping herself upright while hanging underneath a moving ship. The best plan of catastrophe prevention—besides not going outside the ship at all—would be making sure she didn't end up slipping or tripping or getting shaken loose in the first place.

The thought of the boxy parachute now secured just below her shoulders only soothed her anxiety a little bit, though she supposed a controlled fall would be better than a wild plummet.

Neither Sarkans 3's low gravity nor a pile of the tourists' grav-packs would come close to helping if that happened.

Musa seemed to have decided the whole operation was a delightful game. She bustled around, making sure her line of sight was uninterrupted, somehow not getting in anyone's way, in the firm belief that nothing could be done correctly unless she oversaw every single detail.

She even stayed close by while Jemny attached the shoulder light, now stripped of the light itself in favor of the creatively designed speaker setup.

Both Tes and Jemny strapped deceptively small metallic discs around Lina's wrists, elbows, knees, and feet, which Jemny swore were far more powerful than they looked. All Lina could do was trust that once the power was switched on, the magnets would provide much more strength than their palm-sized appearance promised.

Musa nodded at every step, generously granting her approval of the process.

Jemny's work was indeed impressive. She somehow managed to balance and secure the heavy rig so Lina was still able to turn and move without toppling over.

A few solid tugs showed Lina was far more likely to stagger than the rig was to slip off her shoulders.

"Remember where the external components of the beacons are?" Jemny asked yet again.

She'd been describing the exact location for the tiny bits of both the emergency beacon and the tracking beacon the whole time she worked on Lina's suit.

"A series of hair-thin wires on the bottom, tucked into the wells of the rear landing wheels. Once the landing gear drops, assuming it does, I'll have to basically climb inside to get to those with that serious knife right over there."

She pointed to an intimidating dagger half as long as her forearm, with one serrated edge that she'd be comfortable taking on a deep dive in the unlikely event she expected to need to hack apart a shipwreck.

"And?" Jemny prompted.

"*If* the landing gear drops and *if* I can manage to saw through those wires, that should trigger a malfunction in the navigational beacon, which will set off the emergency beacon. Or, I can magnetically scramble up the slippery, smooth surface of this vessel to the top, where I'll find a bunch of sensors that look like tiny red wires embedded in the hull. If I can scrape enough of those off, or chop through them, that sets off the emergency beacon, too."

"Sounds like you've got the idea," Tes said. "Now we just need to get you out there so you can put it into practice."

"You be *really* careful, Lina," Musa said, her face and voice too serious for her age. "I want you to come back inside."

Lina resisted the urge to say she'd much prefer to *stay* inside, and smiled instead.

"I want me to come back inside, too. Thank you for helping Tes and Jemny get me ready."

With her expression as solemn as a middle-aged adult at a funeral, Musa held out her hand for Lina to shake. Then she turned around and walked back to sit with her grandparents.

"Now you have to succeed," Jemny said, her own smile grave. "But you left out one more possible way to do that."

Lina shifted from side to side, adjusting her balance as the heavy, bigger-than-her-head lights mounted to her shoulders moved with her.

"That's because I didn't want to draw bad luck by mentioning it first. My favorite option is I get close to those sensors in the landing gear without having to try to dig them out, then I turn on our very clever feedback blaster. The perfectly matched howl of dissonance blocks whoever's controlling the ship long enough for us to get a message through, or maybe even to change course."

"Assuming they don't catch on to what we're trying to do" Jemny said with a frown, "and decide to crash us for our trouble. Maybe we'll get even more lucky and Ris already has Planetary Security tracking the same frequency all over the planet."

"Or maybe the suspects they've already got in custody will give the others up." Tes yanked the tether attached to the base of one of the ship's seats several times. "Out of guilt or trying to make things easier on themselves. I don't much care which one."

"I prefer the one that doesn't put me at risk of tumbling into the sea. Or crashing into the cliff the spaceport is perched on top of. You sure the tethers won't tangle up the parachute if I happen to need it?"

Tes flashed a smile that almost managed to hide how nervous she was.

"I'm sure. That's one reason I used more than one to keep you from flipping over and fouling the parachute. But there's an easy enough way to make sure. Just don't slip. And even if you do, you'll be tethered to the ship, so all you have to do is keep yourself from panicking. Odds are high you won't even need the chute either way. Ready?"

"After that pep talk? Almost. What happens if I accidentally turn these gigantic lights on instead of triggering the speakers? The whole thing won't blow up, will it?"

Jemny and Pandar had wired the trigger for the speakers into the same palm-unit as the lights. A flat sensor fit over Lina's fingers so the whole thing was within easy reach of her fingertips. But the time crunch and lack of many specialized tools meant the hasty arrangement left two buttons side-by-side.

Hitting the wrong one or both at the same time would be incredibly easy.

"Nothing will blow up if you hit them both at the same time," Jemny said. "You might run the batteries down in a hurry, but by then we won't have much time left anyway. So don't worry too much about it."

Lina couldn't tell for sure from Jemny's voice or her neutral expression, but she thought that was meant to make her feel better. Might as well pretend it did.

"Fair enough. Better get me out there while I can still think."

Jemny looked toward Musa and her grandparents.

"Make sure you're all strapped in in case we run into rough air or anything like that." She turned back to Lina. "And you take care out there."

Lina put her earplugs back in, then pulled her helmet on. The tight fit made her jaw ache at once, but she was sure she'd be glad of the protection even before the feedback really got started.

She nodded, and Tes and Jemny both attached their own tethers around their waists and pulled their own helmets on.

"Comms working?" Jemny's voice came through perfectly clear with the bone-conduction.

"Working fine."

Jemny stepped over to a control pad set into the wall and tapped in the sequence to operate the emergency port. Lina barely heard the alarm that sounded, but she knew it was loud by the way everyone else reacted.

The rectangular door slowly moved to the side.

They were still over water, and moving even more slowly than before, but a gust of warm, sea-scented wind surged through the ship anyway.

Lina carefully sat, keeping the lights-and-speaker rig steady, not wanting to hesitate long enough to lose her nerve.

Swinging her legs around so her feet dangled past the ship's thick hull almost scared her into giving up anyway.

Even the much lighter wind from the ship's slowing velocity felt like it wanted to snatch her boots right off.

The same ladder she and Tes had climbed what felt like years ago unrolled itself, getting driven back by the wind immediately. Despite Lina's doubts that it was strong enough to resist, it locked into place, giving her yet another layer of security in a terrifying situation.

"Just remember to use your mag-pods," Jemny said. "Twist to the side to detach. Powering those up to standby now. That way they'll only take a couple of seconds to start working when you're ready."

Lina didn't feel anything except an odd vibration that seemed to work through her teeth and bones.

"Got it," she said. "Be ready in case I can make this crazy thing work."

Then Lina pulled her mask into place and scooted forward, ignoring the way every muscle in her body seemed to tremble, and lowered her legs through the opening until her feet were steady on the now-rigid ladder.

Even with her hands firmly planted on the floor, her backside still inside, and Tes holding tight to the tether, she felt like she was about to tumble into the water.

With one more smile for everyone not doing such a crazy thing, Lina lowered herself onto the ladder and out of the ship.

CHAPTER 35

EVEN THOUGH SHE knew parachutes and open seas weren't a good match, it was everything Lina could do to keep herself from pulling the handle on her chest.

In her initial rush of exhilaration so fierce it was closer to pure panic, doing anything to change her situation was incredibly tempting.

Only knowing she'd be abandoning Musa, her family, Tes, and Jemny to their uncertain fate kept her focused.

She still had to force her gloved hands to let go of each rung before she could descend another step.

The wind beat against her helmet and mask and the rest of her body, feeling like a thousand tiny drums playing all over her skin at once.

She locked her arms through the rungs and slowly turned.

The belly of the ship was still smooth and unbroken.

No landing gear deployed yet.

Not that it really should be, since they were still a long way out from Mount Bewaker and the spaceport. The ship wasn't even over land yet, and they were aiming for a good ways inland.

Up the side of the ship it was after all.

But not before she tried the vicious feedback outside the protective bubble of the ship.

"Everyone protect your hearing," she said. "Going to test the speakers before I try for the top."

"All protected," Tes said at once. "Good luck."

Lina unwrapped her right hand from the ladder, but before she could activate the speakers, she froze.

Was the button for the speakers on the left side of her palm or the right?

No matter how hard she tried to force her mind to focus and remember, all of Jemny's instructions collided into a blur.

Turning her hand over didn't help, either. Both flat, rounded buttons looked exactly the same, and the harnesses were identical. Made sense, since they came from repurposed parts taken from a suit with the same design.

But that didn't help when it came to what she needed to do right now.

She took a chance and pressed the button closer to her thumb.

The searing feedback erupted, and now it was all she could do to hold on to the ladder rather than covering her own ears.

After several seconds, as long as she could stand even the muted blast, she squeezed the button again to shut down the speakers.

"Anything change? Assuming you can hear me after that noise."

Without the bone conduction, she wouldn't have been able

to hear Jemny's answer over the wind of their flight, even through her own protective helmet and earplugs.

"No break in the comms blackout. And still no control over the ship. Hopefully you'll have better luck up top. You're doing great, Lina."

"I'm just glad to still be attached. Let's see if I can manage to stay that way."

Lina shifted her weight so she could reach toward the flat bottom of the ship with one hand, pretending the thought of letting go of the ladder didn't make her feel like she was going to choke.

"Switch on the magnets to full strength."

The odd vibration from when the magnets had been powered up to standby changed to a tingling current concentrated in her wrists, elbows, knees and feet.

"Switching on," Tes said. "You're ready to climb. I'll keep your tether played out just enough to give you room to move, but remember it's anchored securely in here. You can't fall."

Lina resisted pointing out that of *course* she could fall.

If the tethers came into play at all, it would be because she *had* fallen, and with any luck, they'd keep her from falling any further.

"Don't let it slip."

"Not a chance, Lina."

Rather than stretching her arm full length, Lina reached just to the side of the ladder. Her wrist followed a strong pull toward the silvery hull until it connected with a thud.

"Magnets seem to be working. You're sure they're strong enough to hold me?"

"One of them would hold you in place easily," Jemny said,

"though I wouldn't recommend it. Your body would go past its limits long before the magnet would. We use them for cargo more than an emergency like this. Now I know the advice is normally don't look down, but we're getting closer than I'd like without knowing what we're heading into."

When she did look down—or more accurately forward—Lina nearly lost her grip on the ladder and tested the single-magnet theory.

The ship was still over the sea, but land was close enough to show plenty of details. They'd slowed again, but were approaching Scarlet Beach faster than she wanted to admit.

That stark cliff face pushed her into twisting her wrist to the side to dislodge the magnet, then reaching for another contact point an uncomfortable distance from the ladder. Adding the magnet around her elbow gave her a tiny bit more security.

After a deep breath, she did the same with her other wrist.

Now she really had no choice but to go up the ladder with her feet before shifting her wrists out again.

A few more repetitions of that motion had her nearly full-length along the ship's belly before she was finally bold enough to lift one knee into place.

The magnets showed no signs of slipping even a millimeter.

Sadly Jemny was right about Lina's body taking the strain. Her back complained loudly enough to keep her moving until she clung like an overgrown white-suited spider to the curved side of the hull.

Turned out hanging upright was dramatically better than upside down.

"Still making progress," she said. "About to head for the roof."

"Conditions are steady in here," Jemny said. "Let me know before you activate the feedback again or try to destroy the sensors up there so I can be ready."

Lina once again risked a look ahead.

The ship's gradually rising trajectory promised to take them above the scarlet cliffs rather than smashing into them, but she wasn't about to relax over that small reprieve. The attacker's pattern had the hijacked vessels returning to the spaceport so far.

With a dead body inside on the previous two arrivals, which was plenty of reason to keep moving.

She was surprised and relieved to find it much easier to move once she made her careful way to the ship's roof. The relatively flat surface let her take on a crawling motion rather than dangling upside down or climbing up a wall, for one thing.

And she wasn't quite so convinced that she was about to slip off and tumble to her death on the rocks below.

Perhaps not the most rational feeling, since the unseen controllers could easily flip the ship upside down just to watch her dangle and twist in the wind.

But at this point, she'd take any form of relief and advantage she could get.

A slender fin much like the ones fish on many planets sported rose toward the back of the ship, probably for stability as much as navigation.

Right in front of it, she spotted what looked like a bunch of roads marked in red on an ancient paper map. The sensor wires she needed to do her best to gouge through.

With another glance toward the cliffs the ship was about to pass harmlessly over—close enough that she could see knots of climbing tourists on the face—she crawled back to the fin.

She twisted her right wrist and elbow loose, then pulled Jemny's impressive dagger away from her belt. Tes had rigged one of the tethers around it in case it slipped out of Lina's grasp.

"About to try digging out the sensor wires up here. Any changes down there?"

"Nothing except getting way too close to Mount Bewaker for comfort," Jemny said.

Lina twisted her left arm loose, trusting the magnets on her legs and the ship's reduced velocity to keep her from tumbling off.

The towering gray hulk of Mount Bewaker was indeed visible against the overcast sky in the distance, with a collection of swirling vessels that looked like insects.

"Trying the feedback first, so protect yourselves."

"Go ahead," Tes said.

Lina tried to trigger the howling noise again, but accidentally turned the blazing shoulder lights on instead. She turned away from the glaring reflection against the ship's gleaming hull and switched to the correct palm-button.

She forced herself to count to ten before letting go, blinking against the purplish afterimage in her eyes.

"Please tell me that made some kind of difference."

"Sorry, Lina," Jemny said. "Try to dig out those wires. And be alert in case Planetary Security sends us an unfriendly escort since they won't be able to reach us."

Still trying to blink past the lingering glare, Lina leaned close enough to where she'd seen the wires that her mask bumped against the hull. She braced herself with the magnets on both knees, grabbed the dagger, and dragged the blade across the surface.

Nothing.

It skated across like plastic against glass.

She switched to the serrated edge that looked jagged and sharp enough to saw through steel.

It skittered a tiny bit, but never dug in enough to damage the hull.

"Not getting any kind of purchase here," she said. "Think the dagger will stand up to me using it like a hammer?"

"That dagger would stand up to this ship landing on it," Jemny said. "The hull is every bit as tough. But we're running out of options."

Lina wished she could rub her eyes and try to get the horrid afterimage to dissipate, but she wasn't about to lift her mask or face shield. Even with greatly reduced speed, the wind would scour her eyes and take her breath.

She turned her hand so the dagger's hilt was facing down, then hit the hull as hard as she could.

All she got for the effort was a jolt all the way to her shoulder and a sharp pain in her wrist.

"I don't suppose you have a saw or anything like that aboard?"

"Nothing. But we're about to have company."

CHAPTER 36

Lina turned so fast that she lost her grip on the dagger, sending it skittering along the hull at the end of the tether.

Three much larger ships were fast approaching from Mount Bewaker, with red lights flashing on all three. She couldn't see projections or anything else that looked like weapons, but she had no doubt they carried the lethal force Jemny had mentioned before.

She considered telling everyone inside to put on parachutes and jump. They might have a chance, assuming the big ships didn't shoot them down before they got anywhere near the rocky ground they were passing over right now.

Before she could suggest it, a greatly amplified voice boomed right through her earplugs.

"PLANETARY SECURITY TO APPROACHING VESSEL. ESTABLISH COMMS OR DIVERT COURSE AT ONCE. REPEAT, ESTABLISH COMMS OR DIVERT COURSE AT

ONCE. OTHERWISE WE'LL BE FORCED TO TAKE IMMEDIATE ACTION."

When the noise died down, Lina spoke.

"Any suggestions, Jemny? Should we all jump for it and see what happens?"

"I don't recommend it or I would have already. They'll have targeting systems set to catch anything that falls from the ship in case we try to escape. Or if they decide we're trying to drop bombs."

"Thought so. Will they hear the feedback if I try that?"

"Possibly, but maybe not at this distance. If they don't take us out before we get close enough it's worth a try."

"Then protect your hearing, if you can still hear after that announcement."

Lina tried to trigger the feedback, but nothing happened.

Her heart tried to freeze in her chest.

If the big batteries were already out of power, they might truly be out of options.

She tried again and got a full blast, making herself jump so hard she nearly lost her hold on the ship's tail fin.

She turned her hand over and realized the buttons had slipped out of place while she was trying to saw through the hull. On her first attempt, she'd missed altogether.

Then she squeezed the button for her shoulder lights in the same sequence she'd used during the volcanic ash storm.

Four holds.

I wish to come up.

The ships didn't respond at all, but Lina's mind did.

"Jemny, is there an emergency code I can use with the lights?"

"Yes. An ancient one you might recognize. Three short flashes, three long ones, and three short ones again. If anyone on that ship knows anything in code, that will be it."

Lina squeezed the button again.

Three short.

Three long.

Three short.

Of course. The very old code for SOS that she'd read about when she learned the diving language.

She did it again, just in case the ships swooping toward them thought it was an accident.

The Planetary Security ships were close enough now that she could see they were as red as their own flashing lights.

If they hadn't seen and understood her code, Lina and everyone depending on her were out of time.

But she decided to take one more chance.

This time she squeezed the button for the feedback speakers in the same distress signal code.

The ships kept coming.

But were they slowing?

And wasn't the middle one flying higher now?

As if it was going to pass over them instead of aiming head on?

"PLANETARY SECURITY TO APPROACHING VESSEL. TWO SEVEN SIX. REPEAT, TWO SEVEN SIX."

"I don't—"

"Listen to me," Jemny nearly shouted. "I need you to tap out this sequence, exactly as I say it to you. Understand?"

"Light or feedback?"

"Just do both! Tap out the numbers as I say them, pause and count to five, then tap out the next number. Got it?"

Lina refused to even glance at the ships, not wanting to let her tension get even worse and end up messing up Jemny's very simple instructions. She knelt, letting the magnets around her knees anchor her, leaned one of her elbow magnets against the tail fin, and put the buttons back in place instead.

"Got it. Go."

"Four ... Nine ... Six ..."

The sharp precision in Jemny's voice might have managed to slice through the ship's hull to get at the sensor wires.

She said each number so clearly Lina couldn't possibly mistake it, then paused exactly long enough before saying the next. The string went on long enough that Lina lost track of how many numbers she'd translated into sound and light.

She wasn't sure if her ears were getting numb or the blasts of feedback were losing power, she was too busy doing her best to keep from messing up.

Her focus was deep enough that she was confused for several seconds when Jemny spoke words instead.

"Okay, that's the whole sequence. That was perfect, Lina."

Lina let out her breath in a relieved gust.

She was shocked to notice the three ships had now slowed to a crawl, lights still flashing red.

"Now what?"

Before Jemny could answer, the ships answered for her.

"PLANETARY SECURITY TO APPROACHING VESSEL. DO NOT DEVIATE FROM YOUR PRESENT COURSE. THE SPACEPORT IS AWARE OF YOUR EMERGENCY. BRACE FOR INTERCEPT MANEUVER."

Then all three Planetary Security ships swerved and went into a sharp loop, ending up in an escort formation. One on either side and one above.

Lina laughed out loud, still clinging to the fin and shaking too hard to even consider trying to get back inside yet.

"We did it!" she yelled. "They understand!"

A chorus of shouts rang out over her bone conduction, and she grinned.

"Now get back in here!" Tes said. "I don't want to test those tethers any more than we have to during their intercept!"

"I don't know if I can," Lina said through more laughter. "I think I'm too keyed up to manage it."

"Then hold on long enough to send one more quick sequence," Jemny said. "And let's hope the batteries can squeeze out a little more. Try matching your breath to the numbers. That might help get your nervous system under control."

Thankfully it *was* quick—only four numbers—and Jemny's breath suggestion actually did make a difference.

When she finished, all three ships tilted to the left for a few seconds before leveling off.

"That means they understand," Jemny said. "And that's your cue to get back in here. Now."

So Lina twisted the magnets to detach herself, staggered forward, and knelt to let the magnets pull her toward the hull. The ship had slowed again, thankfully remaining on a level flight path instead of banking hard enough to send Lina flailing over the edge.

As she carefully edged backward, she locked wide-eyed gazes with an older woman in the ship matching their speed on the other side. Lina couldn't tell whether her observer was angry, horrified, or impressed.

When the woman grinned, Lina nodded and grinned back, not caring that her mask hid most of her face.

That recognition and what she hoped was encouragement steadied her enough to get her moving again.

She hoped getting one question answered would keep her going.

"Any change in the ship's control?"

"Nothing so far," Jemny said. "But our situation has improved considerably."

"How are you holding up?" Tes said. "Remember I've got you anchored, but getting you secured in here would be best."

"If I could get myself there faster, I would. Unless you've figured out a way to get me in through the hull instead?"

Tether or not, it hadn't occurred to Lina when she'd climbed up just how much harder it would be to reverse her movement without being able to see where she was going.

Only the thought of turning around and crawling down head-first was more terrifying.

CHAPTER 37

Lina watched the Planetary Security ship to the right as long as she could, then switched her attention to the ship flying overhead when she backward-crawled over the side.

They really were much larger versions of Jemny's ship, with the sun glinting off hulls that might have been made from melted sand from Scarlet Beach. Spotting the same emergency hatch she was aiming for didn't exactly calm her fears, but at least her not-quite-panicked brain couldn't convince her that she'd get to the bottom of Jemny's ship and find a magically smooth and unbroken hull.

The overhead ship helped keep her mind occupied until it was time to shift from crawling backwards-but-vertical to horizontal-and-upside-down.

Which turned out to be the perfect way to realize how much harder and faster her heart could beat.

Lina tried three times to move down low enough to swing her leg up toward the bottom of the ship, but she couldn't do it.

Letting the rest of her body hang loose over the increasingly rocky landscape proved impossible.

A quick glance down made it clear going headfirst still wasn't an option.

So she turned her body parallel to the ground, with her head facing the looming summit of Mount Bewaker.

She barely had time to register that the swirling patterns of scoot and ship traffic had disappeared before Jemny startled her.

"We're running out of time, Lina! You need to get inside and get strapped in!"

"I'm trying! This isn't exactly easy."

"Let me come get you," Tes said, but Jemny jumped in before she could go on.

"No, there's no time for you to suit up. Just drop off if you have to, Lina, and let us haul you in that way. I don't want to scare you too much, but you don't want to be outside when we hit the intercept field."

Lina wasn't sure if it was the words or the tone in Jemny's voice, but the thought of hitting whatever the intercept field turned out to be threatened to freeze her already aching muscles solid.

She gritted her teeth and forced her left hand down and around the curve of the ship, then gasped when the magnet attached to her wrist smacked against the hull.

Only then did she realize her mistake.

The magnets on her knees were on the front, not the side. Even if she had plenty of time, trying to get them moved while clinging to the side of a moving ship when she was already struggling with her fear wasn't likely to work.

She was strong and flexible enough, at least when her muscles hadn't been so recently overused and abused.

But unless she could work up the courage to swing her lower body down and around, she simply wasn't going to *bend* that way.

"PLANETARY SECURITY TO APPROACHING VESSEL, INTERCEPT IS IMMINENT. REPEAT, INTERCEPT IN IMMINENT. BRACE FOR IMPACT AT ONCE."

Tes and Jemny's loud and rising voices blended into painfully loud mush though Lina's bone conduction, only cranking up her fright.

Another unwise glance ahead tightened the vise of tension to intolerable levels.

What looked like a sparkling net of fine golden lines coated with gigantic rubies crisscrossed in front of the spaceport with no room for their ship to pass through.

Lina was certain she was looking at some sort of force field, meant to protect the spaceport from an unexpected or intentional collision.

A force field that wouldn't be kind to a human unable to remove herself from the outer hull of the runaway ship.

And if the likely jolt from impact didn't finish the job, surely the whiplash effect would.

"Jemny, cut power to the magnets!" Lina yelled. "Get ready to haul me inside, Tes!"

The conflicting babble rose for a few seconds, then Tes cut through the noise with a commanding tone Lina hadn't heard from her before.

"I suggest you do as she says, Agent Manhoff, before it's too late. Lina, prepare for retrieval."

"You sure about this?" Jemny said.

"Do it now," Lina replied.

Then she tried to get ready, even though she had no idea what that might mean. The best she could do was try to relax her arms and legs so she wouldn't flail around and hurt herself before she had a chance to collide with the bottom of the ship.

She didn't mean to scream when all six magnets let go at once.

But she couldn't help it.

She curled into a ball as she swung loose around the edge of the ship, squeezing her eyes closed.

Focusing on how she did indeed swing rather than fall helped, but only until she crashed into the far edge hard enough to force the air from her lungs.

On the return trip, she felt Tes yank her upward, and the collision on the other side wasn't nearly as hard.

It was all Lina could do to stop her lungs from taking over all of her bodily functions in their demands for oxygen that her mask fought against.

"Hang on," Tes said, her voice mostly a grunt of effort. "I've got you."

Another hard jerk up, a much shorter swing, and no impact at all.

And finally hands grasping her arms and shoulders.

"Reach up, Lina!"

Lina managed to obey, letting her chest expand as she unfolded herself, and finally getting a full breath.

Which was promptly knocked out of her again when she landed on the floor.

Someone yelled for Jemny to close the portal as they dragged Lina to the side.

"Good thing we retracted that ladder." That had to be Pandar, Musa's grandfather. "You would have crashed right into it otherwise."

Lina reached up to pull off her mask and helmet.

"Hold on, let's get you into a seat," Tes said. "We've all got to strap in."

"Is Lina okay?"

That was Musa, her sweet voice now a frightened wail.

Lina opened her eyes as she was lifted upright, and saw Tes pulling the straps around her body.

"I'm okay." Her voice came out so weak she barely heard herself.

"She's okay, Musa," Tes said, smiling at Lina. "We'll get her mask off in a second and she'll tell you herself."

"PLANETARY SECURITY TO APPROACHING VESSEL. INTERCEPT IN TEN SECONDS. BRACE FOR IMPACT."

"That's got you." Tes moved to the side, and now Lina could see Musa through her fogged-up face shield, seated in the same row, between her grandparents but struggling to get free. All of them faced forward now rather than sitting on the opposite side of the ship. "Hang on."

She helped Lina drag the helmet and mask off.

Lina hadn't realized how stale and sweaty the air in there was until she got a gasp of mostly clean, blessedly cool ship's air.

"I'm okay, Musa, see?"

Musa nodded, then leaned forward and covered her face with her hands.

Trying not to cry herself at that too-adult gesture, Lina looked up to see the same glittering net pattern out the ship's window, much larger and closer now.

"How hard will we hit?" she said.

"From what Jemny told me and Seerit," Tes said quietly, "it's not a question of *whether* we get hurt. Only how badly. Even in here. The impact will be bad enough, but the rebound does the real damage."

Lina turned back to Musa, now wiping her tears and putting on a brave smile. It was impossible to miss the way her grandparents leaned toward her, each with an arm around her.

Affectionate, certainly, and a reasonable attempt to comfort an upset little girl. But just as much to try to shield her from whatever was about to happen.

"Thank you for getting me back inside, Tes."

Tes winked and grinned.

"Thank you for going out there and giving us a chance."

"Brace for impact!" Jemny shouted from the front seat.

Lina closed her eyes again, crossing her aching arms across her chest.

Hoping they all managed to avoid more pain than they'd already fought their way through.

When Jemny yelled again, her voice carried an odd note of triumph.

"Hang on!"

But Lina felt her body pushed *down* into her seat rather than slammed forward.

CHAPTER 38

For what felt like a lifetime, Lina couldn't make sense of what she saw out the ship's window, what her body reported to her brain.

Rather than staring at a vast screen of glittering red-and-gold forcefield protecting the spaceport from an impending collision, she was looking at the deep blue of Sarkans 3's sky, dotted with white and gray clouds.

And instead of being thrown forward and whiplashed back, she felt like a huge, invisible hand pressed her into her seat hard enough that she once again struggled to breathe.

Going by the groans around her, everyone else was fighting the same battle.

Jemny apparently managed to drag in a breath first, because she let out an amazingly loud shout.

"He *did* it! I don't know how, but he *did* it!"

The pressure finally eased, and now the view out the front

window matched the disorientating sensation of the ship *rolling* sideways.

Blue sky twisted to darker-blue sea twisted to rocky gray mountain.

Musa let out what sounded like a piercing scream at first, but then she dissolved into a burst of high-pitched giggles.

"Do that again, Jemny! Spin us around some more!"

Lina's stomach rolled a few seconds behind the ship, and she realized she'd be better off not testing her body any more today if she could possibly avoid it.

"Tell us what you did first," she said with a weak laugh. "So we know whether to feel better or worse."

"Just give me a second to let Planetary Security know what's going on first," Jemny said, glancing back at her with a grin, "so they don't decide to take us out of the sky anyway."

The ship leveled off, now flying along the coast with Mount Bewaker and the spaceport to their right. Jemny made some kind of adjustment so her words sounded throughout the ship and not just into her own comm.

"Planetary Security Agent Jemny Manhoff here, reporting that my ship's controls have been restored. Repeat, ship controls have been restored. I suspect Ris Murray, Director of Planetary Science for the Vatten Continent, is responsible, since he's investigating the recent string of attacks. Permission to land at Mount Bewaker for inspection, and perhaps a different ship? I've got people aboard who'd really like to be back on the ground."

Planetary Security's response—thankfully not over the same booming loudspeakers as before—was lost in an outburst of cheering from inside the ship.

Tes leaned over and hugged Lina, repeating Jemny's words herself.

"He did it! That had to be Ris finding the source of the controllers."

"That or the suspects they have in custody finally admitted the truth," Lina said, grinning herself. "Either way, I'm perfectly fine if I never find out what the Intercept Maneuver actually is."

Jemny let out another great whoop as she stood and turned toward the back of the ship.

"That's the first time I've ever *willingly* given over control of my ship, and I'm damn glad to do it. They're going to bring us in for a landing at the Planetary Security maintenance yard. That way they can make sure nothing was actually planted on the ship to cause that takeover."

Musa piped up, sounding more like the excitable little girl she should be instead of the miserable child who'd been crying only a few minutes before.

"Does that mean we can all get up now?"

"You bet it does," Jemny said. "I expect our landing will be gentle as a sigh, but even if it's not, we've got a few minutes before they bring us in. Apparently we managed to disrupt scoot and ship traffic all over the planet. They want to at least get the word out that all is well on that front first."

Lina got her straps loose, but her legs refused to cooperate when she tried to stand and join in the celebration. Turned out she'd finally pushed her muscles over the edge with her adventures crawling around outside the ship.

She'd ignored too many warnings over the last couple of weeks, and now nothing but hot baths and a chance to relax would solve the problem.

Musa was all too glad to bring a generous share of happiness right to her in the form of a big, tight hug.

"You saved us all, Lina! That was so brave to climb up onto the ship like that."

Lina shook her head even as she returned the hug.

"Thank you, Musa. It sounds to me like Ris came through and kept us all safe."

Tes hauled Lina to her feet, supporting her on one side while Jemny took the other.

"Don't you *dare* give away the credit on this one, Lina. You're the one who told Ris to check the next decrease of energy frequency, remember? *And* who got that pine cone sample, *and* led the way when we discovered the coral reef, *and* warned everyone to get to higher ground before the tsunami hit."

Musa bounced in place, nodding.

"*And* you're the one who showed all of us how to rescue the fishies after the first giant wave." She stared up at Lina, eyes wide, and her voice dropped into a dramatic whispered range. "Otherwise the seas would be empty."

Lina managed a couple of wobbly steps forward and threw up her hands.

"Okay, I give up. I had more than a little to do with all of this. Now we just need to figure out why it all happened in the first place."

Musa stepped beside her, held tilted to one side.

"What's that buzzy noise?"

Lina looked down, then patted her hip pocket.

She'd been so preoccupied with everything else that she hadn't even noticed her comm-stick alerting away to itself.

"I'd imagine that's Ris." She pulled out the comm, which was indeed covered with bright alerts. "Probably about to burst with wanting to answer all of our questions for us."

"Want me to put it on the big screens up front?" Jemny waved one arm that way. "I'd imagine we'll all want to hear what he has to say, and Mount Bewaker Central Control informs me we'll be circling for a while yet."

Lina unrolled her comm and handed it over. After a few seconds, Ris's red face and the spiky mess of his hair popped up in the middle of the forward windows.

"Lina! Where the *hell* have you been for so long?"

Musa giggled and covered her mouth with one hand.

"Right here on Jemny's ship. All over it, really. We're bringing Musa and her family back, remember? You're talking to *all* of us."

Ris had the grace to look flustered as Jemny made a few adjustments.

"Just giving you a visual of the whole crew, Director Murray," she said with a grin back at Lina. "We're heading in for a landing at Mount Bewaker at the moment. Once I secure a new ship, I'll be bringing everyone home."

"Isn't Mount Bewaker still operating under airspace restrictions?"

He frowned when Lina, Tes, Jemny, and Musa's grandparents let out tired laughter. Even Musa giggled again.

Jemny gestured for everyone to sit before she answered.

"We're very aware of the issues at Mount Bewaker. All will be well there soon enough. What can you tell us about what happened while our comms were out?"

Though Ris's pursed lips made it clear to Lina that he very much wanted to ask a lot more questions, he shook his head once and started answering them instead.

"Once I got the current frequency for the attackers' transmitters sent out planetwide, we were able to bring the satellites and every ship and scoot with a sensor array into the search. Turns out there were control modules hidden all over Sarkans 3. They might have been there for years. Very small, most not much bigger than a dinner plate. But they were networked to vastly increase their power and range."

"Everywhere the attacks happened?" Lina said.

"There and in an alarming number of locations they hadn't activated yet. They were set to terrorize the entire planet, and to keep going for weeks or maybe months if they got the chance."

Lina's skin crawled at the idea of more engineered natural disasters and what that would have done to everyone on the planet. And probably to other recreational planets, not to mention those with settlements only for habitation or scientific exploration.

Tes quietly asked the questions before Lina had a chance to.

"But why? And who *are* they?"

CHAPTER 39

Lina glanced at Musa's grandparents, who obviously wished Musa wasn't hearing any of this as much as Lina did.

But Musa gazed fixedly at the screen, and something in her attitude made it clear she was taking in every word. The stubborn way she crossed her arms made it likely she wouldn't take well to being told to put on her adorable set of earmuffs.

Ris might be at the Planetary Science compound, with the cluttered shelves of his office in the background, but neither distance nor his pause and look away from the screen could hide how reluctant he was to answer.

"According to our suspects and everything else we've discovered so far," he finally said, "the attacks were aimed at the *idea* of Sarkans 3. Not just as a leisure world, because there are plenty of those. These people were striking at us as a high-security, high-privacy world."

Jemny shook her head and crossed her arms.

"I'm not sure I believe that's all of it, not with such a well-coordinated and long-planned series of attacks. Were they after anyone in particular?"

Lina's shoulders protested movement after her scramble outside the ship, but that didn't keep her muscles from tensing up at the question. She wished more than ever that Musa were somewhere else instead of possibly hearing about yet another attempt to attack her and her family over technology developed centuries before she was born.

Instead of the scowl or raised voice Lina expected, Ris smiled and inclined his head.

"You've hit upon the most important question, Agent Manhoff, which isn't a surprise. The ones we know of so far were all citizens of wealthy and powerful planets, or worked at some point for an equally influential corporation. There's quite a bit of resentment out there over how individuals with that kind of power can essentially disappear on a planet like this. And quite a bit of fear that more planets that are essentially black holes will be developed for other purposes."

Tes nodded, and she looked more sad than angry.

"That matches what I've heard, either directly or in conversations happening *around* me. You know, when the kinds of guests who assume those of us who live and work here can't possibly be paying attention. Or they assume it wouldn't matter if we were. Please don't repeat this, but at times like this, I can understand where the attackers' ideas come from."

"You hear from the guests themselves?" Musa's grandmother said. "They're aware of this problem?"

"Oh no, not the paying guests," Tes said. "This is from the people who travel with some of them to take care of the unpleasant aspects of vacation. Making resort or activities arrangements or caring for difficult family members or calling for some kind of cleanup. The less-fun parts that make an enjoyable holiday possible. They tend to speak a lot more freely around me than around their employers."

"That's exactly what the witnesses have said," Ris said. "And I'm truly sorry to admit you were right about something else, Tes. Much of the upset is about people who never get reported. The ones who are never tracked or cared for because they've been kept Untraceable in a different way than so many of our guests strive for."

Pandar was next to look at Musa, clearly wishing his granddaughter wasn't listening.

"That's been part of almost every assault on our family," he said. "Both the leaders of the attacks and the poor souls sometimes forced to carry them out have too often been Untraceable. Along with the use of unregistered planets for planning and practice, and the vast wealth they often accumulate for carrying out those plans. I'm afraid the consequences for those involved have often been worse than for us."

Lina leaned forward with her arms across her belly. She didn't want to know more about what led to people and entire planets being kept Untraceable.

She doubted anyone going to such dangerous and illegal lengths did so out of kindness or concern for privacy. And sometimes those kinds of motivations created much worse outcomes than what they'd all just been through.

And too many victims with no chance of being discovered or rescued.

"Do they understand that Sarkans 3 does everything it can to prohibit such activity planetside?" Jemny said. "And that anyone either in that situation or who knows of it is encouraged to report to us without fear of retaliation?"

Tes stared at the ceiling, shaking her head, before looking at Jemny.

"That's just the thing. They *do* face fear of retaliation unless they can somehow afford to settle here or on another safe world permanently. They can lose their jobs or worse if word gets back to their employers. And all of that's assuming they ever have a chance to report or know that's a possibility. Again, I understand why the idea of more high-privacy worlds could lead to fear and anger."

Jemny abruptly got up and paced back and forth across the front of the ship, glancing at the monitors. Even Ris knew to stay silent until she stopped, arms crossed, facing him on the main window.

"This is one of the many reasons I've been agitating for more cooperation between the different groups operating here. Planetary Security doesn't know enough about the challenges Planetary Science faces or what they discover, and vice versa. Sounds to me like the situation is even worse between both our groups and the Tourism Authority."

She turned back toward Lina and Tes.

"I know you've already been through more than you expected these last several days since you met me, and probably learned more than you ever wanted to know about how this planet operates. I don't expect you to answer right away. But I'm asking if you'd be willing to help me *change* this. We all have to communicate more instead of keeping so many secrets."

Before Lina or Tes could say a word, Ris spoke up in a determined voice.

"I'll answer for myself right now. Planetary Security has good reason to operate the way it does in some cases, as does Planetary Science. But without all of us working together, along with Tes and the Tourism Authority, this situation could have been so much worse. I'll do whatever I can to create some sort of regular communication between us, with your help, Jemny."

Jemny smiled and held one hand over her heart as she turned back to him.

"Thank you, Director Murray. *Ris.* Since we're both heads of our divisions, that should give us a good start. But we'll still need Tourism, and I hope Lina and Tes are willing to keep working with me."

"Lina, you're free to make her own choice there," Ris said. "All I'll say is you've done a fine job under an unreasonable amount of stress, and I commend you for that. I do hope you'll still find time for your marine biology. This planet's extraordinary aquatic zones need someone with your skills."

"I'll do everything I can on the Tourism side," Tes said. "It's past time we took what we hear every day in the field seriously enough to do something about it when we can. And I agree completely with wanting Lina to work on both sides if she can possibly manage it. Whether she wants to admit it or not, she's the main reason we got these slow-moving disasters stopped as quickly as we did."

Lina blinked, surprised at the string of compliments, and unsure how to respond while the aftereffects of her terrifying trip outside still lingered in shaking hands and trembling muscles.

As she so often had during all the bizarre events and upheavals, Musa cleared Lina's mind with childlike honesty and a big smile.

"Don't be afraid, Lina. I know you can do it."

Lina sat up straight and smiled.

"I can't possibly refuse all of you. I'll do whatever I can. As long as we all keep working together."

After the rush of hugs and congratulations—and the best hug of all from Musa—Lina asked Jemny to transfer the feed back to her own comm-stick.

It turned out even the excitement of a job well done and the start of plans for the future couldn't quite shut one of the lingering problems out of her mind.

"I have the feeling you've got more to ask now that you're in a quiet corner," Ris said. "And a good idea what this is about."

Lina was hardly in a quiet corner on the relatively small ship, but she was as far as she could get away from the rest.

"Then I'll just ask without trying to explain, and you tell me whether I should be asking Jemny instead. The other hijacked vessels arrived at Mount Bewaker with unexpected passengers, so we were afraid something like that was going to happen to us. I suspect that plan simply got interrupted. Does anyone know who those people were, or why they ended up in that state?"

Ris nodded sadly.

"I knew you wouldn't forget about that. I suggest getting your guests settled back at their lodging before I join you over at Planetary Security. Then we'll all learn more together."

CHAPTER 40

The interrogation suite at Planetary Security Headquarters on Mount Bewaker made the spare and utilitarian classrooms at Planetary Science seem as luxurious as any tourist facility.

Walls, floor, and ceiling of the kind of black that somehow managed to absorb any other colors established a severe decorating scheme that was hardly welcoming.

That surface also deadened sound in an unnerving way that made Lina's ears feel like she was a dozen meters underwater with no protection.

As she sat with Tes, Jemny, and Ris, she couldn't hear herself breathing or moving, much less any of the others. Her underutilized ears focused way too much on her own heartbeat for comfort.

Their matching black chairs weren't as harsh or uncomfortable as she might have expected. Each was infinitely adjustable and seemed to conform to the body like a well-worn and well-loved garment. Or would have, if she'd been able to relax.

Even the air was soothing at the moment, especially after her recent experience of so many harsh conditions all over the planet. Cool but not too dry, and full of a faintly sweet, spicy aroma.

The position reserved for the suspect they'd be hearing from looked more like a comfortable lounge at first glance.

The low-slung, elongated surface had the telltale bulges of grav-packs along its length, and a compact control console sat in an empty chair.

Lina had the feeling the occupant of that inviting-looking piece of furniture wouldn't find the experience the least bit soothing.

They'd said happy-tearful goodbyes to Musa and her grandparents less than an hour ago, trusting their return to their lodging to one of the same automated scoots that delivered new arrivals. More than one Planetary Security agent in the same gray uniform Jemny normally wore reassured Lina that it had been fully inspected.

They'd also showed her the current energy scans from all over Sarkans 3.

Not a trace of the odd grav-drive signature, in any frequency.

But not even the promise of a crewed escort scoot had entirely calmed her worries.

Only the news that Musa had safely arrived—along with a smiling and waving image as proof—finally let Lina relax.

An invisible door on the opposite side of the room from where they'd entered opened without a sound, and a tiny woman who looked older than Musa's grandmother strode in.

Her small stature and diminutive frame did nothing to make her less intimidating.

Somehow the fact that the woman barely came up to Jemny's

shoulder, and yet Jemny stood at attention, only increased the effect.

"Commander Lesovah, thank you for agreeing to speak to us," Jemny said. "I appreciate how busy you are with other responsibilities."

Commander Lesovah's small, lined face broke into a warm smile that surprised Lina.

"I appreciate the sentiment, Agent Manhoff. But since you've been so deeply involved in this investigation, you know better than I do how disruptive these attacks have already been all over the planet. Thanks to you and everyone else here, we have a chance at returning to normal operations much sooner than the attackers planned."

After quick and respectful introductions, Commander Lesovah took the remaining chair, control console in hand. Her bright gray eyes examined each of them in turn, meeting Lina's for several long seconds.

"I understand you all know the basics of what we've learned from the suspects we've detained, so I won't repeat that for you. *You* should understand that the person we're about to bring in was reluctant to talk to us at first. It was only after she learned that we'd captured several others in her group and that we'd discovered and deactivated their control modules that she agreed to cooperate."

She shrugged and shook her head.

"We're still considering her to be an untrustworthy witness. We're not sure about the name she gives either, since she's willingly Untraceable and we can't verify her identity. But so far, everything she's said has been confirmed either by evidence or information from her fellow suspects. Normally, we'd only question a suspect after they're enclosed in the sensory deprivation pod."

She nodded toward the odd lounge contraption, which now looked considerably less relaxing and comfortable to Lina.

"Then only one person would handle all communication with the suspect for consistency. But since she's cooperating, we'll let you speak directly with her if you're comfortable with that. She's made no move to physically harm anyone. And between Agent Manhoff and myself, I assure you, no harm would come to any of you."

Lina answered without a glance at anyone else.

"That's acceptable to me. I want to hear what she has to say directly from her."

After everyone else agreed, Commander Lesovah nodded and spoke in the same quiet tone.

"Send her in."

Someone had obviously been paying close attention, because the same door opened again. This time a much younger woman stepped in, scanned the room quickly, then walked toward the interrogation chair.

She showed no signs of being injured or frightened, but she lacked the solid confidence of a Planetary Security agent.

Her darting eyes never stopped moving, as if she expected a stealthy predator to be lurking in every corner of the room. Her attitude made it clear she didn't assume the predator would win, or that she would.

Lina got the strong impression this woman met any sort of threat by not only taking it seriously, but also by expecting to give it a more than fair fight.

When she sat, her form-fitting black garment blended into the lounge as it adjusted to support her in an upright position.

Commander Lesovah stood and faced her.

"Suspect Three, are you still willing to answer questions with as much candor as possible?"

The woman stared at Commander Lesovah, somehow managing to convey her disdain without crossing the line into disrespect.

"I'll answer questions with as much candor as possible, yes. And I'll say again that you can call me whatever you want, but my name is Marah."

Marah's words came out clipped and fast, sounding like she'd worked hard to conceal any accent.

All Lina cared about was understanding whatever she decided to say.

The commander sat back and gestured toward Jemny, then clasped her hands in her lap.

Rather than feeling a chill when Marah turned her focus on them, Lina got a surprising sense of…ordinariness. As if, had they met under other circumstances, she and Marah would have at least gotten along if not had a chance to become friends.

And none of that mattered after what Marah had apparently been part of.

Lina jumped when Jemny spoke, and sat up straight when she got a look at Jemny's intensely focused eyes and hard expression.

Even though she was every bit as dusty and dirty as Lina and Tes, and her wrinkled and stained clothing had certainly seen better days, right now she was every bit the Planetary Security agent.

One who was determined to get answers.

"Were you involved in the two murders? The dead bodies that showed up at the spaceport?"

Marah looked at Jemny for several seconds, as if she was weighing whether to answer or not.

"Not directly. But I did know what was going to happen. I thought it would be a useful distraction from what we needed to do. So I chose not to do anything to stop them."

Lina spoke without thinking.

"And what exactly did you *need* to do? Destroy ecosystems we don't yet understand? Terrorize those of us who live and work here? Kill people who are entirely innocent of whatever you're so angry about?"

Marah stared into Lina's eyes and slowly shook her head.

"No. This isn't about any of that. This is about stopping the creation of *more* secret, inaccessible planets while we still don't know all the horrors already happening on unregistered worlds. All while no one seems to care about the Untraceable and every-thing they suffer."

Tes sat forward with her elbows on her knees.

"We were simply lucky that more people weren't injured or even killed on Sarkans 3 during your attacks. I can't speak for all of the tourists, but no one working in the Tourism Authority or Planetary Science has been involved in setting up unregistered worlds. Did you expect harming people to draw others to your cause?"

Marah snorted, and her smile was anything but kind.

"Of course not. None of us are here to make friends. The whole point was to try to make at least some of the most powerful people in the system comprehend how it feels to have no control or understanding about what's happening around them. *To* them. Maybe even make them realize they're part of the reason places like unregistered worlds still exist."

Jemny stood and walked silently across the room to lean against one of the blacker-than-black walls, effortlessly drawing everyone's attention.

"So you didn't mind the damage and possible deaths any more than you minded the planned murders. Do you even know who the victims dumped in those scoots were?"

Marah raised one eyebrow and somehow managed to make it clear how little she thought of everyone in the room, along with the dead.

"I know exactly who they were, and they were hardly victims. They were the ones who financed this entire operation."

Jemny didn't so much as twitch, but her gaze darted to Commander Lesovah, who allowed herself her own eyebrow-raised look of surprise.

"That's an interesting claim," she said, not moving from her chair. "Care to explain why you'd kill the ones who helped bring you here and pull off such a difficult series of attacks?"

"At this point, why keep secrets?" Marah's smile was full of an odd sort of relief. "Yes, they arranged for all the advanced tech we'd need, paid for our training and transport, and made sure we had plenty of time to lay the groundwork. They supported our operations for years. They thought we all had the same goal of stopping the creation of more high-privacy worlds, and in a way I suppose we did."

"What changed, then?" Tes said. "How'd they go from your allies to murdered and shoved into hijacked scoots?"

"No, they were *never* our allies," Marah said. "They didn't like worlds like this one because they preferred to know where their enemies were at all times so they could reach them. But they had no problem at all with the unregistered worlds they themselves profited from. Their plan was to keep attacking here and on other secured worlds, and to use what they learned to create more unregistered worlds that they controlled."

Ris rubbed his mouth and glanced from Lina to Jemny before turning to Marah.

"So you took all the help they could give you before turning on them. What would you have done with the ship you hijacked if we hadn't deactivated your control units? Did you forget to throw a dead body on board, or had you run out of targets by then?"

"A successful run without your interference would have made a lovely test of your supposedly impenetrable intercept field, for one thing. If your defenses failed, all the more attention for our little project. If they held, we hoped to learn how to better defeat one in the future. As for targets, we had a list of some of your more powerful guests for future use."

At the calm sound of Marah's voice and the equally matter-of-fact way she spoke about possibly destroying the spaceport and murdering who knew how many tourists, Lina had heard enough.

"And now that you've been captured?" she said. "What did you accomplish besides ending two lives and not managing to kill anyone else? And throwing your own life away in the process?"

Marah nodded and held out both hands as if she were offering to share a meal.

"Not as much as we wanted to, no. But we got the attention

of everyone on this planet, didn't we? I think you'll understand more once you receive our final transmission any time now." Jemny and Commander Lesovah grabbed for their comms, and Marah smiled again, this time in triumph.

Before anyone else could speak, Lina's comm buzzed, and she, Ris, and Tes reached for them.

Tes gasped.

"It's a list of unregistered planets. Dozens of them."

"Locations, populations," Ris said, his voice airy and light. "Even the main industries and trading partners."

"Did this go out planetwide?" Commander Lesovah said in a dangerously calm voice. "Why hadn't you reported this information before now?"

"Not to the tourists. Only to those in security, exploration, and tourism. We tried to report as we discovered the worlds over the years, but we couldn't get the authorities or even the Galactic Tribunal to act in a coordinated way. That allowed the monsters running those planets to relocate and harden their defenses. Now the authorities will *have* to act. Otherwise this report will go out to all registered human settlements."

Jemny showed her clearest sign of real anger by storming across the room to right in front of Marah, who only looked up without flinching.

"If you do that, you'll start a massive war. Individual systems will try to attack the unregistered worlds without any kind of coordination or regard for the planets they drag into the conflict. The Untraceable you claim to care so much about will be killed in the crossfire."

Marah nodded once.

"Exactly so. That's why I strongly suggest Planetary Security on Sarkans 3 initiate communication with the Tribunal. *Today*. You're the most secure but not illegal planet in existence, and your communications are assured to be private. Odds are low there'd be any retaliation from the unregistered planets before the Tribunal can coordinate the response. Especially once you deal with the few security weaknesses we used in our planning."

"And are you *planning* to let us know what those weaknesses are?" Jemny crossed her arms and continued to stare down at Marah. "Or do you find it more entertaining to keep that to yourself and share it with whoever sent this list of unregistered planets out?"

"I don't find any of this entertaining, I assure you. I'm fully aware that I'm not likely to ever leave this planet unless it's to attend a Tribunal hearing. Even if I do, I'll never be in anything close to your luxury tourist accommodations."

Marah took a long, slow breath without looking away from Jemny before going on.

"As far as the weaknesses we exploited, that was primarily done by being present long before you welcomed any guests to this lovely planet. The truth is you've already gutted our capabilities. But yes, I'll explain what I can about the rest."

"Including how to keep this list of unregistered settlement planets from being shared more widely?" Commander Lesovah said. "Agent Manhoff wasn't exaggerating about how disastrous that would be for everyone involved."

"As long as you contact the Tribunal," Marah said, "and get a response that lets me know they're willing to go forward in helping the Untraceable, there will be no further broadcasts. Private as your guests prefer to be, our information suggests there are more than enough leaders and other influential people plan-etside right now to greatly assist in that effort."

Jemny walked back to her chair and sat, her posture no less tense and rigid.

"How will you get the word out to *your* people about that? None of us want to hear about a supposedly accidental transmission later on. Especially not one that might endanger people working to rescue the Untraceable on these planets."

Marah's smile was unnerving, and cold

"I'll give you a coded message for the Tribunal to send if they agree to take action. That will be the first sign to make no more attacks or transmissions. The Tribunal actually *taking* action will be the second. You may not believe me, but I don't want war any more than you or anyone else does. That being said, the growth of unregistered planets and the increasing number of people with no access to civilized conditions might be the one thing worth provoking one."

Lina tried not to shiver with the chill working its way into her flesh and bones. It had been so long since any kind of inter-planetary war had broken out that it was likely no one knew what would actually happen if one did.

She had more than enough to concern her without going that far into the future.

"Are any of the people on Sarkans 3 right now in danger now that the attacks have been stopped?"

Marah held her with that examiner's gaze before answering.

"Not from anyone who's working with me, or anyone or anything else that I know about. The questioners who treated me *so* kindly before you arrived didn't believe me, but we weren't targeting anyone in particular. The only thing that directed the timing of our attack was the high number of influential people on Sarkans 3 right now. It's in everybody's best interests for you to let them know what's happening so they can bring that influence to bear with the Tribunal."

After a long stretch of silence that grew increasingly uncomfortable, Commander Lesovah got to her feet.

"I believe we've all heard enough. Suspect 3—Marah—your cooperation is appreciated. And thank you to everyone else for coming here after such a difficult day."

The door opened silently again, and two Planetary Security agents walked toward Marah. She stood and followed them without a word until she got to the door.

She stopped and turned toward the waiting group.

"If you really want to help the Untraceable, talk to the people on this planet right now who can make a difference. That's all I've been trying to do my whole life. Make something give and start to move. If the change finally begins, it's all been worth it."

And she turned and disappeared through the closing door.

Lina closed her eyes and sat forward, startled when the chair adjusted with her. She didn't move at a hand on her shoulder.

"You okay?" Tes said.

Lina nodded.

"I think I will be." She sat up and looked around the room, where the others seemed to be in a similar state of contemplation. "As soon as I get some rest. Then take the advice to talk to the powerful people I know. I don't like her techniques, but Marah is absolutely right. This is a change that's long overdue."

CHAPTER 41

Lina watched a fresh crop of happy, noisy tourists wandering the crimson-and-silver sands and cliffs of Scarlet Beach.

Blissfully unaware of the near-disaster of the unnatural tsunami just over a month before, they splashed and lounged, climbed and rock-hunted. They had no idea that it was once unheard of to catch sight of the gray bulk of a Planetary Security scoot floating silently above the calm waters of the blue-green sea, so they didn't let it interrupt their pursuits of pleasure and relaxation.

A larger group of tour guides than ever before kept an unobtrusive eye on the proceedings as well. Always happy to assist with future arrangements or make the current day's roster of activities a tiny bit closer to perfection.

If anyone happened to notice how the guides paid closer attention to their surroundings than in days gone past, no one minded as long as they made sure to keep the focus on fun.

Or at least as long as that's what they *seemed* to do.

After all, the recent addition of a Planetary Science special guide to many of the groups added enough interest and excitement to make up for slightly more attentive demeanors among the usual guides. Getting to learn about the most recent discoveries before anyone else certainly turned up the thrill on an already delightful vacation.

Because of those subtle and more overt adjustments behind the scenes, the tourists were free to take full advantage of long and warming days.

They were even treated to a surprise opportunity to help with the restoration of two northern valleys with very different climates than tropical Scarlet Beach. One full of newly planted fir-type trees ready to get a head start on growth before the harsh winter settled back in. The other the chance of a lifetime to study and catalog newly uncovered volcanic deposits.

Tourists visiting both sites learned all about the unusual weather and geological events recently discovered on this most remarkable planet.

The majority of them would enjoy their carefree days on Sarkans 3 without ever knowing about any of the giant waves that had caused so much disruption and terrors, even as they walked through the aftermath.

Lina was endlessly impressed by the power and reach of the Tourism Authority's marketing department. Any group of people who could keep the true cause of such momentous events largely undercover could probably spin just about anything into a happy tale.

What she really wanted to know was how they and Planetary Security had managed to keep the tourists who'd *experienced* the disasters from getting the word out. At least so far.

But she wasn't quite brave enough to ask.

As for her own contributions to the recovery effort, she was all too happy to finally be exploring the painstakingly restored tidal pools at the site of the first disruption.

Digging out the misplaced sand had felt like cheating at first, especially when so much of her training had focused on only observing the natural processes wherever she was.

Not interfering with them.

But in the end, Ris, Tes, Jemny, and even Musa had convinced her that undoing the most unnatural damage they'd all lived through didn't count as interference. The beach deserved the same careful attention as the mountains.

The restoration was its own form of healing, and not only for the land.

So she once again knelt in her rocky pool not far from the towering cliff, enjoying the warm water's caress, and marveling at the amazing resilience of ocean lifeforms.

Despite being buried by piles of heavy, scouring sand, the silky, flowing fronds of violet seaweed were already thriving again.

Sure, they were a bit rough around the edges—like everyone who'd found themselves in the path of a tsunami, an avalanche, and hundreds of years' worth of a volcano's levitating soil. The skin-tickling hairs that adorned the edges of the seaweed hadn't yet recovered fully on the larger strands, though new sprouts along the bottom showed signs of normal growth.

The piney scent of this species was still stronger than usual as well, probably from all those jagged and scraped edges.

But a quick visit the night before had shown the gorgeous purple glow emanating from the leaves was as strong as ever.

And even better, Lina had spotted darting and floating streaks of the same light in the sea's gentle mid-tide currents.

The creatures that had enjoyed dining on her seaweed had survived to feast another day. Probably at least in part because of Musa getting all the adults organized to save the fishies stranded on the beach while they still could.

As if her thoughts had conjured her young friend, Lina heard Musa's high, sweet voice in the distance.

"There she is! I *told* you Lina would be here!"

Lina shifted carefully against the sharp-edged red rocks of the tidal pool, making sure of her footing as she sat on a flat spot. The warm morning breeze felt wonderful as it dried the seawater on her skin.

Musa ran full-speed across the silver-streaked scarlet sand toward her, with her grandparents following along at a more reasonable pace. The bright-yellow sundress she wore over what was certain to be a swimsuit flowed behind her like a girl-sized cape.

She stopped just short of tumbling herself into the pool, giggling and dancing in place.

"Did you find the fishies you were hunting for? The ones with so many *legs*?"

Lina grinned and nodded.

"Look right here in this little box."

She lifted a wire-mesh cage as long and wide as her forearm out of the water. Inside were three coppery creatures, all spines and claws and nine spindly legs, not much bigger than one of her hands. Rather than cowering against the corner of their temporary home, they minced toward the edge, waving an impossible number of deep-orange antennae toward Musa.

The very crustaceans Lina been looking for the day the artificial tsunami pulled the sea out toward the distant horizon.

When the odd adventure of Musa's giant waves began.

"Oh, they're so *prickly*," she said, squatting so she could get a better look. "Will you take them away, back to your Planetary Science building, so Ris can see them?"

Musa had spent several happy days tagging along with Ris while her grandparents were deeply involved in working with the Galactic Tribunal. Both she and Ris had thrived on the time spent together.

"I'll take them there for one night," Lina said. "Then bring them right back here so they can go on about their busy lives."

She didn't mention that bringing them back quickly was vital, since she'd observed both friendly and defensive signs of an approaching mating season in their behavior, even in the cage.

"Sort of like Lina needs to get back to *her* busy life," Musa's grandmother said from the other side of the tidal pool. "You can get in the water, Musa, but don't get so far out that your feet don't touch."

Musa flung the sundress off and toward her grandparents with a cheer, revealing a bright-blue swim tank, then skipped toward the retreating waves.

Seerit wore a matching yellow dress that seemed to float in the breeze, and her smile was as radiant as her husband Pandar's.

"Well, I suppose we've got a few minutes to catch up now," Lina said. "Any more word on the rescues?"

As the descendant of Ivy Cepat and primary heir of the vast corporation she'd founded, Seerit had been instrumental in securing the use of several grav-drive ships—making a point of referring to them by their proper name of Cepat Drives—which greatly accelerated the Tribunal's reach.

Over the past month, a dozen unregistered worlds from Marah's list had been located and their Untraceable populations identified. More importantly, their rescue was underway.

"The ships have reached three more worlds," Seerit said. "And still none of them have been deserted when they arrived. Between the list, Marah and Sarkans 3 authorities keeping chatter down, and the fast ships, surprise has worked in our favor for a change."

Pandan gazed at Seerit with obvious affection, his own loose top and pants the same vivid color as hers.

"Seerit's doing a wonderful job coordinating the flight plans," he said. "She never took enough credit for everything she did for the Cepat Group before her retirement. I daresay they appreciate her more now that she's stepped back into her role than they did when she was on active duty."

"You're right about that." Seerit leaned against him for a second, then held out one hand to Lina. "You'll come visit us, won't you? The invitation stands, and we'll bring you to us no matter where we happen to be."

Lina grasped her hand.

"Of course I will. I wouldn't want Musa to forget all about me."

Seerit rolled her eyes and grinned.

"Not a chance of that. We're not leaving here for another few days, so we'll be sure to see you again. I hope you'll join us at our farewell dinner for all the dear friends we've made here. For now, I think I see your next couple of admirers heading this way. Take care, Lina."

Lina turned to see Tes and Jemny strolling across the sands, and her jaw dropped.

Not because of Tes, who wore her typical bright-pink tour-guide tunic for the first time in a long while.

She'd been overseeing the new cooperation between the Tourism Authority, Planetary Science, and Planetary Security rather than leading groups of her own.

Lina and everyone else saw how clearly her new role suited her, even as she talked about wanting to get back out into the various landscapes all over the planet with gaggles of tourists.

The sight of Jemny in a flowing, springtime-green sundress was what surprised Lina. Even with all the meetings and class-room time Jemny had put in with scientists and tour guides alike, she hadn't strayed from her gray Planetary Security uniform.

Today she even walked barefoot, carrying a pair of sandals that matched her clothing in one hand.

Her sheepish smile made it clear she'd caught Lina's surprised reaction.

"Let's just say part of our new arrangement with the Tourism Authority requires an unavoidable time of *relaxation*," she said, nearly turning the word into an expletive. "Not my favorite change, but one I can tolerate as needed."

"Then let me just say it suits you." Lina did her best to hide her grin as she settled the spiny creatures into the water and climbed out of the tidal pool. "Are you back to tour-guiding today, Tes?"

"Not just yet. I've got a new group of Planetary Security agents to get acclimated to the idea that Sarkans 3 isn't entirely about making sure everyone follows all the rules, all the time. An even more uptight bunch than Agent Manhoff here, if you can believe it."

Jemny sighed and rolled her eyes.

"I already agreed to be your example of how we can survive dressed as tourists, so our esteemed guests won't panic every time we join one of their apparently *fascinating* leisure activities. I didn't say I had to enjoy it."

Much like Tes when she fussed about helping the three groups work together, Jemny's smile took the force out of her words.

"Any changes with Marah?" Lina said.

"Still cooperating," Jemny said. "I'd say she's given us far more information than she promised in return for suggesting she serve her sentence here rather than in a Galactic Tribunal prison. Like she said, she's hardly in luxury accommodations. Our detention facilities weren't meant to hold people long-term. But here she's getting to accomplish something."

The three of them had spent many hours with Marah, discussing the tactics she and her group had used in the attacks, and how they'd discovered so many unregistered human colonies.

None of the other people involved in planning and carrying out the attacks had been nearly so forthcoming. And their current location in the dreadful prisons Marah had avoided reflected that.

Tes nodded. "Honestly, she seems almost…content. Not even Tourism could manage to market her plan for a satisfying life, but she's certainly gotten a lot done for the Untraceable."

"More than anyone has for centuries," Lina said. "She earned her years in detention for certain, but the number of people who owe her their freedom and dignity is hard to believe."

After several seconds of thoughtful silence, Jemny cleared her throat and dropped her sandals on the beach beside Lina's backpack.

"Well, one of my assignments for the day is to get more involved in the day-to-day work of Planetary Science, so I'll theoretically be able to blend in with those groups as easily as with tourists."

Her smirk made it clear she thought that level of comfort might take years.

Lina thought it was a tough assignment, but that Jemny might just make progress more quickly than expected.

"Does that mean you're here to help me study this tidal pool?" Lina said. "There's plenty of room for all three of us since the tide is still in."

"That's exactly what we're here for." Tes dropped her own sandals and knelt on the red sand before swinging her legs into the water. "Ready to get your feet wet, Agent Manhoff?"

Jemny closed her eyes and shook her head before giving up the protest and grinning.

"Lucky for you two, I have a swimsuit hidden away under this frilly mess. Whether it's lucky for whatever lives in that tidal pool depends on you showing me how to keep from stepping on them."

Lina laughed with her friends as Jemny neatly folded the sundress, getting ready to join them in her beautiful sky-blue swimsuit. She kept her opinions about Jemny's sometimes prickly disposition to herself.

"With this particular pool, it's more a matter of protecting your *feet* from their *spikes*. But I think we'll all manage just fine."

ABOUT KARI

Kari Kilgore's wanderlust and imagination lead her all over the world on grand adventures. Her heart and family bring her home to her native Appalachian Mountains of Virginia. From that solid base and with the help of the ever-changing lens of her imagination, she brings those adventures to life in fiction.

Since she always does her best to be a considerate tourist, she plans to do the same when traveling off-planet.

Kari writes romance, fantasy, contemporary fiction, mystery, and science fiction, and she's happiest when she surprises herself. She lives with her husband Jason A. Adams, various house critters, and wildlife they're better off not knowing more about.

The Confidential Adventure Club

For Kari's exclusive free After The End stories and deleted scenes, discounts, early pre-sale releases, adorable pet photos, and a whole lot more not available anywhere else, join us in The Club.

Hope to see you there!

www.KariKilgore.com
www.SpiralPublishing.net
www.ConfidentialAdventureClub.com

bookbub.com/authors/kari-kilgore
amazon.com/author/karikilgore
goodreads.com/karikilgore
facebook.com/kari.kilgore.1

ALSO BY KARI KILGORE

I hope you enjoyed reading *Dangerous Days on a Pleasure Planet* as much as I enjoyed writing it.

For more science fiction ranging from near future here on Earth to life among the distant stars, visit www.KariKilgore.com/ScienceFiction.

Be the first to know about release dates and check out more of my fiction, including almost every genre, at www.KariKilgore.com.

Dispatches from the Galaxy Stories:

Restricted Species

The Becalmed

The Garbage Belt

Plurapod Pathogen

The Changes Cascade

The Storms of Future Past Series:

Dreaming the Storm

Joining the Storm

Into the Storm

Fighting the Storm

Sensing the Storm: A Storms of Future Past Prequel

Storms of the Heart: A Storms of Future Past Romance

Storms of Future Past Books One through Four Collection

The Odd Society:

Independent by Means of Magic

Protected by Means of Magic

The Voices through Time Series:

Songs in the Mountain

Secrets in the Land

Sorrows in the Earth

Walking the Ghosts: A Voices through Time Novella

Novels:

Until Death

The Dream Thief

Hand Me Downs

Protecting Her Own

The Coffee Bomb and the Corporate Spy

The Great Gold Record Heist

Novellas:

Legacy of the Land

In the Pines

DNA Never Lies

The Box of Possibilities

Murder at the Fabulous Feline Emporium

Collections:

Fantastic Women: A Dark Fantasy Novella Trio

Fantastic Shorts: Volume 1

Near Future Forward (with Jason A. Adams)

Fantastic Shorts: Volume 2

Partners in Romance (with Jason A. Adams)

Dispatches from the Galaxy: A Space Opera Novella Trio

Fantastic Shorts: Volume 3

Escape into Romance: A Collection of Sweet Beginnings

Stepping Out of Reality: Short Spells of Appalachian Magic

Facing Down Extraordinary: A Series of Ordinary Heroes

Hacking Cybercrime: Dana Sanderson Short Mysteries

Shadows Mountain Deep: Six Appalachian Crime Tales (with Jason A. Adams)

Investigations Beyond Belief: The Initial Adventures of Deb Powers: Otherworldly PI

Passages in the Real World: Six Stories of Life's Transitions

Fantastic Side Trips: Side Characters Take Center Stage

A Kaleidoscope of Cat Tales: Five Stories of Cats and People Who Love Them

A Tapestry of Holiday Tales: Winter Adventures from the Odds and Endings Bookstore

Uncommon Holidays: A Different Side of the Season (with Jason A. Adams)

Aunties Among Us: Five Tales of Fabulous Women

Four-Legged Heroes: When Pets Rescue People

Partnership in Crime: Six Journeys to Justice (with Jason A. Adams)